SOPHIE RAMO

The Woman who Chases ANGELS

a novel

Jeffrey McClain Jones

For our Rooted group: Nathan, Michi, Janet, Jenny, Jim, Kris, Lillian, Mollie and Wendy

The Woman Who Chases Angels

Copyright © 2021 by Jeffrey McClain Jones

All rights reserved. No part of this book may be reproduced in any form by any electronic or mechanical means including photocopying, recording, or information storage and retrieval, without permission in writing from the author.

John 14:12 Publications

www.jeffreymcclainjones.com

Cover photo from Adobe.com.

Ending the Silence

Sophie Ramos set her thin briefcase on the floor and plunked herself onto the chair by her front door. She was recalling a conversation from when she was a teen, an overheard conversation.

"She'll probably grow out of it. Most people do … grow out of …" The doctor's voice had been obscured by an overhead announcement or something, the way it replayed in Sophie's head. His halfhearted assurance had been intended for her mother. That Sophie might outgrow her *delusions* or whatever they were calling them at that point in her young life.

"Maybe I *should* grow out of it." She snorted a laugh. "Anytime now." She took a big breath. "Maybe not." Sophie was grown. Not a girl anymore. *Young woman* would be generous nowadays. She kicked off one high heel and rubbed her foot. Slipping free from the strap on the other shoe, she watched her customized Band-Aid peel off with the strap. Maybe she should have just turned around and come home without doing the job interview. Hearing that angel talk to her should have been enough to call it a day.

He spoke to her. And she understood.

But why now?

"You'll have other opportunities, Sophie. Don't worry about this one."

As he spoke to her, she'd noticed an aroma. Distinct and familiar. Like incense or some fragrant wood. Something she might find in a shop selling handmade wooden boxes or candleholders. A sweetly satisfying odor. It was welcome and satisfying even in the revolving door of that sterile office building.

She stood next to the chair now. Her moist feet adhering slightly to the wood floor. She wandered through her apartment while still connected to the mental recording of the angel's message.

Staggering through the revolving door into the bank building had been autopilot stuff, Sophie following through on her plan for the day—finding a permanent job. But click-clicking her high heels over the marble floor got muffled under a complaint list about her first personalized angel message.

"You'll have other opportunities." That wasn't much of a confidence-builder.

"Don't worry about this one." Good advice, except it sounded like she wasn't going to get the job.

She had prodded herself to go through with the interview using the argument that she might not know what the angel meant. But even if she really wasn't sure what it meant, her heart still fluttered at the fact that he had spoken. To her.

Sophie probably should have just spun that revolving door all the way around and back out onto the warm, sunny street. Who wanted to do a job interview in August anyway? And for a job at a bank. A bank job.

Anthony had laughed at her when she accidentally said it that way. "A bank job? Really? You're getting that desperate? You're gonna rob banks now?"

He could laugh. He still had his job. He had been working from home and was now back in the office half time with his same employer.

Not Sophie. After catching her talking to one of her angels, her boss had used the office shutdown as reason to cut Sophie from the software development team. Sophie was just grateful Janice didn't poison her chances to get contract programming work during the lockdowns. No negative recommendations, apparently. Janice had been flipped out by Sophie talking to empty space, but there was no evidence she'd shared those misgivings with the employment agency. Sophie hadn't been starving since losing that job.

Standing facing her living room windows, Sophie was suddenly aware of her apartment. She was back home. Again. She had spent way too much time looking at these white walls. So much time staring out these windows. Just Sophie and her usual angel guardians confined here. Getting out was compelling, even out to a job interview.

Seeing the angel she thought of as *the big guy* by the revolving door of the bank building hadn't been startling. Refreshing, really. It was about time *he* got out and about. But then he spoke. Why then? Why not sooner?

In fact, when Janice had caught her talking to that same angel at work last year, Sophie had been teasing him about not talking. A friendly, private joke. But one she should have kept more private, obviously.

Sophie turned toward her bedroom but glanced over her shoulder. That tall golden guy was standing by the counter in her kitchen. Was he going to make her a cup of coffee?

He smiled at that thought, or so it seemed.

Silent, private jokes. Those would be safer in a workplace. If you happened to have an angel accompanying you to work.

Pausing by her bedroom door, she looked straight at him. "What was that smell? I mean, that *aroma* before I went into the interview?"

He smiled on. No answer. As usual.

Sophie shook her head and continued into her bedroom, closing the door behind her. Her crew of angels seemed to accept this as a request for privacy. At least apparent privacy. She was pretty sure they could see through her bedroom door with their angel vision. Speaking through that closed door, she asked anyone who might be listening, "So, I'm not gonna get that job at the bank?" She pulled her suit jacket off. "Well, maybe that's not so bad. They seemed pretty uptight. I don't think I can go from working in yoga pants all day to sitting up straight and having to check my makeup all the time."

Again, no answer. But, of course, she expected no answers. She had never before heard any words from the mouths of the angels she saw. The good ones, anyway. The bad ones were hard to shut up. "Blah, blah, curse this, ruin that, maim, kill, destroy, etc., etc."

But this good guy—her old pal—had finally spoken. It wasn't in answer to a playful question, but a message delivered. He was a messenger, after all. Just like the stories in the Bible. Angels talked to lots of people in those stories. And they answered questions. Like, "How can this be, since I am a virgin?" But even that question had come in response to a delivered message. Maybe Sophie should have asked questions as she spun that revolving door. Maybe that was her chance for a real, interactive experience with one of these angels. Verbally interactive for once.

She hung her charcoal-gray interview suit in the closet and sauntered to her dresser. Baggy cotton shorts were the order of the day, the temperature getting to ninety and the AC in the apartment lackluster as usual. "Hey, I was used to you not talking. *Now* what am I supposed to do?" She pulled the wrong drawer open and switched to the next one up. She was still trying to figure out whether what he had said was useful. In a way, knowing she wouldn't get the job took some pressure off. That led to not trying so hard to impress the interviewer. Sophie probably didn't stress out as much as she usually did in interviews.

With a T-shirt pulled over her head, she aimed her bare feet out the bedroom door and directly to the computer in her dining area/home office. She noted that the flowers potted in front of her computer needed water. What kind were they again? Kimmy dropped them off when she brought the baby over the second time. Regifting. Sophie forgot to note the name of the flower breed. Whatever they were called, the pot of flowers had promoted her dining table/workspace to home garden. A modern combo. A little haven in a tough time.

Her laptop was powered on already. Bumping the mouse on her way to the sink proved that. When she arrived in the center of the kitchen, the big angel handed her the small plastic watering can and lifted the handle on the faucet.

Sophie stared at him. That was new. Watering can in hand. Faucet turned on.

Angel assistance.

What next? And why would she want to outgrow this?

The Obligations of Vision

Anthony texted Sophie again. **"Hey. What are you doing? Are you trapped under furniture or something?"**

Finally she answered. **"Just got back from the interview for the bank job."**

"A clean escape?"

"Got away, but no loot."

"No job?"

"No. But my angel talked to me … finally."

"What? At the job interview?" Anthony considered the possibility that Sophie had suffered a stress-induced hallucination. One thing he knew about her angels was they *didn't* talk to her.

"On the way in. Told me not to worry. I wouldn't get the job."

"What?!?!?!?!" Not to worry sounded good, but not worrying because she wasn't getting the job didn't make sense. Even Anthony was stressed about Sophie not having a regular job. Not getting a job was not something to not worry about. He stood up and walked to his kitchen. He had to get the hamburgers out to thaw a little. At least enough to peel the paper off. **"You still coming to supper?"**

"Sure. Angel didn't tell me I wouldn't be getting supper."

"Ha! Good."

He could see that she was typing more. Maybe a long reply. Then nothing. Changed her mind? Well, they could talk about it more when she came over.

Anthony met her at his apartment door a couple hours later. And she did that thing that added fuel to his conviction that she truly believed she was not alone. She waited for some invisible friend or other to come in the door before she closed it behind her.

"They can walk through doors though, right?" He tried not to sound like he was making fun of her even though he was.

Sophie stared at him for a few quick breaths. "Oh. Yeah. They can. But they do stay out of my bedroom when I change clothes."

"Yeah. You mentioned that before." He pivoted back toward the kitchen, leaving behind any curiosity about what those angels would see in her bedroom when Sophie changed clothes. "But one talked to you today?"

"Yeah. This guy." She flipped a thumb toward empty space next to her.

"Your ... your regular angel guy."

"The guy one. The apparently male one. I have no idea what his name is, so it's just the male-ish one. The big guy."

"Right." After two years of listening to Sophie talk matter-of-factly about her angels, Anthony was still relying on her descriptions of that alternate reality. He had only seen hints and shadows himself. Not that he had ever admitted even that much to Sophie. He stopped by the fridge. "Diet root beer?"

"You don't have anything stronger?"

"Like sugar root beer?"

She snickered. "What about that ginger ale?"

"Yeah. I still have at least one of those." With Sophie not drinking alcohol, he kept sodas for her and a few other friends. "If Ervin didn't drink the last one, that is."

"Has *he* found a job yet?"

"Yeah. In fact, he just did. He's gonna work for the city schools doing this new training program. Coding for kiddies or something."

"Hmm. I wonder if I could do that."

"Teach kids software development?"

She seemed to be consulting the empty space beside her. Getting more job advice? She shrugged slightly and settled onto the stool next to his breakfast bar, her bare legs stretched so her feet reached the floor.

"So why do you think he talked to you now?" Skipping topic introductions when asking questions about angels was fully accepted between them. Anthony could barely recall when that wasn't so.

"I don't know, but I'm totally obsessed with the answer to that question. I really wish I knew."

"Have you called my mama yet?"

"Not yet, but she might not have the answer either."

"Unlikely as it seems, she doesn't actually know everything. Not even about angels."

"No. Not everything." Sophie scrutinized him for a second. "You didn't say anything when I floated the idea of me teaching kids."

He shrugged hard. "What do I know? I never see you with kids." He set his last ginger ale in front of her. "I know Ervin is like a big kid himself. Really big." He tried to inflate himself to match his husky friend's dimensions.

"That probably has something to do with the child thing that hangs around him all the time." She reached for the soda can.

"All the time? Child thing?"

"Oh. I guess I've only seen Ervin about three times, but that kid seems to be stuck to him."

"You never told me about that."

Sophie scrunched her mouth and looked away. "I shouldn't tell you stuff like that, I know."

"Yeah. Now I'm gonna be checkin' Ervin out, lookin' for this child thing you're talkin' about." What started as a tease heated to something more resentful. He really didn't want to know everything Sophie saw.

"Sorry. I gotta work more on confidentiality. Jonathan was reminding me about that the last time I helped him."

"Did that session go well?"

She lasered those dark eyes at him. "Obviously I can't say." Then she grinned minutely. "It went very well. Jonathan and his team know what they're doing, that's for sure."

"Is this gonna be a regular thing, then? You helping him with people he counsels?"

"I don't know how regular, but he was telling me about this other guy who does the demon-casting stuff fulltime." Her eyes were drifting around his living room. "Jonathan wanted to know if he could give that other guy my info. This demon chaser guy has been asking about me."

"Some strange demon hunter guy has been asking about you? How did he hear?"

"I don't know. Maybe *his* angels actually keep him informed." She glanced at the air just over her right shoulder. High over her shoulder. Probably a pretty tall angel there.

"There are other ways to get good information." He turned to pull out the stuff for grilling burgers.

She spoke over the sounds of fridge and food. "Yeah? Like asking your friends in the gamer chat rooms?"

"Ha!" He bared his teeth and growled. "Be nice to my friends."

"Friends like ILivetoSlay13 and HeadRoller77?"

"Hey, those are my buds. You got a problem with that?" He couldn't restrain his grin. And then he let loose a silly laugh. His little-kid laugh. It had been making embarrassing cameos lately after the healing he got at church.

Sophie laughed back. She hadn't made fun of his cackly laugh yet, even when it ended with a dorky snort. She only laughed along.

Later, as they sat next to the little table on his back deck, chewing burgers and sipping sodas, Anthony recalled what Sophie had said about Ervin. "You feel obligated to do something about Ervin having that thing hanging on him?" *He* was feeling obligated. Maybe he could pass that back to Sophie.

"I don't know." She wiped her mouth with a paper napkin and stuffed it back under the edge of her plate. "I see a lot of stuff that I doubt I'm supposed to do anything about. And I know now that I don't see everything. They go invisible a lot. But I see way more than I have time to get involved with."

"Sophie, this is one of my oldest friends. And now I know about this Klingon he has."

"Yeah, but almost everybody has something clinging on. You really think you and I are supposed to be scraping those off everyone?"

"You and I? Maybe not. But you ..."

She shook her head at him, but she didn't look mad. Surely she didn't expect Anthony to become a demon slayer in real life. On the other hand, *she* hardly had a choice about it.

"What should I tell Bagley ... uh, Ervin?"

"Tell him? About his parasite?"

He smacked his lips. "I bet he would freak if I used the word *demon*. But parasite doesn't sound much better."

"So, you don't feel like you have a mission to clean up the whole metropolis, but you feel you *should* say something to your friend." Her eyes rested on him, tinted with something like sympathy.

"Yeah, I guess. Though he'll think I'm crazy if I tell him everything."

"Are you thinking you should say something before he starts working with those school kids?"

"I don't know. Maybe that makes it seem more urgent, I guess."

"I wouldn't worry about it. He can still help kids even with his own whiny child attachment."

"Whiny?"

"Grumpy sad. Nasty spoiled. Dissatisfied. That's how he looks as far as I recall. I haven't seen Ervin in a few weeks."

"And you see so many people's demons that you can't keep track of which is which?"

"Basically." She leaned back. She had packed away the whole burger with lots of fixings and a pile of sweet potato fries. She wasn't a big girl, but she had a good appetite.

And Anthony had that urge again. To ask her about their future. The two of them. More than friends? But this didn't seem like the right time. When would that time come?

He Did What?

Sophie closed the web browser and took a purging breath. Maybe she could just do this contract coding forever. Or at least until she found something entirely different to do with her life. She turned to look at the big guy angel standing with his more womanly coworker. They seemed to be waiting for Sophie to do or say something.

"What?" It had been two days since that guy delivered the message at the revolving door of the bank. Nothing since.

"Crystal will need your encouragement and acceptance. Bring the grace to her that you have received from heaven." That was the she-angel. Her voice rang like heavy bells.

Sophie stared. She restarted her breathing after a few seconds.

Her male counterpart joined the feminine one in bowing, and then they disappeared.

Sophie's phone buzzed where it lay next to her computer. Crystal calling, of course.

"Hey, Crystal. What's up?"

"I, uh … I'm okay, I guess."

"That doesn't sound very convincing."

"I may have screwed up."

"How?"

"I, uh, went to this guy, this healer guy. He said he believed in Jesus, but I'm not sure it's the same Jesus they have at church."

Crystal had been attending the same church as Sophie and Priscilla for in-person services since it reopened in the spring.

"Oh. So, you feel like you picked something up from this guy?" Sophie tried to add some of that bell tone she had heard in the angel's voice. Wasn't that what grace sounded like?

"Your voice sounds strange. Are you okay?" Crystal lowered her voice toward genuine concern.

Sophie laughed. "I was trying to sound encouraging and full of grace, sort of. That's what the lady angel told me to do before you called."

"What?"

"Yeah. I just heard my second little message from one of my angels. They're talking to me now. At least once in a while. Encouraging instructions—that seems to be the pattern so far."

"So, they told you I would call?"

"Let's just say I wasn't surprised to see it was you when my phone buzzed."

"Huh." Crystal paused long enough to worry Sophie about the connection. "But you think I'm okay. I mean, the angels knew about me. They knew I would call."

"They work for God, Crystal. They know pretty much everything, as far as I can tell."

"Oh. That would be nice." Again, she paused.

Sophie wondered whether Crystal was contemplating how nice it would be to know everything or how nice it would be to work for God.

"You think I'm messed up now?"

"What did this healer guy do to you?"

"He put this cross on my hand—you know, where I have that carpal tunnel pain, and he said words in some language I don't know."

"He used a cross?"

"Yeah."

"Hmm. I wonder how that could be bad."

"He sold me this holy oil and told me to rub it on my hand every day."

Sophie squished her eyes shut for a second. "Okay, that does sound weird. Come on over and let's see if I can detect anything on you."

"Thanks, Sophie. Sorry to be a bother."

"Don't worry about it. You're my friend. And there are some angels already working on your case."

"Yeah. That's cool."

Crystal came to Sophie's apartment after her Pilates class. Probably not really in crisis, given the priority she gave that class.

As soon as her friend came in the front door, however, Sophie could see a problem. "There's this guy in robes doing this sort of blessing thing with his hand." She watched the odd priest or wizard guy floating in the corner above the door. "It's like he's floating over you with this string attached. Kind of a wizard balloon, in a way."

"What?" Crystal craned her neck toward the ceiling. "Wizard? Balloon?"

"I don't know. Maybe *priest* is more like it, but not like a real priest at my mother's church. More of an ancient fantasy priest, like in a computer game. Anyway, he's gotta go."

Crystal cringed and nodded simultaneously. Also simultaneous was the disappearance of that floater guy.

Sophie strained her angel optics and tried to detect where that guy was hiding, even looking beyond the ceiling. But he seemed to have cleared out entirely. She could see no strings attached to Crystal anymore. A quick check with her two visible angels, and Sophie was satisfied. "I guess that did it."

"Really?"

"Well, you clearly wanted him off, and it wasn't like a lifelong commitment." She shrugged. "It's not so hard to break off those kinds of short-term attachments."

"Huh. I guess that makes sense." Crystal pushed several blades of purple hair off her face and tucked them behind her ear where the hair was sky blue. Her nail polish was dark pink. Nice combo.

Sophie beckoned for Crystal to follow her to the living room. "So, where did you find this guy?"

"The healer guy?"

"Yeah, not the floating priest wizard guy." They took seats across from each other, Sophie on the couch, Crystal in the slightly springy bucket chair.

"He advertises at the organic grocery store. I've seen his flyer up there for months, I think. I was getting desperate for this wrist to get better. It makes working on the computer painful sometimes."

"Well, I know you've heard people at church talking about doing healing. No priests or wizards attached."

"No holy oil?"

"I don't know. That could be a thing. I'm still pretty new to this. But I can at least try a basic healing the way they do at church."

"I let the ladies in the Bible group give it a try, but it didn't work."

Sophie knew how that felt. The bunion on her left foot was still there, though still not as gross as her mother's was. "It can't hurt to try."

"No. Go ahead. Give it a shot." Crystal leaned back and finally set her sequined purse on the floor. That was when her angel showed up.

Sophie loved to look at Crystal's angel. The graceful, glowing queen reminded her of the part in the Bible about the emerald light around God's throne. Crystal's angel emanated a gemlike glow. "Well, your angel seems interested in the proceedings."

"Really? That should help, I would think."

Sophie agreed. And she remembered what the trainer at church said about faith. Having that angel show up boosted her faith. She stood and took up a seat on the coffee table, close enough to reach Crystal. "Okay, well, I say in the name of Jesus, Crystal's wrist and thumb get healed. Be healed." She held her own hand loosely over Crystal's.

The glow off Crystal's angel was golden-green and flaring now. Sophie could feel warmth multiplying between their hands, more than seemed natural. "What do you think? Feel any better?"

Crystal withdrew her hand and began hinging her wrist. "I think it feels a little better." She nodded. "At least the pain seems duller."

"So, the pain got less. The guy in the class said to try again if you get, like, part of a healing." She raised her eyebrows, requesting permission for a second round.

"Sure. Go for it."

Sophie touched Crystal's hand and essentially said the same thing as the first try. Then she added a prayer of thanks. "Amen."

Hinging her wrist again and twisting her thumb with her other hand in a way that seemed like it would hurt most people, Crystal puckered tightly. "Wow. Huh. I think it's better. Much better, actually. Seems pretty good right now." She raised her eyebrows as if she wondered what Sophie thought about that.

"That's cool. Wow. I didn't know I could do that. Or maybe I didn't know God would do that with me."

"Well, I gotta say, it's not the most unbelievable thing about you, dear."

Sophie snorted a laugh.

A Gentleman Texter

Detta stared at the text message from an unrecognized number. She had assumed it was junk since it came from an unknown number with a different area code, but the contents challenged that assumption. She stood in the doorway between her kitchen and dining room.

"So glad to pray with you, Detta. I appreciate your faith and boldness. Roddy."

"Roddy?" She said it aloud. Then the tumblers clicked into place. Brother Harper was Roderick Harper. He must go by Roddy. But her sister, Loretta, had never called him that. "Hmm." Detta shuffled to her recliner. She needed to be seated if she was going to figure out the process Anthony had shown her for saving someone's number after they texted you the first time. She had done it a dozen times by now. Still, sitting would be better.

Saying he was glad to share in a prayer ministry with her was normal behavior. Sending her a text like that was not so normal. Pretty forward of him. Detta snorted at her own judgmental assessment as she followed one path and then backed up in the phone interface, trying to recall the steps. "I guess he's *particularly* appreciative, is all." She chuckled deep in her chest. "That must be it."

She finished saving Roderick Harper's number, then texted back. **"Blessings to you and your church."** The prayer he mentioned had been for Loretta's struggle with memory loss. Brother Harper was part of Loretta's church. Before hitting send, Detta wondered if she should be more personal. Friendlier. He had addressed her by her nickname and had offered his. But maybe that was just his way. He came from back east, she was pretty sure. Maybe his people did things differently. It didn't have to *mean* anything.

As soon as she hit send, Detta's phone rang. She jumped in her seat. Then she laughed at herself again. It was Loretta calling. "Hello, dear. How are you doing?"

"Don't know if the memory issues have improved at all. And I'm still short of breath. But I'm just takin' it easy. No rush for nothin' these days." Resignation hung heavy on Loretta's voice.

"Oh, sorry to hear about the breathing. But not rushin' around isn't a bad way to be." Detta leaned back in her chair and settled in for a talk with her sister.

Amid Loretta's usual updates on doctor's appointments and cooking adventures, Detta couldn't help wandering back toward that message from Brother Harper. Roddy. It didn't feel like an appropriate name for the dapper old gentleman with the neat salt-and-pepper goatee. Would he mind her calling him Roderick? But when would she call him anything other than Brother Harper? She held the phone away from her face and sniffed frustration at allowing that little meander with her imagination.

Loretta seemed to sense something. "You still with me, Detta?"

"I'm with you, Loretta. I'll keep prayin' for your health. Let me know if you want me to come get you and take you to church with me."

"Oh, I know I should. I'm just too tired to even get my hopes up again."

"I understand. I know how it is." Tiredness seemed to be Loretta's way of coping with her memory issues. Now maybe it sheltered her from her faith issues too.

"You feeling pretty good these days, though?" Her little sister still knew how to be concerned for others.

"I am. I'm quite well, really. Considering the mileage."

Loretta grunted a laugh. "Talk about yourself like you was an old pickup truck."

"Ha. Well ..."

"Okay. Well, I gotta get supper started."

"Just you tonight?"

"Yeah. Leah is too busy for her old mama. Doesn't do me much good to have her back in town now with her keeping such a busy social calendar."

"A girl's gotta get around." Detta was just saying what she'd heard others say. Maybe Anthony would agree with that sentiment when applied to his cousin. But he surely wouldn't want it applied to his old mama.

Loretta seemed to ignore Detta's last comment. Or maybe she didn't understand it. "Okay. Have a good evening, Detta."

"You too." It was an oddly short conversation, as if Loretta had called for something and had forgotten to bring it up. But the sisters had seen each other just yesterday. And that left Detta drifting back toward that prayer time and then to her text from Roddy Harper. Roddy? Really?

She heaved herself up out of her chair and turned her attention to cooking her own dinner. A few nights a week she cooked as if a visitor or two were on the way over, but tonight it would just be her and leftover lasagna. Plenty for three or four if need be, but she wouldn't warm up all that was left.

She stood looking at the fridge. A picture of Anthony and Sophie grinned at her, a photo of a recent trip to a beach. Her boy's grin had turned more childlike the last few months. She couldn't help smiling back. Those two looked happy together. Whatever their together meant.

"What about me, Lord Jesus? What do you think about my interest in Brother Harper? Roddy?"

"Are you interested, Detta?" He often answered her questions with a question, a question they both already knew the answer to.

"Well, I guess I *am* interested. Interested enough to be askin' you about what I should be doin'." She reached for the fridge handle and pulled.

The lasagna was on the second shelf in her biggest square Tupperware. It was a good lasagna. One of her best, probably. But no one else had tasted it. They'd just have to take her word for it. Unless she were to text Brother Harper to see what he was doing this evening. But she would never be that forward.

"Why not?"

She hissed a laugh through clenched teeth. "I ain't that far gone yet."

"It's not a sin to be lonely."

"Huh. Oh, you're meddlin' now, Lord. Gettin' right up in my business, you are." Her chuckle was grumbly in her throat as she set the lasagna on the counter. "I'll just text Anthony and entice him with this lasagna."

That led to only silence from her invisible companion. She suspected the silence was all right. Her Heavenly Father tended to give her some space, especially after introducing something new and strange. There had been a few of those lately. Offering dinner to Brother Harper was out near the visible horizon of strange possibilities. Too far out for tonight.

Detta texted Anthony and then also Sophie to improve her odds of getting a reply.

She wasn't surprised when Sophie was the one who responded with a thumbs up and a smile. The modern version of an invitation acceptance.

What would be surprising would be Detta telling Sophie about her brief temptation to invite an old widower over for dinner. Maybe she was only uncertain about the spontaneity of that other invite. A thoughtful invitation with days to plan would be more like it. But she wouldn't tell Sophie about any of that. Not yet.

"Don't nobody know my trouble but God." She hum-mumbled a line from a song Anthony had sent her recently. This trouble was her own doing. Or at least the temptation of it was.

She sliced enough of the lasagna for her and Sophie, checked for a response from Anthony, and then pulled out a bread pan and set the oven to preheat. Some extra sauce from the fridge would keep it from drying out too much. And there should be salad. That would do it.

A tasty supper and some company. What more did she need?

Convince You or Cure You

Sophie leaned her head on the back of the couch and turned just enough to get one eye on Detta. "You think I should let Jonathan give my name to that demon hunter guy?"

"What demon hunter guy?" Detta blinked hard for a few seconds.

"I told you. That ... uh ... *deliverance ministry* guy and his wife who travel all over dealing with the hard cases. You remember?"

"Okay. I do recall you telling me about that. I guess I didn't think you would do it. Sounds like a lot of trouble."

"Trouble? How do you mean?"

"Oh, I don't know. Somehow the word *trouble* has been crawlin' around inside my head tonight. And the strange thing is, it doesn't come with any kinda fear or worry. Just trouble."

Sophie relaxed and let her eyes wander away from Detta. "Well, trouble is something I've lived with all my life. There's worse trouble I could get into than traveling around and setting people free of demons."

"Yes, that's true. Mm-hmm."

Sophie was hoping for more. Detta seemed distracted. "So, you don't think there would be a problem with me giving that guy my contact info?"

"If Jonathan trusts him, then he must be okay. But I don't know anything about him."

"A white guy, straight church background. Seems kinda boring, really. But apparently he knows something about getting people free."

"What does he need you for, then?"

"Oh, Jonathan was saying this guy—Bruce something—is always looking for ... uh, seers. Someone like me who can see the spirits."

"Okay. Well, he can't be totally wrong if he knows he needs that."

"I mean, Jonathan's like that, isn't he? He's a therapist, and he knows what to do to get people free, but he just doesn't see clearly like I do."

"That's right. Sister Ellen too. She knows what she's doin', but she only senses things kinda like I do. None of those full-color 3D images you see."

"Oh, I forgot to tell you. My angels started talking to me."

Detta leaned forward hard enough to subtract half the tilt out of her recliner. "What? When? What did they say?"

Sophie chuckled at Detta's instant enthusiasm. She filled her in on the action she had missed, trying to be serious even in the face of Detta's girlish interest. To be honest, Sophie had been counting on that wide-eyed fascination from her friend. It was the kind of affirmation she craved. Uniquely reinforcing when it came from Detta.

"Sounds right to me. Your angels are givin' instructions, delivering messages from the throne. That's what they do. They're not gonna joke around with you like you were trying when your boss caught you."

Dropping her chin onto her chest, Sophie expanded with a big intake of air. "I think I'm gonna go crazy if I don't find something to do outside my apartment."

"Like a new job? This Bruce person isn't gonna pay you, is he?"

"I doubt it. I was thinking I could sort of do it as a vacation."

"Doesn't sound like much of a vacation to me."

"I need a change. I need to get out, get away."

"Stir-crazy I can understand. It happened to all of us this last year." She nodded as if answering herself. "I guess it could be good for you to see what that kinda life is like. Doing ministry day-in and day-out could convince you or cure you of it."

"Cure me of wanting to be part of a ministry?"

"A daily, regular part." Detta gave a crooked shrug. "You have an incredible gift, Sophie. Of course you should use it where it's needed most. Do all you can with it." She chuckled. "But I know the limit on that is how much scary stuff you see and the sheer exhaustion that comes with doing that kinda ministry."

Sophie was ready to protest that she wasn't scared, but she knew Detta didn't need to hear it. They both understood the fear as well as the courage to push through the fear. And they both knew the reward of seeing a life transformed. A soul set free. Rewarding and exhausting—that probably described all kinds of jobs worth doing.

"I have enough savings to get me through a month at my own expense. If they can give me room and board, I can do it for longer than a month."

"Well, maybe you shouldn't commit to too long, just in case."

"Yeah. That sounds like a good idea." She wondered if Detta was still hearing the word *trouble* in her head.

When they finished their tea, they kept talking, but not about ministry and angels and demons. Detta started reminiscing about being married. It was a long reach to that part of her life. Sophie couldn't pinpoint what had taken their conversation so far back.

"I could count on him in all circumstances, my James." Detta stared toward the dining room, nodding as if her memories were seated there. "He was no fair-weather friend. I even think he taught me about God and Jesus that way. Like, he showed me an example of what a man could be, how a man could live in a trustworthy way."

After a long sigh, Sophie spoke into a pause. "I can see why you would miss that. And you've stayed single all this time because of that?"

"I was a mother. I had a young man to raise. And ... well, James was a hard act to follow, I guess." Her eyes remained distant, her voice subdued.

"But you've raised Anthony now. And your marriage ended a long time ago."

Detta turned toward Sophie. "Yes. A long time to be single, I know. Would seem longer to you, of course."

Sophie didn't want to make this about *her*, especially with things so uncertain between her and Anthony. She didn't even know what Detta thought of her and Anthony. And she didn't want to lift the weight of finding out right now. She was in no mood for a big decision while so much about her life was up in the air.

The energy for Sophie's visit seemed to have run out. Even Detta's angels seemed a bit dimmed. Sophie said thanks for the supper and gave her hostess a hug by the back door where she had left her sandals.

"Take care of yourself, girl. And make sure you know what you're gettin' yourself into with that deliverance ministry."

"Right. I will. I won't agree to anything without consulting you and Jonathan."

"All right. Sounds good. Good night, Sophie."

Sophie stepped out of the air conditioning into a warm bath of night air, thick in the deepening darkness. Her three angels glowed in that darkness, one on each side and one behind. She noted how their light cast no shadows on the asphalt driveway.

How Much to Tell His Friend

Anthony reached for the front door of the restaurant, but a voice arrested him before he touched the handle.

"Anthony! Over here." Ervin Bagley was seated in the corner of the white tent that covered most of the outside dining area. He waved without standing from his chair. Bagley was easy to see even seated.

"Hey, man. Glad you grabbed an outside seat." Anthony dodged a waitress scuttling toward a side door and picked his way between tables. "Finally got a breeze today."

Bagley wiped a drop of sweat from his forehead. A small darkened spot in the middle of his chest marred his medium-blue polo shirt. "Yeah, it's not bad. Unfortunately I rushed to get here, thinking *I* was late." He cocked an eyebrow at Anthony.

"Ah, sorry. Yeah. There was a controversy at the office. Some VP authorized a project manager to buy an unapproved computer. The whole thing was above my pay grade, but that didn't keep them from dragging me into it." Anthony met Bagley's raised fist with a bump.

"All right, I'll accept your excuse for tardiness. But let's see a note from your boss."

"Or my doctor?"

"That would cover it too." He forced a friendly grin.

"Made you run, did I?" Anthony settled into a chair. "Maybe I should charge you for the fitness training."

"A hundred bucks cover it?"

"Are you feeling flush now that you got that new job?"

"Well, I ain't gonna get rich helping kids learn to code, but they pay well enough to lure me away from some other prospects." A wind fluttered through the semi-sheltered space and tossed a used napkin off a nearby empty table. Bagley stomped on the escapee with one big Nike and then looked down.

Anthony guessed he was debating the health implications of picking up someone else's napkin. And then there was the issue of what to do with it. "You still doing orientation for the job?"

"Yeah. I'm not gonna actually be interfacing with the kids at first. I'll be doing more of the code reviewing and troubleshooting. I don't know if I'll ever really be, like, a tutor or anything."

"I thought part of the point was being a mentor to kids who don't see themselves as future developers."

"That's what they told me, but they also promised I wouldn't have to do too much of the touchy-feely stuff, at least at first. I think that's a precaution for them as much as for me. They need to decide if they can trust me."

"Sure. That makes sense." Anthony paused as a busboy delivered water and stooped to pick up the stray napkin. "You don't sound anxious to get involved with the kids."

"Not directly. And maybe not all by myself. I think it might be okay to be working alongside, like, high school teachers who don't know so much about coding. You know, soft skills next to tech skills."

"Yeah. I don't think I'd be too anxious to deal with high schoolers either. That takes some special superpowers."

"Pretty intimidating, really."

As the waiter took their drink orders, Anthony recalled Sophie's words about the kid-thing attached to Ervin. That attachment might be keeping him from being comfortable dealing with kids. Maybe it was keeping him from being the adult in the room, sort of.

"You still with me?" Bagley was scowling, his eyebrows tightened over his wide-set eyes.

"Oh, sure. Just thinking of why we're so freaked out by working with kids."

"It's a big responsibility. And guys get in trouble doing stuff like that all the time."

"Oh. There is that. I was picturing you working with boys, but I guess there are girls too."

"That's part of the point. Getting underprivileged kids into computers, and girls especially."

"Right. Kids who don't identify as geeks yet."

"Uh-huh."

Anthony considered if he should say something about what Sophie had seen clinging to his friend. He had no clear exit strategy if he started, but he was really worried about Bagley. "I told you about Sophie's special skills, right?"

"Sort of. She sees ... like ... spirits. So, she sees ghosts and stuff?"

"Uh, not really ghosts. More like angels and demons."

"Right. Okay. I assume that's why you two aren't hooking up."

The complexities of Anthony and Sophie's relationship ground him to a halt for a few stuttering seconds. "Uh, I don't know about that. I don't know that we're not at least ... dating, I guess you could say." He shook his head sharply, breaking out of that mental somersault. "No, I wasn't talking about that. I was just thinking of something she said about ... about seeing something ... about ... well, about you."

"Me? Like seeing what?" Bagley's voice sounded like he had a literal frog lodged in his throat. He cleared it and lifted his water glass.

Anthony hit pause. The waiter was back with a soda for Ervin. They gave him their appetizer order. Anthony lifted the menu to confirm his meal choice, but the waiter scooted away.

Debated taking that pause as an excuse to drop the subject, Anthony reviewed how much he had said already. He had surged into it out of frustration over his relationship with Sophie, probably. But dropping it now would be too awkward, even for him and Bagley.

"I know it seems crazy, but I really believe she sees stuff. And I've seen it really make a difference for some people—to know what's hanging around them. Maybe they can even ... like ... get free of things."

"What the **** are you talking about?"

Anthony winced at the profanity. The word didn't bug him as much as the realization that he had lunged into a very sensitive topic with the delicacy of a defensive lineman. While he contemplated his missing exit strategy, a basket of chips arrived with a selection of salsas. Then they ordered their main course.

As the waiter walked away, Anthony reached for a chip. "Uh, this is good salsa. Sophie likes this green one." He dug a big scoop of the hot *verde* sauce. Way more than he needed.

"You brought her here?" Bagley reached for the chips but kept his eyes on Anthony.

Anthony breathed through his mouth, trying air cooling. "Actually, she was the one who told me about this place." He sipped his water. "The food is mostly Mexican, but they do some authentic Puerto Rican dishes too. That's her, half Mexican and half Puerto Rican."

"So, you guys really *are* dating?"

A load of betrayal was already squashing Anthony into the metal patio chair. He surged from under it, hoping brutal honesty might work as an antidote. Honesty about his relationship with Sophie, at least. "I don't think she would say we're dating. And I really don't know if I'm what she needs. She's so hardcore. I mean, especially with that spirit stuff I was mentioning." He set his eyes on the potted plants just outside the open flap of the tent.

"Yeah. I don't think I could get into that. Too intense." Bagley made a noise that probably represented a backspace over something more he might have said. He clearly thought Sophie's gift was too weird.

Anthony was certain Sophie was *not* too weird for him, but he wasn't so sure that he wasn't too wimpy for her. He had just added evidence of the latter, retreating so awkwardly from offering Bagley something. But what would he be offering, anyway? Insight? Freedom? Anthony wasn't ready to be the one who actually brought that kind of freedom. He had recently referred one of his friends to folks at his mother's prayer group, but that was far short of bringing deliverance to lunch with him.

They drifted away from talking about Sophie, though they still talked about women and relationships—mostly Bagley's concerns and aspirations in that realm. And the rest of Anthony's meal was tainted by guilt and by the burn of that initial nervous scoop of verde sauce.

Meeting the Demon Hunters (Virtually)

Sophie entered the video meeting and waited to be connected to her hosts. She had talked to Bruce Albright on the phone just briefly after a longer conversation with his wife, Deborah. Sophie was glad to see them both appear in the video window when they accepted her entry.

"Hello, Sophie. Good to see you even if it's not in person." Bruce was a moderately handsome man with regular features, nothing outstanding. His haircut was standard-issue church leader, from what Sophie had seen on the forty-something pastors and counselors she had met. Bruce looked a bit like Jonathan, though not as bony, and with darker eyes.

Deborah leaned toward the camera a little. "Hi there. How are you doing, Sophie?" She was a slender, pale woman with big dark eyes and medium-length brunette hair, sharply styled. She reminded Sophie of other comfortable white middle-class women who accepted the benefits of their demographic without an obvious sense of entitlement.

"I'm good. I still haven't found a full-time job, so that leaves me open to spending some time working with your … ministry. At least for a while."

"Good. I'm glad you're open to it." In the glow of what must have been a laptop screen, Bruce's moderately tanned face took on a bluish tint. "We've been talking about how we might do this. We have a home base here in Florida, as you know, but we mostly do ministry for full-time pastors and parachurch staff members at this facility. We were hoping you could help us with someone who would best be served near where *they* live."

"We serve some people who have issues that are connected to their location, so it's best to meet them there." Deborah said that with little drama.

"Okay. I guess that makes sense."

"So, would you be willing to meet us in another city and stay there for a few days? We would provide accommodations for you."

That was different than what Sophie was picturing, but that picture had been sketched mostly out of her own imagination. "I can travel. That's not a problem. I can take a break from the contracting job I'm on just about any time."

"We generally only plan a few weeks in advance. Much of what we deal with is urgent crisis ministry." Again, Deborah stuck with an even tone, though her voice warmed with compassion in a way that kept her from sounding clinical.

Bruce followed. "We would like to have you meet us in Iowa. There's a woman there who has a very complex history. There's been some confusion about what all she's connected with, so we could use your help."

"When is that?"

"End of next week." Bruce looked apologetic, as if he feared that was too short notice.

"Okay. I can do that. I can fly there, right?" She didn't know much about Iowa or its available airports.

"Yes. We can pick you up at the airport in Des Moines. Ross can book you a ticket." Ross was their administrative assistant, from what Sophie could tell.

"Oh, okay. That sounds good. I'd like an aisle seat, if possible."

"Excellent. Glad you said that." Bruce's enthusiasm was probably not about aisle seats.

Deborah responded. "Yes, we can get you that, I think. And we can put you up in the hotel where we'll be staying. We have a conference room rented there for the ministry time."

"Sophie, you should know that this town outside Des Moines, near where we will be working, has a disturbing spiritual history." Bruce's face hardened with those bluish shadows more sharply defined. "We suspect that history may impact what we hope to bring for this woman."

"Disturbing? How?"

"For example, about thirty years ago, there was a fire in an orphanage. Several of the children died. There's some controversy around how the fire started. There may have been staff there involved in … illegal activities. So much of what we know is based on rumors, so I don't want to repeat any specifics. But indications are that this woman's oppression may be influenced by that spiritual legacy. And it's a legacy that goes even farther into the past."

"So, not mostly a personal history, more a local history?"

"Well, there are also some obvious personal causes. She has engaged in some risky behavior. But those regional spirits may be adding some power to her oppression."

Sophie raised her eyebrows at Bruce's deft protection of his client, as well as his restraint against speculating. "Are you working for the woman with the problem, or for someone else?"

"A local pastor called us for help. Their church is paying our expenses. Basically room and board. We have supporters who contribute to our organization for our general living expenses beyond that. Salaries for me and Deborah and Ross."

"I think I talked to Ross the first time I called your office."

"He travels with us sometimes, but he was in Florida that time you called."

Deborah leaned toward the camera again. "We have a couple of friends in the Des Moines area who are going to help us as well. Supporters from way back who do this kind of ministry around there."

Sophie tried not to obsess over whether she was being sucked into a secret network of demon hunters. Bruce and Deborah seemed so normal. How weird could all this be?

"When you meet these people, you'll feel comfortable with them, I'm certain. They are very stable and experienced ministers." Deborah seemed to be reading Sophie's thoughts. Though maybe it was all right there on her face. The downside of a video call.

"Okay. That sounds fine."

"I assume you don't need any of the personal details or history of the woman we're ministering to?" Bruce was both asking and assuming, apparently.

"That's right. I'm fine with just meeting her when I get there. It probably helps if I come in cold. Or fresh." She didn't retract that awkward answer, despite sounding like she was describing a salad.

"Good. That's what I thought."

Was it truly *good* that Bruce didn't have to reveal personal information about the woman, or was he just glad Sophie was behaving within expectations, within the working parameters of his ministry?

Deborah piped in. "Ross will email you the flight information as soon as we get it."

Sophie wondered who this Ross guy was to them. Just an employee? He had sounded young and nervous on the phone. The opposite of these two seasoned leaders. At least that's how they came across.

Soon after ending her video call with the Albrights, Sophie checked her texts. There was one from Priscilla. She hadn't talked with her for over a week. Sophie tapped on Priscilla's icon in the messaging app and selected audio call.

"Hello, Sophie."

"Hey, Priscilla."

"What have you been up to?" Priscilla sounded like she might be driving.

"I was just on a video call with some demon hunters who are buying me a plane ticket so I can meet them in Iowa to help this woman oppressed by some area spirit having to do with a bunch of dead orphans."

A pause. Priscilla was breathing. Sophie could hear that. But she wasn't speaking.

"'Cilla?"

"Ha. You know, if it was someone like Anthony or someone from church who said stuff like that, I would laugh hard. But this is you, and I know you're serious. And this stuff still blows me away."

"Sorry. I kinda needed to get all that off my chest. Believe it or not, I'm freaked out by all this too. Still."

"Yeah. I believe you. Huh. So, who are these demon hunters?"

"Well, not really demon hunters. *Deliverance ministers* is what Detta called them."

"Right. But she's so old school." Priscilla's voice took on a humorous harmony. "I mean, I think it would be better to call them demon hunters. That sounds so much more relevant."

Sophie hesitated. "You're joking, right?"

"Ah, pretty much. But really, *deliverance ministers* doesn't sound so much less weird than *demon hunters*. It's just older. More churchy. Time to get more relevant, don't you think?"

"What does our church call 'em?" Sophie stuck to the serious side of the topic. And she silently congratulated herself for not calling it *your* church.

"Oh. I don't think we have any of those. Either of those—demon hunters or deliverance ministers. Not that we don't believe in demons, of course. As you've seen for yourself, folks do kick some out every once in a while. But they do it different, right?"

"Yeah. What I've seen is definitely not like Detta's prayer group. Maybe I should talk to Pastor Julius about it."

"You can just call him Julius. And you *should* talk to him. I'm pretty sure he knows about your gift. He was in on arranging that thing with the woman from Africa."

"He was. That's right. I should definitely talk to him. I probably should have done it a long time ago."

"You've just been with this church, like, a year and a half."

"It seems like a long year and a half."

"Yeah. It does."

Ready for a Relationship?

Detta stared at Roderick Harper's contact entry in her phone for at least a minute, trying to decide how to address him. Then she gave up and opened the texting app. She wouldn't have to address him at all in there. She had learned that you could spot the rookies in text messages when they added your name to the top and theirs to the bottom like they were sending a letter.

What to say? She tapped a clean nail on the screen a few times. **"How are things at the church?"**

She paused over that. Was it dishonest? She wasn't really contacting him to find out about his church. Detta was hoping to get some tea with him somewhere. Inviting him to dinner was too forward. She had figured that much out. Dating, or anything even vaguely like it, was what other people did. People like Anthony and Sophie. She was still figuring it out for herself.

Detta said a short, silent prayer for Sophie and then a longer one for Anthony while she decided whether to send that text.

Then a text came in. From Anthony. **"Can I come over for dinner tonight? Need some advice."**

"Huh. Well, I'm sure I got some advice for you. But I better pray first to be sure it's any good." She didn't send that. Neither did she send that text to Roderick Harper. Or Roddy.

"**See you at 6:30.**" That was the one she sent. Then she had to go back and check to make sure she hadn't sent that to Roddy. No. It was to Anthony. Okay, her heart rate could go back to normal. She shook her head and chuckled at herself.

Detta set dinner on the picnic table on the patio. Not too windy this evening. The temperature was dropping down to eighty, on its way to even friendlier territory.

"Fried chicken? You haven't cooked me that for a long time." In the kitchen, Anthony kissed her on the cheek and grinned into the frying pan.

"Not the healthiest thing to eat. Maybe I should get one of those air fryers."

"I could get you one for your birthday."

"Not gonna wait to surprise me?"

"You're too old for surprises."

"You think I might have a heart attack over receiving a brand-new air fryer?"

"I'm sure stranger things have happened." He took the plate of corn on the cob from her and carried it, with the salad, out the back door.

She followed him with the plate of chicken. She hoped the fresh greens in the salad would counterbalance the fatty, fried food. Redemption of a kind. "Can you crank that umbrella a bit? I think it goes higher. It just got too hard for me."

Anthony turned the crank on the umbrella that was planted in the middle of the round red picnic table. He got half a turn out of it. "How are you feeling these days, Mama?"

"You worried 'cause I couldn't crank that umbrella all the way up?"

"Not really. It *was* pretty hard. But it did remind me to check how you're doing. Do you have a plan for when it gets too hard to do things for yourself?"

"Do I have a plan? Who have you been talking to?"

"I had lunch with Ervin Bagley. His grandma is still living on her own in her eighties. They're worried she's gonna fall and hurt herself or something, but there's no way she's gonna go live in a home."

Detta slipped around the end of one of the small benches and situated herself in the shade of the umbrella. "I don't know anybody else's business, but isn't there someone in that family that can take her in?"

"She doesn't want that either. Maybe even less than moving into a nursing home."

"Huh. You afraid I'll be that ornery when my time comes?"

Anthony finished dishing his salad. "Actually, I was having a hard time picturing you being cantankerous like that. I assume you'll just go on being the wise and reasonable mama I've always had."

"Ha. You butterin' me up for something?"

"Can't take a compliment? You might wanna work on that, Mama."

"Butter on one side, grill marks on the other. Too bad I boiled the corn, otherwise I'd look just like 'em."

He paused with a drumstick in one hand and scowled at her. Then he smiled. "Okay, I get it." He shook his head. "Seriously, Mama, you might need to work on accepting praise from folks. I know they got me working on that in my men's group."

"Sure is a blessing, you goin' to that group and workin' on your stuff. I really admire you doing that."

"What about you? Are you getting help like that from your ladies' Bible study?"

"Hmm. Maybe we could learn a thing or two from these new men's groups. I think we could do a lot more to sharpen each other. There's plenty of sparks, but I'm not so sure the iron is really sharpening the iron most of the time."

"Accountability. That's what Vic and them are always talkin' about. You have accountability in your group?"

"Oh, you know we do. No one of us is gonna let any of the others get away with *anything*." She cut into the chicken breast on her plate. Clear juice rose into the cut and disappeared back into the steaming meat. Just right. She could push the crispy skin aside. Her doctor would just have to be satisfied with that.

Anthony was eating skin and all. He set a stripped drumstick on his plate and grabbed another paper napkin from the ceramic holder in the middle of the table. "I bet the guys in my group are more diplomatic than your group."

"Diplomatic? Well, could be. Mm-hmm." She chewed another bite of chicken as she wondered what the ladies would say if she mentioned Brother Harper and her romantic thoughts about him. Then she looked at her son. What would *he* think?

"Can we talk about the advice I need? Or should we wait until after we eat?" He set a plump chicken thigh on his plate and wiped his hands again.

"Oh, no need to wait for a ceremony. Won't be one around here, as usual." Detta tipped her head and considered her next bite of chicken. "What's on your mind?"

"Sophie."

"That's nothin' new. What about Sophie?"

"*Me* and Sophie."

"Okay. That narrows it down quite a bit. Are you two an item, as they used to say in my day?"

"It still *is* your day, as far as I'm concerned, Mama." Anthony chomped into his corn.

Chewing and thinking, Detta assumed.

"I wonder if I'm ever gonna be what she needs in a man."

"What she needs? Or what she thinks she needs?"

He stopped chewing and wrinkled his brow at her. "What are you saying?"

"I'm just wondering myself. Does Sophie know what she wants in a man? I don't think you or I can answer that. But I'm not seein' her work real hard on figuring that out herself just now."

"So, you're saying it might not be a good time to try and work out our relationship, like some kind of commitment? Becoming more than friends?"

"How much of this have you discussed with her?"

"Probably less than you and I've covered during this one cob of corn." He proceeded to finish off the half cob.

"Have you figured out yet whether you like her *because* of her gifts or in *spite* of them?"

"Oh. Well. Hmm. I haven't really thought about it directly. More like slid around it about a million times."

"I can understand that." She turned back to her salad, stabbing rhythmically with her fork. "Sophie's gifting is unique. Some of the rules that apply to the rest of us don't apply to her. It's sorta like if you wanted to go out with a famous actress or rock star. You have to account for the big chunk of her life that's dominated by her talent."

"Too bad she's not making bank like an actress or a rock star."

"She told me she has enough saved so she can take time off to do some work with a deliverance ministry."

"Yeah. She has savings, I'm sure of that. Though not millions. But that's not really your point, is it?"

"No. I guess you were making a joke that I took too seriously." Detta crunched at some celery and lettuce and considered that she might have missed his teasing tone amid her chewing racket.

"I hear what you're saying though, about her gifts. I know you're right. And I guess I've only known her as a girl who sees angels. Or a woman who sees and hears angels. Did she tell you they started talking to her?"

"She did."

"Pretty cool."

"Yes. Very cool, I'd say." She quirked a half smile at him, just short of winking. She sat up straighter and let her fork settle next to her plate, reaching for the salt. "I don't think I'm really giving you any good advice this time."

"I don't know. You asked the important questions. And maybe you confirmed what I already know. That there isn't anyone who can answer my questions except me and Sophie."

"Mm-hmm. That sounds about right."

Just Julius

Sophie stood in the little waiting area next to the coffee maker and the bulletin board. That board had clearly been neglected. Nothing newer than 2017 on there as far as she could tell. Proof that an analog bulletin board was a thing of the past.

Julius Nichols was probably twenty years older than her, but she wouldn't call him a thing of the past. He looked like your basic computer nerd, really. His glasses were parked crookedly halfway down his nose, and he was smiling, as usual. It was a cheeky grin, like he was trying to imitate a chipmunk without the required chubbiness. "Sophie, how are you doing? Can I get you some coffee?"

"Uh, no thanks. I'm good."

"Well, I hope you don't mind me getting a refill." He held a smallish white mug in one hand. "You can head in there and find a comfortable seat." He swept his free hand toward an office with an open door next to a tall window.

"Okay. That's fine." She shuffled past him and through a small maze of tables and chairs to his office door. His name plate had been customized. *Pastor Nichols* had been crossed out with white correction tape and a handwritten *Just Julius* had been attached under it on a rectangle of gray cardboard. She tried to guess whether Priscilla had met him in that office and said the thing about not calling him Pastor Julius with that in mind. Or maybe it was just his thing. This church was pretty casual about issues like that. In contrast to Detta's church.

Sophie sat in a leather chair with padded wooden arms. It made a scrunching sound when she lowered her weight into it. She wore black jeans and a loose cotton blouse. Modest attire for a pastoral meeting. She checked to be sure no cleavage was showing just as Julius swept into the room behind her.

"Comfortable?"

"Very. Nice chair."

"Isn't it? Marcy found it in a consignment shop downtown. She's a bonified treasure hunter." Marcy was his wife, Sophie was pretty sure.

"Yeah, that's cool. My apartment is about half furnished with Salvation Army stuff."

He grinned at her as he sat down. His light blue eyes were usually wide open, like he was waiting for someone to laugh at a joke he just told. "So, I was hoping we would get a chance to talk. I've heard some amazing stories about your gift for seeing angels."

"That's what I wanted to talk to you about. About using my gift for ministry."

"Like, for deliverance ministry?"

"Sure. I guess that is the obvious thing."

"Yes. Though I would think a worship leader might want to hear some specifics about angelic activity in a service. We might look at doing something with that."

Sophie was having a hard time getting out of low gear, stalled over how readily this pastor just assumed she was legit even though she had never made any effort to convince him. Clearly, he was responding to what others had told him.

She hadn't been hiding her gift all this time. And he certainly knew about at least one situation she'd helped with—a woman plagued by a nasty animal-spirit thing. Sophie was nodding, but that was more a placeholder than an answer.

"So, what did you specifically want to talk about?"

"Well, I'm thinking of spending some time helping Bruce Albright and his wife with their traveling deliverance ministry." She paused for some sign of recognition from him.

"You mind if I Google them?" He tipped his head toward his laptop.

"No. That would probably help." Maybe he really was the geek he appeared to be.

Julius typed, backspaced, and typed some more. Then he grabbed the mouse and started scrolling, finally clicking on something. "As with lots of good ministries, you have to get past the haters to get to some real info." He kept his eyes on the screen even as he explained himself to Sophie.

She hadn't done a web search for Bruce Albright and company, relying entirely on Jonathan's recommendation, a direct link to their website, and the utterly normal conversations she'd had with Bruce and Deborah.

"Looks like a mainstream evangelical ministry with endorsements from some folks I recognize. And they're part of a bigger ministry that addresses more than just deliverance."

"That's good, right?"

He nodded and looked at Sophie. "Sure. But what makes you want to sign up with them?"

She assumed he meant *sign up* in a generic sense. "I do like helping people get free. My part is pretty easy, really. I've worked with a counselor in the city who I met through a close friend. And the transformation in people is ... well, it's kinda addicting."

Smiling, Julius nodded more emphatically. "I know what you mean. But why this group? Why would you want to work with a ministry so dedicated to addressing demons?"

"I guess because it fits my gift so well."

"You can really see things, can't you?"

"I can."

"Anything to report in here?" He raised his eyebrows like a kid asking for a new toy.

Sophie took a deep breath and glanced toward the corners of the room. "I suppose you always have those two that are hanging around there and there. They look like guards to me. But I also see this beautiful woman standing behind your chair. She strikes me as a messenger. Now that I focus on her, I can see her whispering into your ear."

Julius shivered visibly. "Whoa! Yeah. Okay. Wow. I can feel the confirmation of what you're saying." He took a few seconds to slow his breathing, sliding his glasses up his nose a bit.

She waited while he recovered, blinking away a little tear from the corner of her own eye.

He sniffed once. "Wow. Thanks for that." He took a deep breath. "So, huh, why not just dig in here and do what comes your way?" He glanced over his shoulder. Was he hoping to catch a glimpse? "I'm just wondering if it would be best for you to go with these folks on their traveling deliverance missions."

"You do deliverance ministry around here, I know. But how regularly?"

"Sure. We do it whenever needed. We don't back off when we run into a spirit that has to be kicked out. But we don't put out a shingle for it either." He leaned back and settled his elbows on the arms of his office chair. One sleeve of his beige button-up shirt was coming unrolled. He didn't seem to notice. "For us, it's just part of the prayer and healing ministry that our people do. All kinds of people." He stopped and stared at Sophie. "But ... you have a particular gift. And I can understand you wanting to take it to a new level." He cleared his throat. "Do you have people you're regularly in touch with? People who keep you grounded and help you sort things that come your way?"

Sophie immediately thought of Detta. Jonathan and Ellen did that for her too. And Anthony and Priscilla to an extent. "I do. I have a few trusted people. Including my mother."

He grinned with half his face and nodded contemplatively. "I believe you do. I have a good feeling about you, Sophie. I sense that you're a warrior who has settled into a vital secondary role right now. And I believe that's okay at this point. But you have a calling, I think, that will eventually take you more to the front of ... to a leadership role in the ministry you do. You're learning now. You're being equipped. And you're shoring up the people around you who you'll need for support later."

Staring with her mouth slightly open, Sophie recalled hearing people say things like that to others in the church. It was like a word of encouragement or even a prophecy. "You see all that?"

"I think so. I don't always see clearly, not perfectly. But I have a strong impression about you and your future. I bless the process, and I will pray for this adventure with the

Albrights, that it will build you up and not tear you down in any way."

"Thanks. Uh, thank you for praying for me. I really appreciate it."

"You have folks who pray for you regularly?"

"I do. My friend Bernadetta is part of a prayer group. She calls them prayer warriors. She makes sure they all keep praying for me."

"That's great. Exactly what you need."

Though his few skeptical questions about the Albrights left an aftertaste, Sophie departed Julius's office greatly encouraged. He had reinforced some of her own hesitation about her mission to Iowa, but he seemed as willing for her to give it a try as she was. And it was very encouraging to hear his words about her future as well as his promise to pray for her.

It felt like she received a new piece of armor that afternoon.

What Her Mother Wants

Sophie had missed dinner with her mother for two weeks straight. She was determined to fit into her mother's busy professional schedule, so they met on Friday that week.

"Sorry to take you away from your social life on a Friday." Her mother kissed her on the cheek as Sophie came in the front door. A billowing breeze pushed in after her.

"Oh, that's no problem. I wanted to be sure to see you before I go on this little trip next week."

"The way you say that makes me worry. Should I be worried?"

"Of course not. You're not ever supposed to worry." She patted her mother on the cheek and smiled. "But, to be real, I am a little anxious about it myself. So, I suppose you will be too when I tell you what it is."

With a large inhale and a resigned tilt of her head, her mother led the way to the kitchen. "Supper is almost ready. Tell me what you're doing."

Sophie sat down and explained the opportunity to work with the Albrights, though she didn't call them demon hunters. And the venture was surely going to trouble her mother enough without Sophie saying anything about the dark spiritual history of the Iowa town. So she left that out.

"Is this, like, a time for you to practice and advance your skills? I don't think you really need that, do you?" Her mother had settled all the food on the table. She was looking around the kitchen as if to confirm she had everything.

"I don't think of it that way. I just heard Jonathan explain how the Albrights need help from folks like me—someone who can see what's going on in the spirit realm. They already work with people they trust who have some gifts, but he thought my level of seeing would be extra useful." Sophie slid two tamales onto her plate.

"Because the people they minister to are extra troubled?"

"Maybe that. Some of that, I suppose." Sophie scooped beans and rice onto her plate. "I think part of it is just for me. Not finding a good job yet and not really knowing what I want to do with my life. I mean, I'm leaving things unsettled between me and Anthony too. I know he wants more. He at least wants to talk about it being more. But I keep putting him off."

"Oh. Well, you're not going to solve *that* by traveling to Iowa."

"It will give me some space from everything and help me decide what I should be doing. A ministry like the Albrights' could be the kind of thing I was made for."

"Are you considering doing this all the time? I'm not sure that would be good for you, Sophie."

"I know. My pastor said something similar. But I'm not committing to anything. Just testing it out. Maybe these aren't the kind of people I should work with. Maybe I should be doing this kind of work but doing it with a different ministry."

Her mother sighed and put down her fork. She hesitated as she reached for her water glass. "I'm glad you're getting good counsel from your pastor. And I know Detta is always helpful. These are not things I have a lot of experience with. So, I am glad you can ask others for wisdom."

Sophie smiled at her dear mother. "You're the one who taught me what wisdom is. I want to hear what you have to say. You *know* me. And you know all about my gifts. I come to you for wisdom too, Mama."

Sitting back to contemplate Sophie for a second, her mother squinted slightly. "I expect you will have a ministry of your own someday. I expect you will be a leader, not assisting others in *their* ministry so much. And I will keep praying that you are protected as you find your way into that. You are a warrior, Sophie, and I know I should not stand in the way of that."

The parallel with what Julius had said sent a tremor up Sophie's spine. She laughed self-consciously. "Ho. That was just like what my pastor said to me. I felt like he was sort of prophesying about my future."

"Prophesying? I don't know about that. But you are right. I do know you and I have seen what you are capable of."

On the way home, Sophie took a call from Kimmy.

"I may have made a big mistake. I think I really am too old to start being a mother." Kimmy's voice was tattered and unusually deep.

"Is there something I can help with? You want me to watch Betsy this weekend? You and Jack can go out and relax."

"Huh. Thanks, Sophie. That's so sweet. Actually, tomorrow my mother is coming over to watch her for the afternoon so we can do some shopping. But thanks for offering. Maybe next week."

"Well, next week I head to Iowa for this ministry opportunity. So maybe after that."

"Ministry opportunity? What's that?"

"Well, it's some of that stuff I've been doing around here, you know ..." Among all Sophie's close friends, Kimmy was the one who knew the least about her ministry work. Kimmy still wasn't part of a church. She had been busy getting married and having a baby while Sophie was finding her place in a church.

"Uh, okay. I don't need to know the details. It would probably just make me even tireder. Just keep praying for Betsy like you did. I appreciate that."

Sophie had taken a lesson from some friends at her church who prayed for a newborn and her family by blessing the baby's room, including welcoming angelic protection. She could see the baby was protected but could also see the value in verbally affirming that protection. And Kimmy and Jack had welcomed Sophie's blessing. They weren't active churchgoers, but they were accepting of Sophie's faith.

"How is Betsy doing?"

"She's a bit cranky. We suspect she's allergic to something I'm eating. Wheat or dairy maybe. I'm starting to cut back on dairy this week to see if it helps."

"Oh. Sorry to hear that. Well, I'll pray for all that too."

"Thanks, Sophie. Thanks for being a really good godmother."

"Right. None of that wicked godmother stuff from me." Sophie slowed her car to a stop at a light. She averted her eyes from a pair of surly demons standing on the corner as if waiting to waylay passersby.

"Ha. Yeah. None of that. When do you go on your mission?"

"Uh, I leave Thursday for a few days. Not absolutely sure how long."

"You getting time off?"

"Yeah, I can take off. I'll work through the weekend to finish a project by Tuesday or Wednesday, but it all works out."

"Good. Sounds good. You sound really healthy."

"Thanks. You sound tired. But that can be healthy when you're a new mom."

"I hope so. I just may be too old for this."

And they were back to where they had started the conversation. Sophie said a silent prayer before hanging up and another after. She took her godmothering responsibilities seriously.

Literally Chasing One

Anthony stood up when Sophie pushed through the screen door of the coffee shop. It was still early, moderately cool outside. The shop door was open, inviting a breeze to the tables spaced over the shiny oak floor. Sophie looked relaxed and happy. Her hair was almost to her shoulders now, and she wore it loose today. She rarely appeared worried about her looks. No makeup as usual. But a fresh smile for him.

He kissed her on the cheek the way he had seen her mother do. She had never objected. "Howdy, girl. How you doin'?"

"I'm doin' fine, pardner." She smirked at him. "What did you order?"

"Tall American."

"Tall, dark, and handsome American."

"Yours truly."

She also didn't seem to mind him flirting. She gave as well as she got. "I'll get a latte." She snickered and headed for the counter.

He had debated ordering her a latte, knowing that was her pre-lunch drink of choice. But she didn't always order it the same way. Extra shot? Caramel or vanilla? Sophie was a little unpredictable. On lattes as well as other things.

Setting his phone aside when she finally arrived back with her *medium* latte, he smiled at her. That was another option he might have gotten wrong—size. She wasn't looking at him just then. Sophie was easily distracted. Usually by things only she could see. This current preoccupation seemed particularly intense. She was squinting at the space just behind him.

"What did you say?" She wasn't talking to him. She was looking past him and higher. She asked again. "Wait. What did you say? I wanna understand what you just said." Sophie set her latte on the table and looked as if she was about to grab some guy by the lapels.

Anthony peeled himself out of his shock and looked over his shoulder. Of course there was no one he could see. He checked around. No one else seemed to be disturbed by Sophie talking to the air above his head. Before he could even form a whole word to question her, Sophie strode toward the door.

"Wait. Please, tell me what you said." She was leaving.

Anthony grabbed his phone and stood to go with her. Then he looked at the two paper cups of coffee on the table. He grabbed them both. The screen door was just slamming when he got to it. He glimpsed the heel of Sophie's running shoe heading west on Korsten Street. He fumbled with the door until he got an assist from a skinny guy trying to leave after him.

"Thanks, man."

"Better hurry to catch her."

Anthony eyeballed the guy for a second, but he didn't have time to figure out if the young Caucasian guy was making fun of him.

Sloshing travel cups in both hands, he cranked up his speed walk, as if he were late for the train and too cool to run. Running with two full coffees wouldn't be cool.

Sophie was pausing at the next corner, checking for traffic. At least she was aware that there was traffic to consider while chasing an invisible stranger. That was a little reassuring. But then she started sprinting. She called again, "Wait, please. I didn't catch what you said. I wasn't listening."

Anthony slammed on his brakes and sloshed a bit of his coffee up through the sipping hole onto his right hand. He nodded apologetically to a guy in a sports car turning the corner in front of him. Then he was off at his fast walk again. He could still see Sophie. She hadn't changed direction. But she was almost a block ahead by now. He dodged pedestrians coming at him and tried to keep track of her.

A city garbage can caught his attention. He said goodbye to both coffees and wiped his hands on the back of his jeans as he accelerated to a jog. He was too far behind to stick with being cool.

"Soph—" He stopped himself from calling when he saw her duck into an alleyway. That new direction concerned him more, but he was sure she wouldn't hear him calling until he reached the corner of that building. By the time he reached that turn, he was stoking frustration at the angel Sophie was chasing. Why wouldn't it just stop and repeat the message?

He couldn't see Sophie around the dumpsters and stacks of pallets in the alley. Then he heard pounding.

"Hey. I can't walk through a door like you can. This isn't fair—" Sophie's complaint stopped abruptly.

Fortunately, Anthony saw her when he rounded one of those dumpsters, assured that she had stopped her complaining of her own volition. She stood in front of an open door. A small East Asian woman was looking up at Sophie. The eye contact was a strain for one party. The old woman's back was severely hunched, and Sophie was a head taller than her.

"Come. Come." The old woman gestured, and Sophie followed.

Anthony landed at that door just in time to keep it from closing behind Sophie. He briefly entertained the wild possibility that the old woman was the one Sophie had been chasing. Couldn't these things shapeshift? Well, maybe not. That was only in movies. And that was aliens.

The corridor into which he stepped was warm and dark. A yellow light shone from an open door several paces down the hall.

Sophie suddenly appeared in that lighted doorway. "Anthony, come on. I need your help."

He raised a hand to his chest but stopped himself from saying, "Who, me?" He was surprised she knew he was still behind her. But then, Sophie knew a lot of things that he was surprised to discover.

She waved for him to follow her, gesturing in much the same way the little old lady had beckoned her.

Anthony followed Sophie into a room in which two young women sat on cots. One was scowling in a way that seemed unnatural. Strained and intense.

"She has this spirit clamped on her, and it seems to be, like, locking her down. And the angel I was following is, like, poised over her for action. I assume he wants us to start the action."

The scowling girl grabbed her stomach and began to moan.

"The spirit is grabbing her insides."

Anthony was glad for the vague anatomical reference. He didn't want the exact details. "What are we supposed to do?"

"You know. It's like that time with Kimmy, when she had that thing grabbing her on the throat."

He did remember that time with Kimmy. It was at least a year ago, but he would never forget the panic and then the relief when Sophie's friend stopped turning blue and breathed easily. At least he wouldn't forget that incident unless he was going to have to keep doing stuff like this with Sophie.

"Okay. Just tell me what to do."

Sophie pointed to the floor in front of the small woman who had long black hair and dark almond eyes. She pinched those eyes closed again, moaning with pain.

"In the name of Jesus, I command this afflicting spirit to stop harming this girl." Sophie leaned down. "What's your name?" Then she looked up at the other young woman seated on the cot behind Anthony. "What's her name?"

The second girl said something to the first girl in Chinese, presumably, and then said to Sophie, "You can call her Amber."

That answer froze Sophie for a second. Anthony assumed she was assessing whether a made-up Anglo name would suffice for this kind of work.

"Amber? Are you with me?"

The girl looked up at Sophie. "It hurts. Can you help?"

The old woman said something very rapidly, probably in Chinese.

Amber seemed to be responding to the old woman. She spoke in a low, groaning voice. "I was honoring one of my ancestors and this pain started. Grandmother says he was not a good man, and I shouldn't have been honoring him."

Anthony recognized his own confusion in Sophie's face, but she shook it off and started from there. "I break the power of this ancestor spirit off Amber right now. The ancestor spirit and the afflicting spirit grabbing her must let go of her right now." She cocked her head back slightly. "The angel is, like, wrestling that spirit." She glanced over her shoulder at Anthony. "Pray. Pray like your mother would."

He almost busted a laugh at that description, but he knew exactly what she meant. He started praising Jesus and declaring him Lord of this situation and calling for his glory to fill the room and to fill Amber and Sophie and all of them. He basically just let his mouth run. Not to say his mother did it that way, but he felt like he had plugged into something, maybe something his mother had installed in him. Hopefully it was something like faith.

"You say it, now, Anthony. Tell the afflicting spirit to let go and leave without hurting anyone." Sophie looked at him and then scowled for a second toward a pair of burning incense sticks on a shelf above the cot.

With his mouth already rolling fast in neutral, it wasn't so hard for him to repeat what Sophie was saying.

Then Sophie piled on. "Yes, Lord. I bless your angel, your messenger, to win this fight. And I claim this space for you and your glory." Her authoritative tone gave Anthony more confidence.

With that rising confidence came a sort of freshness in the air.

"There it goes." Sophie smiled at Amber.

The girl took a deep breath and raised her head. She almost smiled.

But that celebration ended quickly when the old lady started flapping her arms and spouting words in whatever language she spoke. Then she barked and fell to the floor.

Sophie grimaced and shook her head at Anthony. "I don't know why she went down, but it must be okay. That angel I was following is with her, and my angels are, like, watching with their arms crossed. *'No worries'* is what I see on them."

"Really?" Of course Anthony barely even qualified as a novice in these things. Why couldn't it be okay for the old lady to hit the deck like that? Actually, she seemed at peace now. A childish grin on her face revealed a lot of missing teeth, but it seemed a genuinely restful smile.

"Are you okay, Amber?"

"May Lei. My Chinese name is May Lei." She nodded. "I am much better. Grandmother has faith. She is under the power of God now. She could not have God on her like that if that the ancestor was with us still."

Sophie's nodding was a bit loose, like she was reserving the option of going horizontal with her head bobble. But she was smiling, maybe forcing a smile. Her discomfort at this point was actually reassuring to Anthony. But that was probably selfish of him.

Speaking of selfish, now they would have to go back and buy coffee all over again.

A Strange & Assuring Intro

Sophie walked down the concourse away from the gate where her flight had deplaned. When she approached the windows where she could see cabs and shuttle buses, she looked around for a familiar face. As familiar as any new face could be in the airport's required medical mask. There was a young man staring at her. He waved and called her name. Was that Ross? She hadn't seen his face, not even in photos on the web. Deborah had said, "One of us will meet you at arrivals." Apparently, Ross counted as one of *them*.

She approached him despite the large belligerent beast standing behind him. That monster appeared to be accompanying Ross, though not exactly attached the way spirits often were. Sophie forced herself to focus on the young man instead of the demon. "Hello. Sorry I didn't recognize you."

"Not until you heard me speak, anyway." He had pale skin, bulgy eyes, and straight brown hair that was a bit mussed up in a stylish way.

She laughed. His voice did sound familiar.

"Just the carry-on luggage?" He looked at her small rolling case.

"Yep. It's enough for the weekend."

"Yeah. It shouldn't take more than a few days. But your return flight Monday is refundable, so we can switch if we have to."

"Great. That works." She followed his lead toward a revolving door. "Have you guys worked with people who took more than a few days to get free?"

"Oh, yeah. All the time. But Bruce and Deborah are counting on you speeding things up for us." His eyes squinted as he grinned.

"No pressure."

"Right. *Our* flights aren't set until Tuesday."

"Huh." She looked over her shoulder and reassessed the big bruiser that stayed immediately behind Ross. She could see two angels following just behind the grumpy ghoul. That order was all wrong. Should she say something? Of course she should say something. But when?

"Are you looking for someone?"

"No, just checking the … surroundings." All three of her angels were fully visible. They seemed to be positioning themselves in a line that blocked the big bad guy from her but not from Ross. She really wanted to talk to them about this configuration, but it didn't seem like an appropriate setting for an angel question-and-answer session. And who knew if they would talk to her?

She decided to try a circuitous approach to Ross's problem. "How often do you get to take a break? This must be pretty intense work." They slowed to a stop next to the curb outside the terminal.

"I get time off at holidays and whenever I'm feeling stressed or anything."

"You ever get, like, residual effects from the spirits you deal with?"

"I'm mostly taking notes and observing, not really in the hot seat. So they usually ignore me. Bruce and Deborah take turns in the lead depending on who they're dealing with and what the need is."

"You said *usually*. I bet they don't always ignore you. The spirits, I mean."

They were stepping onto a shuttle bus when he figured it out. "Wait. Are you seeing something that's ... with me?" He whispered the last two words despite the noise of the bus and the absence of people right next to where they had settled themselves.

Sophie assessed Ross to guess how he would respond to what she was seeing. "You seem to have, like, a stalker. He follows you and seems to be getting in the way of your angels."

"Angels?" His voice cracked as he crossed the line from stage whisper to full voice. He checked the handful of other passengers as if worried they had heard him.

"I've noticed that folks who do active ministry like the kind you do often have more than one visible angel. I'm also pretty sure I don't see all the holy angels at any given time. I can't say for sure about the unholy kind either."

The slow calculations he seemed to be doing internally surprised Sophie. How long had he been doing this work? How much did he really know about the spirit realm? And how much did he trust what she was saying? Lots of questions. But she held onto them while he appeared to run through a few reboot cycles.

"We can talk about it with Bruce and Deborah. Maybe that would be better." Sophie tried not to sound patronizing. She was certainly several years older than Ross. And he seemed a bit out of his depth.

"No. I mean, yeah. That makes sense. We should do that." He cast an eye over one shoulder.

"Straight behind you. Always straight behind you, as if to keep you from noticing him. He's, like, embedded in the side of the bus now."

Ross stared at Sophie with his eyebrows straining upward. "But I don't see … I mean, why would he have to hide? I've never been able to … to see any of that stuff."

"Sometimes I think what I see is mostly symbolic. I mean, these things aren't like us. They don't have to move as slow as us or be limited by physical things. So, I feel like lots of times I'm just getting a sort of message about what matters rather than an actual video feed of physical realities. They're spirits. This one seems to just stay out of your line of sight, basically."

He took a deep breath and stood up quickly. "This is our stop."

Sophie hesitated, a bit shocked at Ross standing up so quickly. As much as she was trying to sound casual, that big stalker was actually making her nervous. Shaking her head at herself, she grabbed the handle of her case and followed Ross off the bus.

"So, you think that one is always directly behind me to symbolize that it's staying where I can't see it or, like, be aware that it's there?" He spoke loudly as a jet took off nearby.

She was impressed that he got right back to that point, let alone that he understood the implications. "I think that's right. Or something like that."

"Huh. Is that normal?" He pulled his disposable mask off.

She twisted a grimace after removing hers. "*Normal* is an idea I'm tempted to address now and again, but I generally resist that temptation."

He barked a laugh. "Huh. I guess that … that would be a problem."

This was another of those moments where Sophie couldn't help marveling at how readily someone believed what she was saying, no matter how outside the box it was. Jonathan must have strongly vouched for her, and Bruce's team must really trust Jonathan. That was all she could figure.

At the hotel, after introductions, including a hug for Sophie from Deborah, Ross jumped right into what Sophie had been telling him. "She says I have a large demon following me wherever I go."

Sophie didn't remember saying anything about the spirit's size. What did its dimensions really matter? Size was probably symbolic too. But Ross might have calculated the size of the beast by the angle of Sophie's gaze. The thing did appear to be about seven feet tall and almost as wide. She offered a small sideways smile. Maybe it was an apology for getting in so deep so quickly. But she wasn't sure she needed to apologize for anything.

"Really? Following?" Bruce evaluated Ross from a safe distance. "Not, uh, attached?"

Sophie looked at the thing. "What comes to mind is something about an *assignment*. Does that word make sense?"

"Assignment. We've heard of that." Deborah stepped closer to Ross and grasped her husband's arm as if to pull him in with her.

"Yes. That fits." Bruce adopted a more aggressive tone. "It's an assignment from the enemy to mess with Ross and his ministry."

"But what about you guys?" Ross looked from Deborah to Bruce.

Sophie was only now slowing herself to consider whether the hotel lobby was the best place to discuss all this. She watched an elderly couple bickering. A small demon floated between them, as if it were filtering what they said to each other. She focused on the assignment guy and caught him waving his arms as if conducting an orchestra. Another symbolic gesture. Pretty obvious. The beast following Ross was orchestrating a bit of chaos in the lobby just then. That might have been his role in Ross's life in general. To stir things up around him, even if it couldn't attach itself directly.

"Can we get somewhere more private? This stalker guy is stirring up trouble in the lobby." She lowered her voice and hunkered closer to the other three.

Deborah, Bruce, and Ross all stared at Sophie. Their locked gazes were all the same. Stunned but not doubtful. It was like an "Oh, yeah" sort of pause.

"Sure. We can go up to our suite." Bruce stopped staring and glanced toward the elevators.

Bruce and Deborah's room was literally a suite, but not a luxurious one. It wasn't a fancy hotel, part of a moderately priced chain. Even its suites were generic and dull. The four of them entered a small sitting room. The most interesting things to see there were the gathered angels. The gang of demons was unimpressive, easily upstaged by the seven or eight angels.

The most captivating of these was extremely large. He looked like a bearded man, and he sat in the corner of the suite, too tall to stand in that room. He seemed to be in charge. And he reminded Sophie of the time she had seen what she still thought of as Jesus in her apartment.

"Are you an angel?" she asked him without speaking aloud.

The giant nodded and smiled. That was the sort of angel communication she was used to.

"Well, do the angels at least outnumber the demons in here?" Bruce stood in the middle of the room watching Sophie's preoccupation with things he clearly could not see.

"They do. And they're much more impressive."

"Okay. Let's break off that assignment before we do anything else. We don't need any interference as we go about our business."

When Sophie checked Ross, he was standing alone with his hands in the pockets of his skinny jeans. She hadn't noticed his little bit of paunch hanging over the waistband until then. His shifting eyes reminded her of a kid at a new school waiting for someone to befriend him. Sophie followed the urge that stirred. She took two small steps and rested a hand on Ross's shoulder. "It's gonna be fine."

She glimpsed Deborah and Bruce exchanging a small smile between them.

"Ross. Take a seat, will ya?" Bruce pulled a chair away from the little round table near the tall windows.

The curtains were open far enough to show about a third of the view. Not a very exciting view. Just a highway interchange and a few gas stations and restaurants. They were on the eighth floor near the top of the hotel.

For Sophie, that view was suddenly obscured by a huge, angry face. She blurted a fragment of a scream, then clapped a hand over her mouth.

"Something else?" Deborah was next to Sophie, replacing Ross, who had taken a seat.

"A really big one. I assume a ruler in this area."

"What does it look like?"

"A very angry old man. Just plain wicked."

"Hmm. Is it unusual for one to look like an old man?"

"Actually, I think it *is* unusual. I don't remember that impression before. Or at least nothing comes to mind now." She had to force her voice to maintain a steady altitude.

Bruce had stepped next to them, nodding. He didn't even bother to look out the window. "Okay. In the name of Jesus, I command all local spirits to stay outside this room and in no way interfere with the people or spirits inside." He turned to Ross as soon as he finished.

Deborah followed up. "We claim the blood of the true Lord Jesus Christ over this hotel room for now and as long as we have authority here. We will not allow any new spirits to come in or affect the people in this suite in any way."

For the most part, Sophie was right at home. She had heard Jonathan, Sister Ellen, and Detta say things like that. She had even said similar words herself. What stood out was the apparently rehearsed clarity Deborah and Bruce sustained throughout. No emotion, just business. Their tone was unfamiliar but somehow comforting. These people were pros.

The rest of the session proceeded with practiced scripts and easy unity between Deborah and Bruce. The cooperation between them was also confidence producing. Even Ross started to relax as Bruce investigated how the assignment received access to him, then broke all connections.

Bruce and Deborah's voices each fluctuated just slightly on one or two occasions. Sophie could sense their attachment to Ross and guessed that personal connection dented their professionalism just a little.

The demonic choreography around the ministry time was nothing more than a little distracting. Sophie had grown less fascinated by the dramatics of all sorts of demons. Little of it appeared to affect Ross, though he did start to sweat visibly just before the big burly guy finally took off. It had apparently gained access to Ross through a recent association with a young woman. Sophie was glad to not discover any of the details of that relationship during the session. She was not a counselor and had no ambitions in that direction.

Ross was inhaling yet another big breath and wiping at his forehead when the first smile bloomed on his face. He had a boyish smile. Though Bruce and Deborah were probably too young to be his actual parents, the scene at the end of the ministry session resembled mom, dad, and son finished with the hard chores of the day.

Bruce had rolled up his sleeves in the middle of the process—an ironic act, given how effortless the work seemed for him. That effortlessness was certainly increased by Sophie's contributions, assessing the status and confirming the movement of the spirits.

When the big stalker flew out the window—without breaking glass—he took with him three subservient spirits. One of those looked like the joker in a deck of cards. Curious. Nonetheless, Sophie didn't say anything about that.

Calling it a Calling

"When did you know this was what you would do full time?" Sophie sat in a corner booth in the hotel restaurant across from Bruce and Deborah. Ross sat to her right, as quiet as a person exhausted by a long journey. Probably not the trip to the airport.

Deborah looked at Bruce before answering. She set her iced tea on the table and wiped her hands on a paper napkin. "We were pastoring in Florida, a denominational church. I was the typical pastor's wife in the modern mode. In charge of this and that. And a lady who was part of a Bible study I led had come out of the occult. She was actually a professional palm reader at some point. She got converted at a big evangelistic rally in the area and found our church after that."

"I remember how befuddled we were after the first Bible study where she started manifesting demons." Bruce had that small, knowing smile on again. He was looking at his plate, not at Deborah.

Rolling her eyes just briefly, Deborah resumed. "Yes. We were both baffled. I mean, Bruce had not covered that in seminary, and I could only tell him what I was seeing. Like, she had this way of switching her eyes. I think we've seen it a time or two since. It was like she had an extra set of lids almost, that changed the color and texture of her eyes. Like a lizard or something. That was so outrageous that I refused to believe I was really seeing it at the time."

"But there was a woman in that group who saw it and knew what it was." Bruce glanced at his wife and nodded at the memory.

"Charlotte Fuller. She was a former missionary in Papua New Guinea. She knew what was going on, and she even had some ideas about what to do with it. She managed to get that woman—I'll leave her name out—to come back to the group and start to talk about what was happening. The woman did come back the next week, but only about half of the others in the group showed up."

"You can't blame them. None of us had a grid for that stuff at the time." Bruce looked up at the server carrying their main courses and offered a greeting smile.

Deborah didn't let the arrival of the food end her story. She recalled the process of searching around their denomination for someone who knew what to do for the woman. Bruce shook his head when she recounted how many of the leaders in their Protestant denomination suggested they contact the Catholic church.

"We did end up learning quite a bit from a couple of priests. One we never met. We just read his books and listened to his podcasts." Bruce cut into his fish with his fork.

"They didn't call them podcasts back then though." Deborah grinned at him, teasing probably.

"So, you helped that woman and then you thought you could just go on helping others?" Sophie found the chicken breast she had ordered was hard and dry, overcooked.

"Actually, the other priest who helped us, the one we did meet, gave us some hands-on instructions for setting the woman free. That included sending us to observe the lay ministers who did most of the actual deliverance for their parish." Bruce looked at Deborah as if to hand the story back to her.

"We got to watch those folks operate, and it seemed we just had to learn the rules so we could do it ourselves. Find out how a demon got access, break off that access. It was all new to us, but it all made sense once we got a good look at it." Deborah seemed uninterested in her food. Perhaps it was as bad as Sophie's.

Bruce swallowed and interjected. "And that first woman we helped had friends who started coming to the church. Eventually a couple of them also needed some form of deliverance." He gave half a shrug. "After that, we became the go-to people for our denomination. It wasn't that no one else had ever found the need before. They just referred people to psychiatrists or Catholic priests before."

"So, you two brought it in-house. Then you started helping folks from other church associations?" Sophie was working on her green beans and mashed potatoes. Not much hope for that chicken.

Deborah took another stab at her salad. "We ran into some resistance in our own denomination. We started benefiting from the gifts of people outside our faith tradition. That offended some, but we didn't let that stop us. We discovered along the way that we need folks like you, Sophie, to be sure we know what's really happening."

"You know other people like me?" Sophie regretted that childish question, including the slight crack in her voice.

Deborah smiled the motherly smile she had aimed at Ross before. "We have had the privileged to work with some very gifted seers or discerners, whatever you want to call them. But I expect none of them have the level of gifting and the calling you have, Sophie."

Nodding solemnly, Bruce evidently agreed, but he conserved his words. Maybe he hadn't seen enough yet to pronounce any conclusion about Sophie's skills.

Ross had become more animated by then. "I always wondered if they kicked you out of ... the denomination."

"We were invited to find another setting in which to pursue our calling." Bruce sounded like he was quoting a solemn document.

"They were gentle about it. And we were clearly ready for the change." Deborah added that amendment with a consoling tone.

"The biggest worry at the time was the finances. Devon and Carissa were barely teenagers. College still ahead and all that." Bruce raised his fork as if tallying those considerations on an invisible board.

"You have grown kids?" Sophie was recalculating their ages.

"Thank you for being surprised." Deborah lowered her face and her voice and gave some more attention to her dinner.

Bruce took a break from eating, most of his fish gone by then. "Anyway, we found a Christian psychiatrist who was starting this organization that primarily treats pastors and missionaries. He found a place for us in his interdenominational ministry. He also helped us raise money for support. A lot of our old friends in the denomination still contribute these many years later."

About the time Sophie had finished eating as much of her supper as she could, Bruce looked around the table. "Dessert, anyone?"

"No, thanks." Sophie declined out of habit as well as an expectation the desserts would be no better than the chicken.

Deborah looked at her sporty watch. "Oh, it's later than I thought. We should get some rest. We see Maris tomorrow at nine."

"Maris? That's the woman?"

"That's the woman." Bruce nodded once.

"Okay. I am tired." Sophie breathed a small, self-conscious laugh. She had already carried her things to her room. Not a suite, but the king-sized bed was a generous provision. And she didn't expect to do much more than sleep in her room. Probably Deborah had given it some thought. She and Bruce seemed like people determined to do everything thoughtfully and thoroughly. That worked for Sophie. And it seemed to be working well for lots of troubled people.

A Ripple on the Surface

When she pulled back the curtains the next morning, Sophie discovered she had a better view than Bruce and Deborah. A line of trees, a retention pond, and farm fields greeted her, backlit by the rising sun. She hadn't slept particularly well and was up early. The sunrise was almost worth it. She stood in her long T-shirt holding the curtain open, watching some kind of large bird rise from that pond. Maybe it was a few blocks away. Maybe half a mile. She couldn't judge distances out there in the wilds of Iowa. No sidewalks, no train stops, no buildings bigger than a gas station.

A swirling sensation forced her to grip the curtain more tightly to keep from reeling. Something had passed before her eyes. Was it near her? Was it way out there in the dawning light? The sky was more golden than red now, but that was probably just the natural sunrise progression. Something unnatural had disturbed her, had perhaps disturbed the atmosphere around the hotel. It reminded her of the time she had attracted the attention of a giant spirit propped against the building where she used to work. Back when she had a regular job.

The thought of her old job soured her mood. Worrying about her work on top of the task that lay ahead was too heavy to carry without a grimace. At least an internal scowl.

She got started on showering and dressing, ignoring the goings-on outside, turning her back on the bigger events that might conspire to affect her much smaller life. She ignored them while conscious of the inevitable ineffectiveness of that strategy. Ignoring them never made them go away. At best, she would buy some time.

    Sophie settled in at a table for four, wondering if she should expect to see the rest of the team in the restaurant this early. Very few of the tables were occupied. A cute older couple were talking in low, confiding tones two tables away. She tried not to listen or even to watch the charming interaction. They must have been at least in their seventies. Pale and somewhat hunched, they nevertheless gave an impression of life and health.

    How much of that impression was natural observation and how much spiritual discernment, Sophie was determined *not* to figure out. At least not until she had her morning coffee.

    Breakfast was buffet style. Sophie followed the watering hole path between tables to the coffee station first. Intimidated by the self-serve latte machine, she just went for fresh-ground coffee.

    The old man of that couple swept up to the juice station a few feet away. "I recommend the cranberry. Very good." He winked at her before filling a new juice glass with the ruby liquid.

    She didn't make a sound, nor even an acknowledging gesture. She was too stunned by the muscular figure shadowing the old man. A golden angel dressed for war. At least dressed for wars fought in millennia past. He had shiny covers on his forearms. What were those called? She knew what a breastplate was called. And a shield.

"You see one, don't you?" The old man glanced over his shoulder as he stepped closer to her.

The angel stepped closer as well. Sophie shivered.

"You must be Sophie." He raised his eyebrows. "I think you have three with you."

"Three?" She turned to find her three familiar guards just behind her. The one she thought of as the warrior was armored more elaborately than she had ever noticed before. This unsettled Sophie even more than it reassured her. That the old man had recognized her had started the unsettling. "Uh, Sophie. Yes. Who are you? You know Bruce and …?" She had forgotten Mrs. Albright's name.

"Deborah. Yes. I'm Ivan. My wife is Lee. We've done ministry here a few times. They have a good buffet. Is Ross with them?"

"He is. He's here somewhere." Sophie couldn't shake off the sleepwalker feeling. The old man had initially struck her as one of those seniors who started a conversation with anyone he came across. The angel, on the other hand, gave the impression of a champion ready to crush any enemy he came across.

Ivan smiled permissively at her tongue-tied awkwardness and headed back to his wife and their table.

Sophie scalded her tongue with a fast slurp of coffee. She winced and added more half-and-half to cool the fire. Pulling herself out of her mental skid, she grabbed a tray and carefully set her coffee in one corner. She loaded the tray with a fruit cup, oatmeal, eggs, and sausage. By the time she was fully alert, she was on the way back to her table with a pretty good looking breakfast.

Bruce and Deborah entered the restaurant after Sophie was seated and eating. She glanced from them to Ivan and Lee. That drew Bruce's attention to that other table, and generous greetings began between the two couples. Sophie watched from under her eyebrows, determined to get through her eggs while they were still warm.

Eventually, Bruce and Deborah joined Sophie at her table. She was deciding whether to finish the oatmeal and the sausage when they sat down. She opted for another cup of coffee instead, to keep her occupied as the others ate.

"So, uh, Ivan can see spirits? Or he just senses them?" Sophie only asked after the old couple had finished eating and left for a walk outside.

Bruce finished buttering his blueberry muffin. "I always had the impression that he knows what's in the room in an intuitive way. Seeing hasn't been the way he describes what he knows. And Lee has a strong sense of sympathy for the folks we minister to." He bit into the muffin.

"Sympathy?"

"She can usually tell us what's going on emotionally with our people." Deborah bobbed her head side to side. "And that's crucial when they're unable to communicate clearly for themselves. Lee's insights have proved true many times."

"Yeah, I guess that would be helpful." Sophie reran moments from ministry sessions she had been involved with. "I mean, you wanna get the person invested in what's going on, but sometimes that's really hard to do." She remembered to start on her second cup of coffee before it turned tepid.

"How many sessions have you done with Jonathan?" Bruce checked Sophie from under his eyebrows, still intent on his breakfast.

"Almost a dozen, I think."

"You've worked with other folks, I assume?" Deborah leaned back and lifted her coffee cup.

Sophie nodded. "And on my own once in a while. Or with whoever I can recruit in the moment." She thought of Anthony following her into that alley last week.

"Really? Sort of in the heat of the moment?" Bruce might have been impressed. Or maybe that was skeptical. She couldn't read him very clearly. Unlike Lee, insight into the emotional state of the humans around her was not one of Sophie's gifts.

"Yeah. I'm used to just ignoring what I see around me. I rarely intervene. But sometimes it's ... I just can't resist. Like when one of the angels gets me involved."

"I suppose it's hard to refuse an angel." Deborah's tone was wistful. Did she wish angels would tell her when she could set someone free of the creepy critter clinging to them? A lot of people wished they could see the good angels. Sophie hadn't met many who wished they could see the other ones.

"The angels usually don't talk to me. Only a couple times recently have they done that. But I can often tell what they want me to do. I guess body language is pretty universal."

"Universal including angels?" Again Bruce seemed amused, but maybe not in a sympathetic way. Was he laughing at her?

That was when Sophie spotted something strange next to her coffee cup. She had seen spirits of all sizes. This was one of the smallest she had ever noticed. It was peeking out at her and suddenly froze when she returned the attention. Then it vanished in a poof of smoke or dust or something. Pixie dust? "What the ...?"

"Huh?" Bruce and Deborah turned toward Sophie simultaneously.

In their eyes, especially Bruce's, Sophie saw only curiosity, none of the accusation or mockery she had been imagining. The little imp might have had something to do with that distorted perception.

"A small accusing spirit. I think it was trying to mess with our communication."

Both Bruce and Deborah just nodded with tight lips. They had probably heard it all before, if not seen it.

Their first meeting with Maris was in a small conference room on the first floor of the hotel. The fifty-year-old woman with short blonde hair and a bright smile entered the room a few minutes late. She had a twenty-something woman with her.

"Maris, this is Sophie and Ross. You've met Ivan and Lee, of course."

Maris reached back for the younger woman with her and pulled her in close. "And this is my daughter, Heather."

Her daughter didn't resist being drawn into the circle, but her lips remained locked. She only nodded her greeting.

Sophie shook Maris's hand distractedly. Usually by the time Sophie met with people who required special deliverance ministry, their distress was obvious. Maris showed none of the erratic behavior that often started a deliverance session. She wore smart designer glasses with dark red frames that lifted a hint of red from her hair. She had deep smile lines, and the smile that carved them was winning and true. This was not who Sophie expected to meet this morning. She looked at Heather, wondering if the younger woman was actually the one they should be ministering to. Heather remained stiff and might have even twitched a time or two.

"So, are you the one who can actually see those things—angels and demons?" Maris spoke with the curiosity of a science fiction fan discussing the possibility of a UFO sighting. She raised her head as if reading Sophie through the bottom half of her glasses.

Sophie nodded. "Uh, yeah. I can." Her answer was muted by the fact that she could see nothing particular on Maris or her daughter. She was, however, seeing a similar disturbance to the one that rattled her early that morning. It was like someone was wiping a hand over the surface of the world, disturbing it temporarily like it was a glassy pool.

Maris seemed to be watching Sophie as if testing how much she could see. Was she manipulating Sophie in some way? Was she manipulating spirits? Something about Maris resembled the new-age guru who tried to recruit Sophie a few years ago. Maxwell Hartman. There was a sort of pressure in the air around Maris that reminded Sophie of him.

Perhaps oblivious to all that, Bruce took charge. He directed people into the center of the conference room and invited them to sit in the collection of comfortable chairs. He and Ross scooted one of the conference tables farther to one side as the others settled into seats.

Sophie did not sit. She wanted to delay that in case she decided to run for the door. But why was she even thinking about running?

Before she could answer that question, a burst of electricity, like a palpable pulse of light, blanked out the room. Everyone startled in unison. Someone screamed. Then Sophie blacked out.

What Has She Gotten into?

Detta wanted to scratch an itch, but couldn't decide where it was located. She scratched her head, a finger inserted through her Afro to her scalp. It was almost like the irritant was inside her head. Did she need to scratch her brain? She shook her head sharply and scowled at the thought. "What's goin' on here, Lord?"

As soon as she asked that question, Sophie's face came to mind. Something was up with Sophie. Sophie was … she was disabled. Or even paralyzed. Those were the odd thoughts ricocheting around Detta's head.

Pulling out her phone, Detta sent a text to the prayer group. Prayer requests were a daily occurrence among her friends. She resisted the temptation to use all capital letters for this one. Anthony had warned her not to do that. **"Sophie is helping with deliverance ministry in another state this week. I sense she needs us to intercede for her right now. Please pra!"** She almost cursed when she saw the typo, but the prayer warriors would know what she meant. And they would surely recognize her urgency.

Then she thought of texting Sophie to see what was wrong. Tapping a fingernail on a front tooth for a few seconds, Detta decided against possibly distracting her young friend. Instead, she sent a message to Anthony. Maybe he knew something. Anyway, he would want to be praying too. **"Sophie needs us to pray, I think. I have a feeling she's in trouble just now."** Detta left out the list of unanswered questions she was accumulating. Her boy would tell her if he knew anything.

"Okay, Mama. Will do."

That was generic, but Anthony was at work. Maybe he would have to go into some kind of network closet or something and pray there. Though, of course, he could just pray silently wherever he was.

Detta extracted her mind from that little muddle and settled back in her recliner. "Well, Father, I guess you're the one who told me about this. And you know I'm ready to do my part. You're already working to support Sophie, of course. Send whatever help she needs. Fill her with your Spirit, Lord. Give her your wisdom. Encourage and empower her for the fight. Prepare her and equip her for the battle." She let those words rest in the air around her, listening for a response, for an urge to go on, inspiration to say more.

In her imagination, she could see Sophie lying on a floor in a plain room, not much decoration, not much furniture. There was a blinding light around her. And not a good kind of light. It was like a sparkly bomb had gone off and knocked her to the ground. "Get up, Sophie. Get up and fight back. You can do it, girl. This is your fight to win." Sitting there in her recliner, Detta didn't even know if she had said those words aloud.

"You hear me, Lord. Even if those are just my thoughts. And you see Sophie right where she is. Help her to get up. Help her to contribute her part to that ministry." Then something else seemed to need addressing. "Help Sophie and the other folks there to see what's hidden. Reveal what's really happening, please, Lord."

Detta's phone had been buzzing as she prayed. One message and then another. Text messages coming back. The sisters were praying. Two of them said they had sensed an urgent need to pray for Sophie *before* Detta texted. Sister Carter said she saw Sophie getting up off the floor.

"Ha! You're all over this, aren't you, Father? Go get 'em. Beat that enemy down and cast him out. Yes, Lord!" She hooted and laughed at herself before getting back to praying.

Ten minutes later, Anthony texted. **"Any news on Sophie? She's not answering my texts."**

"She's probably in the middle of a deliverance session, remember."

"Okay. I wondered if that would start already. Not waiting until later tonight."

"Why night? Deeds done in the light, my dear."

"Okay, Mama. You know best." He added a hug emoji.

Detta chuckled at that reply from her boy. "Well, you got a place in this too. If you're gonna be with Sophie for long, you gotta take up your place in a fight like this." She didn't text any of that to Anthony. She wanted to focus on praying for Sophie instead. Her son's relationship with that gifted woman would only be a distraction right now.

For almost an hour, Detta prayed and responded to texts from the group. Then she prayed some more as she went about her housework.

What Hit Me?

Sophie could recall the first time she'd worked with Jonathan and Sister Ellen. It was in the psych ward at a Catholic hospital. One of her fears back then had been that she would be a liability. That something would happen to her that would make her a problem instead of part of the solution for that troubled young man. Lying on the floor looking up at the ceiling tiles in the hotel conference room, it seemed that one of her harshest fears had come true.

Ross offered her a hand. He had a mischievous grin on. "You okay?"

"I don't even know." She allowed him to help her up, regretting her answer. It was a true answer, but more vulnerable than she wanted to be with this group of strangers. She wasn't hurt. In fact, she had felt no intense physical sensation during the whole … incident. Experience. Happening. Whatever she would call it inside her own head. She wasn't willing to open the curtain any further to the others.

They were all standing and looking at her in exactly the way she dreaded.

"It's no problem. Really. I'm fine." She wondered just how much Bruce was regretting bringing her into this mission.

Then she focused on Maris. Her eyes were not her own. Everything about the pleasant, middle-aged woman was the same except her eyes. Not her eyes. There Sophie saw accusation. Rage. Violence.

"You have no power over me. You cannot harm me or anyone else in this room." She flinched just slightly as she spoke to the spirit that was using Maris as its mask.

Now the team members all turned toward Maris. She shivered and nearly collapsed, staggering to retain her balance. Her instability didn't seem real to Sophie. Was it just for show? Who was putting on that show?

"Okay, I see we have met some of our enemies." Bruce sighed in a way that seemed more about relief than frustration. He did cast an inquisitive glimpse toward Sophie. He looked at Lee next, probably wondering what she was seeing.

Bruce had struck Sophie as tight. Keeping tight control. A tight team. Surely she had shaken some of that with her theatrical collapse. She prayed silently about her fears. *"How could they knock me down like that?"* She didn't really expect a clear answer. Perhaps it was a protest more than a fact-finding prayer.

Deborah stepped sideways and settled a hand on Sophie's shoulder. Was she praying silently for her? That's what Ellen or Detta would be doing in that moment. Her mother would be muttering some memorized prayer. But Sophie couldn't tell if Deborah was like any of those women. Was Lee? The older woman kept her head bowed. Probably praying.

Sophie returned to considering the explosion of electric light that had knocked her off her feet. Had she just imagined others reacting, even screaming? Could that little scream have been only her? When she got up, she had found them all staring as if something had happened to *her*. Not as if something had happened to all of them. But maybe it was just a matter of degrees—something affecting all of them, but her the most. She wanted to ask, but Bruce was busy orchestrating the room and the people in it.

He settled Maris in a roundish armchair flanked by couches and love seats. She continued to wobble, breathing rapidly. It still looked like playacting to Sophie. Deborah and Heather sat on opposite sides of Maris. Everyone else took seats around the rough circle.

Though she was listening, present in the room, Sophie didn't attend closely to the memorized prayers and statements Bruce and Deborah took turns speaking over the group and the room and even the hotel. They were staking out the territory for the work God intended to do that day. Sophie understood that. But she was not entirely comfortable with the scripting of so much of what they were saying. Jonathan and Ellen used prayers that had become familiar to her, certainly very familiar to them. But she never heard them reciting the way Deborah and Bruce were doing.

Next to her, Ross was taking notes. She could see his references to the particular prayers and pronouncements in shortened form. These were standard elements of their ministry times, obviously.

Sophie was here to help. To participate, but also to learn. These ministers had a national reputation and over a decade of intense experience. She could learn a lot from them. Yet they had invited her because she brought something she could *not* learn from them. Something they could not do for themselves.

She resorted to silent prayers of her own as she listened to the sort of liturgy that now included getting Maris to declare her willingness to receive freedom through the people gathered there and the grace of God working in them.

Maris acted as if she were willing. She said the words. Maybe that was enough.

Ross marked the times when major segments of the ministry took place. Looking over his shoulder was how Sophie kept track of the passing minutes and hours. They spent an hour and a half going through the things Maris needed to renounce to begin the process of her liberation. Sophie knew it was largely up to Maris how much they accomplished today or any day.

After that ninety-minute session, they took a break. Coffee, soda, and snacks were supplied by the hotel. Sophie opened a diet soda with caffeine. The liturgical pace of this first meeting had dulled her. She assumed that was the cause of her grogginess. Natural weariness or even boredom. Probably. She continued to pray silently.

When they were supposed to resume, Maris did not return.

Heather was there, and as confused as anyone. "I thought she was headed back here. I saw her in the restroom." Heather's eyes were wide, her words short and defensive.

"It's okay. We can wait." Deborah took a seat, and others followed her example.

They waited. Finally, after ten minutes, Heather checked her phone. She stood and exited the room without saying anything, but she didn't get far outside the door before she started talking. "What are you doing? Where did you go?"

Bruce sat with his elbows propped on the arms of his chair, his fingers interlaced beneath his cleft chin. He pursed his lips. Was he praying, or just waiting for what came next?

The Woman Who Chases Angels

"She still wants it." Deborah spoke at quarter volume. Confident. Relaxed.

Bruce nodded mutely.

Heather was still close to the door. "But how could you get lost? You were just down the hall."

Sophie looked at Bruce and then Deborah. Had Maris gotten lost trying to find the small conference room? That was no more believable than any of her playacting as far as Sophie was concerned. But she put the brakes on that attitude. The spirits working against Maris might be coloring Sophie's opinions.

"Where are you, then? What's around you?" Heather's voice was just barely audible. All the people in the room seemed to be holding their breath to listen.

"We need to go and get her." Lee raised her head and looked around the room as if awaiting confirmation. She was a slight woman who had perhaps been athletic in her day. She didn't appear frail, but a natural deference seemed to diminish her physical presence most of the time. She was asserting herself now.

Ivan nodded steadily next to her. "We can do it. She trusts us." He looked at Bruce.

Sophie knew that Ivan and Lee had met with Maris before, interviewing her and her daughter in advance. Sophie wasn't clear how often this happened, but she wasn't surprised at the old couple's assertion that they had a rapport with Maris.

"Okay. See if Heather wants to go with you." Bruce looked around the room. "The rest of us can break. Watch your phones. We'll text if she's ready to meet again before lunch."

"Maybe no lunch for her." Ivan was helping Lee out of the love seat they had occupied.

"Maybe." Bruce's eyes just grazed Ivan and Lee before he locked eyes with Deborah.

Sophie had been in one session where Jonathan was quite insistent the spirits could not induce vomiting in the person needing deliverance. It was sometimes an issue. She didn't know Bruce's policy on that, though there was no obvious provision for anyone in this room being sick. No bucket.

Bruce interrupted her squeamish musing. "What do you think, Sophie?"

"I saw something in her eyes that seemed like it had a very strong hold. And I felt like that spirit was manipulating her most of the time." She inhaled sharply when she finished, a bit surprised at her own clarity.

"Okay. That fits what I was sensing." He spoke to the old couple as they reached the door. "Does that fit what you were seeing?"

Ivan nodded, checked with Lee. He spoke deliberately. "She wants help, but she still doesn't have control."

"We'll go get her." Lee grinned with her lips tight.

As they left, Bruce turned to Sophie again. "Do you know anything about the spirit you saw?"

"There's something beyond her, something beyond this hotel that's stirring the air. I also sensed that the one looking at me through her was a commander. A leader of some kind."

"Okay. We knew that was possible." He checked with Deborah and then Ross.

Sophie could hear a low-volume discussion outside the door. Heather seemed to be comfortable with Ivan and Lee. She was crying. Lee's comforting voice seemed to settle her some. Most of the words they were saying stayed outside the door.

Was everything else staying outside? Bruce had claimed the space, asserted spiritual authority over the room. How much could Maris bypass that by cooperating with the spirits connected from outside?

"What color was the one you saw on her?" Deborah turned toward Sophie. Apparently it was a simple question. A normal question.

"Color?" What did Deborah know about colors? What did she know about how Sophie saw these things?

"Did it leave an impression?"

"The eyes were black and gold. Like a dark ruler." She had been learning to sort her experiences according to their symbolic meaning. Size and color were only symbolic as far as she could tell—and from what she had learned in conversations with everyone from Detta to Ellen to a priest named Brother Glendon.

Ross started writing.

"What do you know about the colors?" Sophie was curious why Deborah had taken that route.

"Sometimes it helps. It gives us clues about who we're dealing with." Bruce glanced at Deborah as if for confirmation.

Sophie pressed a little harder. "But do the demons really conform to a system?"

"A system? I think so. But the system we're more interested in is the one given to the seer. That one comes from God, for the most part. And we've seen a consistent pattern across a large number of sessions. I think it's really about language and communication." Bruce pursed his lips briefly.

The Woman Who Chases Angels

"You are given the sight so you can do something about it. What you see helps you—helps us—know what we are dealing with." He faced her more squarely. "It's not *our* system. It's God's. We hear it and see it in a language we understand, fortunately. And that language includes symbols related to color and shape and size."

Sophie smiled. "Good. I've been understanding things that way more and more lately." In that moment, exactly what they had agreed on wasn't nearly as important as the affirmation she was feeling. They were still relying on her. And she was in synch with the team.

The others rose, following Bruce's lead, and shuffled out of the conference room. The three in the hall were gone by then.

Did You Lose Someone?

Detta stopped debating and called Sophie. If she wasn't available, then she wouldn't answer.

"Hello, Detta. How are you doing?"

"I'm quite fine. I was calling 'cause one of the sisters in the prayer group had a message for you, I think."

"Really? A message?"

"About someone you lost."

"Lost? Huh. Well, the woman we're supposed to be ministering to *says* she's lost. Her daughter and two others are going to find her."

"Well, you can tell 'em to look behind the kitchen. I don't know if that makes sense, but that's what she said."

"Wow. Okay. I'll see if I can get a message to them."

"Good. Well, let me know if that helps."

"Sure. I'll call you back."

No goodbye. Just silence. But Detta knew the pressure Sophie was under. She had been there with her a few times.

It was only two minutes later when Sophie called back. "I got word to the folks looking for her. I don't know if they found her yet, but I wanted to talk to you while we wait."

"That all sounds fine. How's it going? Aside from the woman getting lost, of course."

"I got knocked down. Blasted off my feet. I didn't get hurt, but I knew it was one of the fallen angels that did it to me."

"Hmm. That's unusual, isn't it? You haven't been laid out by one of them before—as far as I know."

"Right. It is new to me. And no one else hit the floor. But it was like a sudden explosion."

"Yes. I see. They're trying to shake your credibility."

"The spirits?"

"Mm-hmm. The folks you're working with want to rely on you. The spirits want you to look *un*reliable."

"I don't think it worked. Bruce was asking me what I saw and taking my word for it when I told him. No hesitation that I can see. Though I saw plenty of hesitation from this woman we're here to help."

"Yes. They're usually not one hundred percent convinced even when they reach out for help. That goes with the territory, I expect."

"So, I shouldn't worry that it knocked me down?"

"Not really. Did the minister in charge address that?"

"He did a lot of praying and binding, all memorized and carefully worded."

"Carefully worded? I guess that's worth something. There's a thing about these spirits. They follow laws. You get the words just right, and they have to listen. It's slow and difficult that way, but I've seen it work."

"As opposed to just getting revelations and having angels lead a charge into the fight."

"Ha. Something like that." Detta tried to guess Sophie's real question. "You know, Jonathan and Ellen and the folks at our church tend to be more spontaneous about this kinda ministry, so we don't do a lot of written prayers and such. But that doesn't mean you can't team up with folks who do it differently."

"No, I know. I didn't expect it to be just like a midweek service at your church." Sophie might have snickered.

"Not like one of those Saturday night prayer groups I brought you into?"

"No. Not like that." This time the chuckle came through clearly, but she sobered quickly. "Here's a text. Oh, they found her behind the hotel. Near the kitchen. You should tell your friend it was right on. And very helpful. Now we can get together again before lunch."

"Fine. That's fine. Very good. So glad we could help."

"Thanks for getting into the fight with us, Detta."

"Of course, dear. We're always in this fight together. All of us. Praise the Lord."

"Amen. Thanks, Detta. Talk to you later."

"Blessings, girl. Talk to you later." Detta looked at her phone. Call disconnected.

But she was gonna stay connected. No phone required.

A Glowing Web

Sophie watched Maris enter the conference room under her own power, Ivan and Lee following. Heather was not in the room yet. Sophie recalled a session at Detta's church that had involved two young men running into the night to find a runaway subject of a ministry session. They hadn't managed to carry that girl back to the church because they were stopped by a skeptical police officer.

Perhaps Maris and Ivan could carry Lee, the slender old woman. But the two old folks were probably in no shape for carrying or physically restraining someone like Maris. Most of the sessions Sophie had observed banned physical resistance. Not battling against flesh and blood, after all.

More visibly subdued than before, and perhaps sincerely so, Maris apologized to the group. "I don't know what happened. I was suddenly confused. I … well, I don't know exactly what happened."

"Don't worry about it, dear." Deborah took her arm and led Maris back to her seat.

When she caught Sophie's eye, Maris shook her head as if they had some kind of understanding. Did they? What kind of understanding?

"Confusion." Sophie said it without meaning to.

"Yes." Bruce didn't have to ask what she was talking about. "In the name of the true Lord Jesus, I command confusion to shut down right now. You cannot access the mind of anyone in this room. You must stay silent and inactive until I tell you you have to leave."

That was something Sophie had seen before. The leader didn't tell the spirit to leave right away. Sophie guessed it was a matter of Bruce choosing his battle. Maybe he didn't think it would be worth struggling to get rid of the confusing spirit at this point. Later, apparently.

Lee was grinning at Sophie in a grandmotherly way. Neither of her grandmothers had ever smiled so proudly at her—for a whole list of reasons. What was Lee's reason for her obvious pleasure? Maybe gratitude for the tip about where to find Maris. Sophie offered an accepting grin, not sure what she was accepting, but rebuking herself for overthinking it.

The next thing she was aware of was a dimming of the lights. She couldn't be sure whether it was a physical dimming, but everyone reacted to something.

Then Lee grimaced and clutched her belly. "Oh, my."

"What is it, dear?" Even as Ivan asked that question, his face hardened to fierce resolve. "You get off her right now. You inflicting spirit, let go of Lee right now in the name of Jesus."

Sophie could hear Lee muttering prayers under her breath. She glanced around the room. Everyone except Maris looked disconcerted. Bruce's eyes were bigger than Sophie had ever seen them. Deborah's hand was over her mouth. Ross was frozen with his legal pad and pen in hand. What to record? Chaos at eleven o'clock?

For once, Sophie asked to see more. "Show me what's happening, Lord." And that was when she saw the web.

The entire room was crisscrossed with a glowing web, pale gray with alternating pulses of red. Maris was at the center of that web. It stretched from corner to corner and ran at least once through all the others in the room.

Where was Heather? To Sophie, that question seemed like a diversion. What did it matter? But somehow it seemed significant.

"There's a sort of web that crisscrosses the whole room, and it's linked to all of us through Maris. She knows it's there. She knows what she's doing. And something about Heather is also a problem right now."

A cackling like the Wicked Witch of the West split the room. Sophie almost laughed back at the cartoonish affect. It came from Maris, of course.

Maris suddenly sat up straighter. She stared intensely at Sophie. "Can you see them? I can't control them." Her eyes appeared to be clear, and clearly frightened.

Sophie saw six or seven foreign heads poke out of Maris's neck and shoulders. She shuddered at the grotesque deformity that presented.

Bruce started to respond, but Ivan spoke first from where he was holding Lee. "Just tell it to stop, Maris. You have to say it aloud. You have your own will. Exercise it."

That explanation probably implied a longer conversation Ivan had had with Maris in the past.

Maris did respond as if she knew what he was talking about. "I want control. I don't want these spirits to be in charge anymore." Her voice shuddered. She gulped audibly, then pitched forward onto the floor.

When they gathered around her, Heather came through the door, letting it close loudly behind her. "I couldn't get in. Was it locked?"

Sophie hadn't noticed anyone knocking or even wrestling with the doorknob, but she had been fully focused on what was happening inside the room. She wasn't entirely comfortable with either Maris or her daughter. When she looked more closely at Heather now, she saw an image of Maris imposed over her, like a miniature version of her mother embedded in her chest just below her collarbone. That started another shiver in Sophie. And she didn't know what to say about it. It was rare to see a spirit that looked so much like a living person, but so much about this morning was unprecedented for her.

Despite how bizarre the day had been so far, everything seemed to settle down after that. Bruce took charge again with more prayers and more commands to forbid interfering spirits. He led them in a group prayer that seemed to unify them, including Maris. This latter impression came to Sophie despite Maris remaining on the floor curled in a fetal position. Their unity was best represented by the angels in the room gathering around them in a perfect circle.

That web disappeared. Sophie assumed it had been shut down, at least for now.

After another half hour of reviewing, exchanging perspectives on what had happened so far, they agreed to adjourn for a lunch break.

"Everybody take a deep breath and release it slowly." That was how Bruce ended the session. They all complied, including Maris, who was now seated in her usual spot.

Sophie was surprised at how much that large release of breath settled her. It was a fitting end to the calming process Bruce had already started by taking charge and getting everyone together on one page.

They all exited the room under their own power, headed to lunch.

The Sound of Weeping

    The afternoon session ran smoothly under Bruce and his system, with Ross taking notes. On occasion, the latter was asked to read back previous notes to clarify what they had covered. Sophie wondered if she was needed for this part. She told herself it was building character, this waiting to be useful.

    The quest for feeling useful had been a long one. For most of her life, she'd experienced much more of that liability feeling. Even when they hired her at the marketing firm to do coding, she'd wondered who would cover for her when she freaked out. Would her boss learn to tolerate her weirdness? Could she even accommodate Sophie's craziness? The meds didn't banish all the freak factor.

    Admittedly, she did land a job that could be held by an eccentric. And she managed to become a contributing team member. She was in her midtwenties by then. It was the first time she felt like a contributor. It was a contribution to the development of marketing applications and websites. She was part of a team selling hotdogs, mustard, or shoes. But it was a team.

    Sophie had grown up thinking of herself as a liability, but she also knew her mother would never abandon that liability. Sophie could survive as a burden, but she longed to be an asset, at least to her little family. She imagined finding a man to marry her, contributing grandchildren to her mother, and adding back to their diminished lineage. But that had remained a fantasy. Someone else's fantasy, probably.

Nothing in her life settled that rattling piece into place, that need to truly be needed, until the first night she worked with Jonathan and Sister Ellen. Sophie and her gift had provided obvious aid toward the spiritual liberation of a very troubled young man. She pulled it off without incident. Without letting them down even for a moment. That experience of the parts fitting and working so well, even powerfully well, transformed Sophie's life. It transformed the way she saw herself. Not as a crazy girl, but as a gifted woman. A woman of substance.

She awoke from those musings when Maris began to growl. That disturbance to Bruce's system was not, however, nearly so bizarre as the huge head rising from the floor. The head was so large that only the top half of it fit beneath the ceiling. Was this like one of those giants she used to see when she worked downtown?

Bruce seemed frozen. His eyes shot wildly around the room as if he knew there was some massive disturbance nearby, something beyond the growling of the woman sitting in the middle of the conference room. But he clearly couldn't find it. He couldn't find it because it was all around him, from Sophie's perspective.

"Oh, it's a very large ruling spirit." Lee sounded like she had just found a snapping turtle in her backyard. *How odd. How interesting.*

Sophie wasn't so comfortable with the discovery, but she could probably see the rising beast more clearly than any of the others.

Lee stood up. She was looking at Bruce, but he was unresponsive, staring at a coffee table behind Maris. Lee faced Maris. "You can stop this now. You can renounce your power. Do it, Maris. Do it, now."

Power? What power? Sophie had gladly sheltered herself from the details of Maris's past life. Now she wished she knew more. Most immediately, she wanted to know about the sound of crying that seemed to be wriggling up the walls on every side.

"I renounce those old powers. I break off all influence from the rituals we did. I don't want that evil power." Maris's voice cracked sharply. Her tone was like nothing Sophie had previously heard from her. Something seemed to be driving Maris to cooperate again. Could she see that giant head? Could she hear those ghostly wails and sobs?

Sophie watched as small hands reached up the walls, hands attached to the children who were crying. Brown hands. Darker than her own. Who were those dark-skinned children?

Maris started chanting something in a language Sophie didn't know. She thought it sounded like a North American native dialect.

"What kind of school was that? The one that was destroyed?" Sophie shouted at the walls, hoping her words would bounce to someone who had an answer.

"Before it was an orphanage, it was an Indian school. A native school." Ivan was turned toward Sophie, a knowing look on his face. He generally seemed to know more than he was saying, and he always seemed ready to connect with what Sophie was seeing.

"There are children crying. Native children crying out."

"It's not the literal children, it's spirits that have gathered around the terrible things done at that school." Ivan was standing an arm's length from Lee, who had not returned to her seat after admonishing Maris.

Maris spoke clearly again. "I don't want it. I don't want ..." She huffed. "I don't want to benefit from the power accumulated out of violence and oppression."

The air snapped like a giant static spark. Bruce shouted something Sophie didn't understand. And the atmosphere began to sort. Ivan commanded the spirits gathered around the suffering of those native children to leave that place. Bruce commanded the ruling spirit to back down, to release its hold on Maris. And Maris crumpled to the floor again.

Words were flying. Spirits were retreating. But two people were still standing. Lee and Ivan stood side by side over Maris's fetal form. Deborah was bent over her chair with her eyes closed. Bruce had graduated from his paralysis to a sterner stare. He eventually sank back in his seat and took a chest-expanding breath. Then he prayed for God's peace to come and fill the room. He commanded enemies to back off again, and Deborah added prayers for peace. Again, she and Bruce seemed to be relying on a formula for their prayers, but they spoke them with increased personal conviction this time, and perhaps some desperation.

When the spirits retreated, Sophie sat back and panted for several seconds. Lee and Ivan helped Maris to her feet and then into her chair. When all were settled, Deborah led them in a prayer of thanksgiving. Then Bruce followed with a prayer for direction.

It was past three o'clock as far as Sophie could tell, though she couldn't have accounted for where the time had gone. She could see Ross's notes, notes now settled on the love seat between his leg and hers. He had cataloged their progress, times included.

"Let's break for today. No session tonight?" Bruce surveyed the group. No one argued.

Weary smiles, back pats, and some stretching brought each individual back to life. Sophie kept her eyes on Ivan and Lee, hoping to debrief with them. But she needn't have worried. Once Heather and Maris were out of the room, the others gathered back in their seats. Sophie sniffed at herself for not assuming they had more work to do.

"What happened at that school? It was … a boarding school? For native kids?" Sophie scooted back farther in her seat for better back support. She had probably been slouching during the heat of the session.

Ivan nodded deeply. "In the nineteenth century, native children were taken off the reservations, away from their people. The purpose was reeducation. That orphanage was a native school a hundred years before the orphanage fire. A school designed to wipe out native cultures." He paused as if to allow others to contribute. No one spoke. "As far as I can tell, some folks around here noticed some powerful evil forces gathering in that place. Folks who decided to take advantage of the portal to darkness that that school opened."

Bruce clearly knew about all this. "What we didn't know was the extent to which Maris had gotten connected to those ancient spirits. At least ancient by American historical standards."

"So, the children I heard and saw, they weren't the actual children? Not, like, … ghosts?"

"No. They were probably spirits taking on the form of the children to intimidate you and set you on edge." Lee grimaced apologetically.

"Set me on edge?" Even as Sophie replied, she had a sense of what Lee meant. The creepiness factor of all those wailing children had left a mark on her heart. Apparently that was the point. "And that giant head. The ruling spirit?"

Bruce explained. "Given how long these spirits have ruled this area, they have expanded their influence and certainly grown in power. People in recent decades have been doing pagan rituals at the site of the boarding school and orphanage. Some sort of abuse at the orphanage probably added to that dark power. The rituals might have started while it was still occupied by children."

Ivan snorted and shook his head. "People. It's always people who give the demons their power."

Deborah was looking at Sophie. She tipped her head to the side. "You didn't want to know the personal details, but I guess we could have told you more about the historical background. Sorry to leave you out."

"Oh. I don't really mind. In a way, it makes it easier for me to trust what I see. Without that history, I had no reason to see native children or hear their screams." She shivered at the memory of it. That prompted shivers in at least two of the others.

"Let's take a break and get some rest. Do something relaxing and fun. Take a nap. Whatever recharges you. We can talk more after supper." Bruce surveyed the group. "Should we eat together in the restaurant here?"

"I recommend the catfish." Ivan grinned.

Awake Too Early

Sophie woke early the next morning. Very early. She lay in the hotel bed for hours. In her best moments, she prayed. In others, she calculated how long she would have to wait to call Detta. She also wondered about the angels.

During the various explosions and invasions the previous day, she had only been peripherally aware of the angels in the room. They were always there, usually visible to her. Keeping her attention away from them was nothing new. She hadn't really ignored them. In fact, she had, at one point, counted fourteen angels in the small conference room.

She had noted as many as seven angels that seemed to accompany Bruce and Deborah. That crew seemed fluid in their shadowing of either or both of the Albrights and even appeared to cover Ross. Ivan and Lee seemed to have almost as many, though Sophie had only actually counted five angels clearly attached to them.

Yet, despite that fully staffed guard, stuff still got out of control.

Sophie recalled a conversation with Jonathan after a quick and successful ministry time with a teenage girl.

"I wouldn't get hung up on the number of angels, Sophie." He was gentle as always even when correcting her. She usually only thought of it as correction when she later considered what he said. "God can do anything with or without angels. And this is the age of humans taking back territory from the enemy in the name of Jesus. Angels are helpful, but they are only here to assist. Of course some of us are doing work that seems to obviously benefit from their presence, but the presence that really counts is God, his Spirit. The Spirit of Jesus."

She wasn't hung up on the numbers any more than she cared about the size or color of angels. But she aspired to be like Jonathan, who *was* enamored with another kind of Spirit. The Spirit of God. There was that moment in her first session with Ellen and Jonathan when a demonized man shouted that the Angel Michael was in the room. It was Ellen or maybe Jonathan who countered with a reminder. "That's not so impressive. The Spirit of God himself is here!" Something like that.

On the other hand, holy angels were impressive. And powerful. So, how could the dark powers around Maris so thoroughly mess with the people in that conference room? Maybe Sophie should pay closer attention to the holy angels to get a better sense of what was happening.

She rolled to her other side. That was when her three angels became visible to her. The room was still dim before sunrise, and the usual crew glowed golden in various shades. Then a fourth one appeared. This angel had a reddish tinge and somehow seemed older. How old were angels? Here was another thing Sophie could get hung up on. She shuffled that question aside and studied the new arrival.

"Who is that?" She was looking at the new angel but not addressing her particularly. This one was taller than the other three, her face like bronze but still glowing.

"Just as there are regional spirits working for the prince of this world, there are regional spirits working for our Lord

The Woman Who Chases Angels

and his Christ." That answer came from her big male angel. Her first guardian.

"This is a regional spirit on the good side?"

Her angels all nodded, and the new angel bowed.

"We show you this so you understand."

"Understand what?"

The lovely feminine angel that was always with Sophie answered. "God has provided all that is needed on every level. And there are many levels involved here." Something about the way she spoke those words, then closed her mouth and raised her head, told Sophie those were the final words on the subject.

Did Sophie understand those words?

God has provided. The angel started with that. Then she essentially emphasized that things were complicated. "Many levels." Sophie might have ordered those bits of info the opposite way. *It's complicated, but God has provided.* No. The angels started with God's provision. While not denying the complications.

Then a thought entered her head. *"Look at Heather."*

"Really?" The angels had faded into the walls, but Sophie wasn't addressing them. She didn't assume that new thought came from an angel. God's Spirit was in her. She expected his Spirit had fed her that new direction.

What would it mean to look at Heather? Well, Sophie could see things on people, of course. She had checked Heather a few times. There seemed to be a disturbance around her, but then there generally was a disturbance whenever Maris was around. Sophie had assumed she was seeing an echo of the turmoil around her mother when she looked at Heather. But maybe Heather had a more active part in the struggle. Wasn't that the implication?

Sophie would look. She would look with discernment and hopefully not suspicion. She prayed toward that end and fell asleep praying.

A knock on her door woke her. "Huh?"

"Sophie? Are you awake?" It was Deborah. "We've all eaten breakfast. Are you getting up?"

"Uh, yeah. Sorry. Getting up now." She swore at herself, then apologized to the angels, who certainly heard that. Shaking her head, she wobbled out of bed and hustled to the bathroom.

Within ten minutes, she was in the small conference room. Damp, uncaffeinated, and hungry, but she was there. Maybe it could count as fasting. Depriving herself of a blow dry, coffee, and food felt like penance. Not that Sophie had done a lot of official penance in her life. Beyond those irritations, the alert about watching Heather loomed as unfinished business.

But Heather was not there. What happened the previous afternoon when Heather said the door seemed to be locked? Was that real? Had she faked that? Or was she being manipulated by something?

"Heather's not feeling well. She might join us later." Maris looked subdued. Older, maybe. She might not have slept any better than Sophie had, judging by her grayish complexion and still-damp hair.

"I ... I was feeling like we needed to see what was going on with Heather today. That was before I knew she wasn't going to be here." Sophie's voice grated like she was fifty years older than when she went to bed.

As Sophie spoke, that fourth angel appeared in the corner of the room. The regional angel was nodding. She struck Sophie as wise and experienced. What did that mean? These beings were thousands of years old, certainly. They had the wisdom God gave them. But this one's appearance perhaps carried a particular message. Maybe the message was only that the team was being provided a senior angel here. A supervisor angel? Detta would have a better word for it. Sophie paused to regret not getting to call Detta before the morning session.

"Well, we can check on her later to see how she's feeling." Deborah didn't show any surprise at Sophie's assertion. Maybe she had received the same message, though perhaps not accompanied by a visiting angel.

"I feel like—" Maris blurted that as if fearing everyone would leave before she had a chance to speak. "I feel like I should repent ... uh, *renounce* a couple of relationships that weren't healthy. Including with Heather's father."

Was that real progress? Sophie consulted the area supervisor angel—there had to be a better term—who was nodding in a sympathetic way.

Then Maris jumped from her seat and sprinted toward the door. "Wait, what am I doing?" She turned back to Deborah, who was two steps behind her.

Sophie had risen after Deborah and was trying to decide whether to follow.

A bat-like thing appeared, its talons stretching toward Maris.

"Somebody sent a spirit to scoop her away." That was the best Sophie could do to interpret what she was seeing.

"It's him." Maris spoke dully, almost automatically. "Heather's father. She might have been talking with him."

Skin crawling with electricity, Sophie could feel the truth of Maris's speculation. Maybe this was the part about watching Heather.

The regional angel appeared next to Maris and raised a hand toward the flying demon.

"There's an angel prepared to snatch that new demon away. She's a sort of ... a ruler angel, I believe."

Bruce was at Sophie's shoulder now. "In the name of Jesus, I command the attacking spirit to leave right now. I break off any connection between this room and Heather's father, Hollis, in the name of Jesus."

The ruler angel grabbed the demon around the throat.

Sophie rooted her on. "Go for it! Get that thing out of here in the name of Jesus!" Once her words spilled out, Sophie cringed at the unorthodox outburst, but Bruce just stood beside her, nodding.

The tall angel launched out of the room with the demon.

Sophie shivered one more time. And she was close enough to Bruce and Deborah to see them also quake slightly.

Lee spoke up behind them. "Praise the Lord. Praise the Lord."

Sophie echoed that.

Bruce stepped back toward the circle of chairs. "Amen."

And Deborah took Maris by the hand and led her back to her seat.

Family Ties

Another round of renunciations, prayers, and breaking of ties filled the rest of that morning, which had gotten a late start in part because of Sophie. This felt like slow progress, though it *was* progress. Perhaps Sophie was just tired. And perhaps she was feeling some urgency about Heather not being there. Sophie had her orders. Waiting to follow them added to her jitters.

As the team sat together at lunch, except Ross, who went for a walk before eating, Sophie got a chance to tell Bruce and Deborah what the angel had told her that morning.

Bruce stared past her for a moment. Then he looked at Ivan. "What do you think? Does it ring true that Heather was manipulating some of what's happened?"

"It could be." Ivan looked at Lee.

Lee gave a nod. "I've been watching her. She seems to be cooperating with some sort of spirit that is resisting. I wasn't sure if it was just her personal resistance or if she was trying to interfere with Maris's progress. This seems like an answer." She offered another of those grandmotherly smiles to Sophie. It was better than caffeine.

"All right. Who's gonna talk to Heather?"

"Maybe Sophie and I can." Deborah looked at Sophie, a question mark raising one eyebrow.

"Sure. I'd like to be there to see what I can see." Sophie resisted laughing at her own awkward wording. She also dismissed a quickly rising fear about what might happen if only the two of them confronted Heather.

Deborah texted Heather, who answered immediately. Sophie and Deborah rose from the lunch table and headed for the elevator.

"I don't suppose I have to say that I'll do most of the talking." Deborah's motherly smile was almost as winning as Lee's grandma grin.

"No. I have no problem with that." Sophie's return smile was confessional. Deborah seemed to understand her well enough. Sophie didn't doubt that she exuded uncertainty if not fear. "I'll just watch and signal you if there's something you need to know. Otherwise you can always ask me."

"That sounds perfect."

In the ultraquiet hallway on the eighth floor, Sophie followed Deborah over dark red carpet that seemed to be concealing pillows beneath it.

Deborah knocked on the door, and Heather answered it a few seconds later.

"Hi, Deborah. Mom said you would want to talk to me. I guess I screwed up. I know now that I shouldn't have called my dad this morning."

Sophie could feel Deborah relax a little. Heather seemed to be making this as easy as possible. When Sophie saw that Maris wasn't in the room, the tension tapered even more.

"Yes. It turns out he's still playing an unhealthy role in your mother's life." Deborah followed Heather into the room.

"Yeah. I know he still really believes in all that stuff."

"The pagan rituals?"

Heather motioned to the bed next to the one she settled onto. Then she looked at the chairs pushed up to the little table in the corner. "Sit wherever."

Into Sophie's head came the thought that this room hadn't been cleaned properly. Or maybe a better term was *cleansed.* She focused on a greenish film that appeared to cover most of the surfaces. The Bible on the nightstand was one exception. Again, her vision had obvious symbolic implications. Maybe too obvious. She had to resist rolling her eyes at herself.

Sophie sat on the other bed as Deborah pulled a chair away from the table. That chair allowed her to sit close to Heather, facing her directly.

Heather hadn't answered the question about what "stuff" she was referring to regarding her father. Deborah leaned forward in the chair. "Do you know if your father is actively sending things our way? Spirits intended to keep your mother ... in line?"

"Oh, I don't know exactly what he's doing. But I know he hasn't, like, repented or renounced anything. Including control of Mother."

Puckering and nodding, Deborah glanced at Sophie very briefly.

Sophie assumed that was a casual look and not intended to prompt a response from her, but she was seeing things move. There was even something moving inside Heather. It reminded Sophie of the serpent she'd seen in Detta's chest a couple years ago.

Despite her previous agreement to let Deborah lead, Sophie spoke directly to Heather. "How are you feeling? Is something bothering your ... insides?" Sophie put her hand on her own stomach about where she could see something slithering inside Heather.

"Yeah. Just a little …" Heather glitched like someone interrupted by a burp. Then she bared her teeth just briefly. "Uh, just a … a little stomach thing." But then her demeanor changed drastically, from pained to very friendly. "Thanks so much for asking, Sophie. That's so considerate of you."

The syrupy response didn't fit anything Sophie had heard Heather say since they'd met. She didn't have to have angel sensors to know something strange was happening to Heather. The fact that whatever was on her had affected her personality so dramatically tightened Sophie's breathing.

"How are you feeling otherwise?" Deborah leaned in a little closer.

Heather turned to Deborah. From that angle, Sophie could see only her profile, but the way she recrossed her legs and leaned toward Deborah told Sophie enough. As soon as the word "seductress" formed in Sophie's head, she could see a shapely female form rise from Heather like a curl of steam. *Steamy* seemed an appropriate label just then.

"Oh, I'm feeling very, very fine." The throaty voice coming out of Heather was theatrically seductive, bending and worming into Sophie's ears.

Her mouth open to address what was happening, Sophie stopped when Deborah asserted herself. "Seductive spirit, I command you to back down. You cannot affect this conversation. I bind you in the name of Jesus."

The cackle that burst from Heather's mouth was not the high-pitched Wicked Witch voice that came out of Maris the previous night. This was a deep, world-weary laugh, like a woman who had seen it all and was above it all. "Oh, you don't have to worry about any of that. Heather is not going to cooperate with you. Your religious efforts will be useless."

Says the demon. Sophie had heard boasts like that before. Deborah had certainly heard many more.

Instead of keeping up the imperious persona, however, Heather pitched backward onto the bed as if trying to drive her head into the mattress.

Sophie jumped off the other bed. Standing there, she wondered why she had jumped up. Was she preparing to run?

Deborah maintained control, at least of her own reactions. With dogged verbal prying, she coaxed Heather to talk to her, to get control of her own words.

But Heather's body repeatedly resorted to writhing in a suggestive way. When Sophie shook her head at that grotesque display, Heather suddenly opened her eyes and locked on Sophie. "You want me, don't you, Sophie? Come here ..." A gurgling in her throat stopped the blatant seduction attempt.

Sophie hit back. "I refuse to let you into my head or my spirit. I bind your ability to speak to me unless I tell you to, in the name of Jesus." She was aware of Deborah still focused on Heather. She could also sense three or four angels crowding around Deborah as if to prop her up.

"Heather, we need you to take control. I want you to renounce your loyalty to your father and any unholy influence he has over you." Deborah wasn't touching Heather but was leaning over the bed.

Sophie wasn't sure it was generally okay to renounce paternal loyalty, but in this case it seemed like a good idea.

Suddenly Heather went still, except for heavy breathing. That seemed natural, given the struggle she had endured so far.

"Heather?" Deborah sat up straighter. Sophie could see one of her angels touching her lower back. Sophie said a silent prayer for Deborah's physical endurance. "Heather, what's going on?"

"I'm tired of it." She moaned that answer. With her hands over her face, Heather released a stream of sobs that nearly broke Sophie's heart.

Sophie paused to note the deep sympathy those tears were stirring in her. Whatever was in Heather had been trying to manipulate them from the start, so she paused to check if her warming sympathy was healthy. A silent prayer and a check-in with her female angel seemed to assuage her suspicion. Still, Sophie kept her distance.

A hand on Heather's wrist, Deborah was praying consoling prayers. Then she switched to shutting down more enemy activity. A bit more writhing, a gagging fit, and more weeping accompanied various stages of the binding and renouncing that followed. Heather did her part while still supine on the bed. Deborah made no attempt to move her.

The digital clock on the nightstand read 2:47 when Heather finally sat up. Sophie wondered what the others in the group were thinking about their long absence.

Heather finally looked at Sophie with human eyes. Her own eyes. Exhausted but normal.

The room seemed more secure. That green film was gone. Sophie imagined the angels scrubbing the walls and furniture while she and Deborah were focused on Heather. But she suspected it had more to do with Heather severing her unhealthy connections with her father.

That was a man Sophie never wanted to meet.

So How Was Your Day?

Detta was sliding a pork roast into the oven when her phone rang. "Hang on. Give me a minute. Don't wanna roast myself here. Hang on." She stood up as quickly as she dared and closed the oven door in one motion. She had done that maneuver thousands of times. "Hello?" She hadn't bothered to check who it was.

"Detta, it's Sophie."

Detta stopped herself from looking at the screen now, an odd thing to do after the fact. "Sophie. How has your day been?"

Sophie laughed. "Well, it has been a wild day. I'm laughing because I just made a joke about asking that same question to the rest of the folks in the group. We ended up ministering to two people simultaneously in separate rooms. Not planned that way."

"You're takin' care of yourself, though?"

"I didn't get much sleep last night, but I did meet a new angel and got a message that helped us know what we needed to do today."

"Well, that's handy, I'd say."

"Yes. Very handy." Sophie sighed. "I do need to take care of myself though. This is stressful."

"More than the ministry we do around here?"

"I don't know. I guess it feels like more work here because I don't really know these people and their system. Maybe I'm not cut out for going around working with strangers."

"No, that wouldn't be best for you in the long run. You'd have to be part of a team that you trust. Get to know them and their ways."

"These other folks are part of a team. They've worked together before." She sniffed, maybe a laugh. "I guess I'm glad they let me be on their team. They really have been supportive and trusting."

"They trust your gift?"

"Yes. No question about that. Jonathan must have told them things. They seemed to trust me from the start."

"Yes. I imagine his recommendation carries a lot of weight."

"It would with me."

"Sure. And me too." Detta paused. "How much longer there in Iowa?"

"At least another day. I think my part might be done by then. There's more pastoral work for Bruce and Deborah to do with this woman, and there's some other work that has to be done by local people." Sophie paused. It seemed she wanted to say more. "We're doing something risky tomorrow."

"More risky than deliverance ministry?"

"Ha. Well, it's part of it. We're going to this abandoned building where people have done pagan rituals in the past. And maybe even recently. It has a very wicked history, but Bruce thinks this one woman at least needs to go there and be part of ... sort of renouncing what lives there."

"Spirits, you mean?"

"Yes. Spirits that hang around there. Maybe *live* isn't the right word."

"No. I suppose not." Detta hummed for a second, keeping her place in the conversation. "It makes sense sometimes to go to a particular place. Of course spirits can't be contained in a place like we can in these old bodies. Well, mine is old anyway. So, you shouldn't worry about that, as long as the people you're with are full of faith and have the gifting they need for the ministry."

"I think they're gifted, but they're different than the folks in your prayer group and Jonathan's group. Maybe that's part of what makes me more nervous here. They have their systems and their methods, and those clearly work eventually, but it does seem to take longer. Like you said when we talked before."

"Yes. That way's not for everyone, but it makes it sort of predictable. At least as much as it can be. Predictable works pretty well for some folks."

"Hmm. I wonder if I need the wilder kind of wide-open thing that happens in your church."

"You callin' my church wild?" She raised her voice playfully.

"I'll deny it if you quote me."

"Mm-hmm. You better renounce it right now."

Sophie laughed, but even in her amusement, she sounded tired.

"You doing more ministry tonight?"

"No. We're gonna get together and sing some worship songs before bed. One of the guys plays guitar, and Bruce thought it would be a good way to recharge."

"Oh, that sounds real good. Good idea. Yes, I bless that. And we're havin' one of our Saturday night prayer meetings, just a few of us. We'll bless the Lord and do some praying for you and your team."

"Oh, good. I appreciate it, Detta. I feel like I'm well covered. Having you and the prayer warriors backing me is even better than three or four angels in my hotel room."

"Really? You sure about that?"

"Definitely. Well, I should try to get a nap before supper. Thanks for talking."

"Of course. Blessings, girl."

"Thanks. And bless you too."

Detta pulled her phone away from her ear and saw that Sophie had disconnected. She set her phone down and checked the oven to be sure she had the right temperature. A blue jay on her patio made the gentle trilling sound she had heard between jays. She thought about Sophie off in another state facing an enemy that was not confined to any state.

"Well, Lord, thanks for blessing Sophie and her group. More of that, if you please. And I know you do."

Into a Dark Place

The worship time that night probably helped Sophie sleep more soundly. That and the exhaustion of missed sleep and a stressful couple of days.

At breakfast, they gathered around a pair of tables shoved together. Everyone except Heather.

"She's not going to the orphanage with us. I don't think she's ready for that. And I doubt it would mean as much to her as it will to Maris." Deborah looked across at Maris as she said this.

Maris nodded but didn't say anything. She had been subdued during worship the previous night as well. Sophie hadn't heard a lot of detail about what happened while she and Deborah were with Heather, but she didn't feel the need for specifics on Maris's progress. She trusted Bruce and Ivan and Lee implicitly.

"I'm not going either." Lee set her empty orange juice glass on the table. "I was outside that place once, with Ivan. It's too emotionally intense for me."

"Lee is sensitive to the human suffering that's left its mark on that place." Ivan slipped his arm around his wife.

Sophie had heard of people who had a sympathetic soul, who were able to sense the pain of others.

"Are you gonna be okay?" Deborah exuded sympathy when she turned that question toward Sophie.

"I think so. I generally sense spirits, not so much people and emotions."

"That's what we thought." Bruce looked satisfied. With Lee not among them, they would rely even more heavily on Sophie's insights.

After breakfast, Ivan drove the six of them in his van. It smelled of incense and olive oil. Sophie couldn't explain exactly why, but she liked the combination. She also liked riding in a vehicle she didn't have to drive. She rarely rode with another driver. Anthony drove once in a while, but she took the wheel almost as often as he did when they traveled together. That riding along feeling inspired her to take some deep breaths and relax like Bruce had urged them to do that first night. Was that the first night? How long ago was that?

Recalculating the length of her visit led Sophie to the fact that it was Sunday. Was it odd to do this kind of ministry on a Sunday morning? Shouldn't they all be in church? Calendars seemed to lack significance in the middle of this mission. Maybe it was like being at war.

Ivan steered the van off the frontage road they had been on for about ten minutes and onto a battered drive that hadn't been paved for decades by the look and feel of it. But even the bouncing rumble over the rough road was pleasant in a way.

"Are we there yet?" Ross was seated behind Sophie. He spoke softly so only she could hear.

She laughed at his joke. How did he know she would think it was funny? Probably not everyone in the van would.

Maris was gripping the back of the front passenger seat, looking like a skydiver about to bail out. Deborah, next to her, was holding a side handle, but Sophie could see no white knuckles on her grip. Up front, Bruce was saying something to Ivan, but Sophie couldn't hear it above the squeaking of the vehicle and the crunching of gravelly pavement.

The structures they approached separated into three buildings when they reached the driveway that curved in front of the central structure. Sophie looked for surviving glass in any of the windows. There were a few that reflected the blue sky back at her, but only a few.

"How long has this place been abandoned?" Sophie projected her voice, maybe a bit too loudly, as they slowed to a crunching stop.

"About twenty years. Probably more." Deborah turned around halfway to answer. Then she reached over and patted Maris.

Maris's voice was tight as copper wire. "I've been here a dozen times in the last twenty years. It always seemed as run down as this." She made a low noise like a nervous laugh.

Sophie was nervous too. Why was Ivan parking so near the entrance? The front door gaped—a toothless mouth ready to swallow them. Surely this wasn't a legitimate parking place. Then again, having the van this close would make a dashing escape a bit easier. Shaking free of those wayward thoughts, Sophie was glad she didn't have to cover them with nervous laughter. She was keeping her crazies to herself.

Until the world outside got crazier.

Out of all the windows she could see, tentacles reached. Unfurling and flexing, stretching toward them.

"Oh, I ..." She didn't mean to speak. She looked at Deborah, who was holding her nose as if someone had just opened a septic tank.

The side door of the van was open. Maris was still playing skydiver. She wasn't going to jump. She had braced both hands against the doorframe. Sophie assumed she wouldn't be able to push the stouter woman out even if the van were on fire.

Then Ivan prayed. "We're here for your glory, Lord. Make the way straight in front of us. Protect your people. Protect your mission. Thank you, Lord."

Bruce sounded a hearty "Amen," and those tentacles withdrew.

Deborah released her nose, and Maris relaxed her grip on the doorframe. She remained in her seat, however.

Pushing past Sophie first and then Maris, Ross led the way out of the van. His movements were natural, not those of a claustrophobe escaping the confines of the back seat.

"How is everyone doing?" Bruce had opened his door but paused to turn toward the people seated behind him. He offered his wife a tight-lipped grin. He furrowed his brow at Maris and gave Sophie a nod.

They each affirmed their general welfare and followed Ross out of the van.

Sophie checked for her phone as soon as she hit the ground. It was halfway out of the back pocket of her jeans. She slid it to the bottom of her pocket. She could feel the sweat under her arms as she did that, a warm breeze turning cool where it revealed that nervous dampness. Swallowing was unusually difficult. But Sophie wasn't going to confess any of that to the group.

Deborah sidled up to Sophie. Her voice was low and warm in Sophie's ear. "You speak up if this place gets to be too much for you, dear."

In that moment, Sophie could picture Deborah aged and mellowed like Lee. Missing Lee probably prompted that comparison. Turning toward Deborah, Sophie smiled. "Thanks. I'll take you up on that if I need to."

With a small squint and slight flex to her smile muscles, Deborah turned to consult her husband. Her hair tossed in the wind, and she pulled it away from her face. The couple spoke in hushed tones and both focused on Maris.

Maris was wandering toward the front door like a zombie. One of the slow, brainless zombies in movies Sophie had watched with Anthony.

Sophie put herself in gear and caught up to Maris. As soon as she did, she saw a chain of spirits stretching twenty feet from the front door of the institution. They were trying to get a grip on Maris, who stood still below the first concrete step.

"Back off." Sophie waved one arm at the dark spirits. Doing so seemed to surge her own angels into action. They barged ahead and scattered that chain of demons.

Behind her, Sophie heard Deborah say, "It's started already."

Bruce's steady voice replied, "Of course."

Something about that "Of course" disturbed Sophie, but she expected it would do no good to investigate why. Her last conversation with Detta, about whether Sophie fit in with this group, rested on a sort of sideboard in her mind waiting to be picked up on her way to somewhere else ... later.

For Sophie, anywhere else seemed an attractive destination. She was seeing layer upon layer of spirits through the gaping door and the broken windows. It reminded her of the mansion occupied by Maxwell Hartman, who had tried to recruit her into his group of psychics and spirit manipulators.

She shook Hartman out of her head and considered the symbolic significance of those layers. Her spirit senses were being overwhelmed by the sheer number of creatures crawling the walls and haunting the halls. But the layers seemed significant right now. Which layer was Maris attached to? That seemed a strategic question.

Perhaps it was a divine prompt. She could sense the Spirit of God stirring in her, as if preparing for battle. Something in her said, *"Bring it on."* But that part wasn't going to convince the rest of her to say such a thing aloud.

Ivan stepped past Maris to the front door. He stood next to it like a doorman in the city. But his face was somber. This was no role play. The rest of the group tromped slowly up the stairs, crowding around Maris. Sophie couldn't discern whether that was for Maris's protection or their own. Strength in numbers.

The ceiling of the lobby for the old orphanage and boarding school was oddly high and ornate, though it was plainer than the grand entry of Maxwell Hartman's mansion. Again, Sophie shook Hartman out of her head. Here they were, hundreds of miles from home. What did he have to do with this place? She stepped out of that little cloud of questions and led the group to the reception desk at the far end of the lobby.

Sitting at that desk was a dark spirit that glowed from orange to blue like it was burning natural gas. Sophie's three angels stood to her left and right. She felt covered from behind by the other angels and people with whom she had entered the building. Then she caught a flash of flaming bronze from her left, and the tall warrior angel she had met at the hotel quickly displaced the orange and blue demon behind the reception desk. The angel's face was fierce, but she didn't say anything or even seem to acknowledge that she had accomplished something by seizing that strategic seat.

Maris moaned and clutched at her chest. "What was that?" This added to the evidence Sophie had collected that Maris had extra insight into the spirit world. Perhaps she had developed that sensitivity in this building.

"Is this the spot where we should work?" Bruce was looking around the lobby.

For a brief moment, Sophie imagined what Bruce was seeing. A broken railing. Piles of plaster. Scattered glass. Displaced wall trim. Cobwebs. Graffiti on many of the flat surfaces. It was an ugly space even without the demons.

"Where are you connected?" Deborah was looking at Maris.

Sophie expanded the question. "There are layers here. Can I assume it's the latest spiritual layer you're connected to?"

Maris's blue eyes had been wide until Sophie asked that. She squinted tightly and shook her head. That move corresponded with a winged demon swooping toward her.

"Confusion spirit, I command you to stay away from Maris." Sophie instinctively waved a hand at the diving demon.

"We need to establish protection and safety right now before we do anything else." Ivan was at the back of the group, but not a full pace behind anyone. They were still bunched together in the center of that dusty expanse.

"Yes. Of course." Bruce started one of his liturgies. Nothing he said startled Sophie. Nothing seemed questionable or inappropriate. But she still felt something was lacking.

When Bruce finished, Ivan spoke up. "I think Sophie should lead in declaring victory for the angels she sees around us. She sees. She believes. Her faith has power."

Sophie's knees nearly buckled at the impact of Ivan's words. She barely noticed Bruce or Deborah's response. She just launched right into it. "I declare that the faithful servants of the Most High God are victorious here because we are here in the name of the Lord Jesus Christ." She paused as all the angels she could see started to shine brighter. "This place is safe territory as long as we are here. These angels cannot be beaten or bypassed by the demons in and around this place. In the name of Jesus, we take authority over this institution and declare Maris safe right now." Those words flowed from Sophie much more smoothly than she would have expected. It was as if the Spirit of God had something to say and was willing to use her to say it despite all her weakness and doubt. Maybe that was what faith felt like. Something poured into her just because she was open to it. Perhaps Ivan's words had opened that tap.

Tap seemed a relevant image because Sophie was feeling a bit tipsy. She was just a little outside herself, beyond the borders of all her comfort zones. And her angels glowed brighter out there on the fringe of her normal daily experience. Suddenly aware of the others staring at her, Sophie turned to Bruce and nodded.

Deborah spoke next. "Maris, are you ready to say that you break off all unholy connections with this place and all the unholy spirits here?"

It was a familiar formula, but surely Maris needed that prompt. She was shaking slightly as if shivering with cold, though the temperature was over eighty by now. Maris attempted to repeat what Deborah had said. The jumbled version she spoke was shrill and ended in a choking sound. Then she fell to the floor among the broken bits of hardware.

Sophie gasped at what she saw there on the floor.

House of Pain

When she was a girl, Sophie used to play with dolls. An odd assortment of babies, princesses, and soldiers. The latter included a wooden soldier inherited from her father, who had inherited it from his father. She didn't play with them in the conventional way. She understood that early. Her cousins let her know.

At their house on the holidays, Sophie would watch, stunned, at the silliness of their games. Getting married? Baby dolls and army men? But she was the one declared stupid for acting out the sadness and sickness she imagined each little person had to overcome. The dolls and soldiers seldom did overcome, but at least they had mothers to comfort them in their pain, emotional or physical. It was the emotional pain that offended her cousins most.

Jessica, a year older and infinitely wiser than Sophie, hissed at her when she witnessed a toddler doll sitting in a corner in a time-out. "That's not how you do it. That's just ordinary. Just like real kids. Not like a game."

Reality had always been an important goal for Sophie. Acceptable reality. Not the unbelievable things she alone could see.

In the lobby of the former orphanage, grown-up Sophie watched as two spirits that looked like injured children wrestled in and around Maris's chest. They seemed to be struggling not with each other, nor with Maris, but against someone else. Someone who was trying to touch their private parts. Sophie had never acted out that scenario in her game of dolls, though she had seen signs of kids struggling with spirits like the ones tangling with Maris.

"Get them out. Get them off me." Maris's voice was as squeezed as it might be if two children were physically sitting on her chest.

"What is it?" Deborah grabbed Sophie's left arm and pressed her fingers into muscle and bone a bit too hard.

"Children. Children being abused."

Maris released a scream that filled the lobby and echoed down unseen corridors.

Ross put his hands over his ears and looked like he would turn and sprint for the front door.

Bruce puffed his chest as if collecting a breath to blow out his birthday candles, but he remained stuck in that posture.

Dropping to his knees as quickly as a man in his seventies could, Ivan landed next to Maris.

Sophie directed him. "Two children, about nine or ten. I think they are girls. They are dirty and badly dressed. There is no beauty in them."

Maris wailed. She began sobbing with athletic intensity, as if she were the puppet of catastrophic pain. She was the doll in this game of emotional woundedness.

"This isn't just about her. This is Maris bearing some of what went on in this place." Ivan spoke to everyone and no one. Then he directed commands to the spirits that were torturing Maris, but he did not send them away. He seemed to think they had some right to be here. Some link to Maris that had to be addressed separately. That fit, for Sophie, with the way these spirits had ignored the commands she and Bruce had issued already. Whatever was happening to Maris bypassed the authority the team had claimed for this place.

Hovering over Ivan's shoulder now, Deborah began another series of commands, breaking ties and settling Maris's place in the protective care of God and Jesus no matter what wounds lashed her to these spirits. "All tortured and abused spirits, let her go right now. Let Maris's emotional wounds be isolated under the protective care of the true Lord Jesus Christ." That's how Deborah finished.

A spirit staggering next to their little scrum cackled insanely. He had fake long hair and a beard. He looked like an actor in a poorly staged church play. An actor portraying Jesus. He was *not* the one true Lord Jesus Christ. He was an impostor. He laughed drunkenly.

"Be gone. You have no power over us." Sophie waved her right hand at him, and he vanished. Sophie's warrior angel landed in the place the fake Jesus had abandoned, as if to occupy that conquered territory.

A clattering down one of the halls startled Sophie, though the reaction of the people around her probably startled her even more. Everyone made some involuntary sound, though none of them actually screamed. Ross came the closest. Sophie was too focused on the intrusion to laugh at his girlish squawk.

"What was that?" Ross was the first to speak.

Sophie's big male angel was the first to move. He pivoted and raced toward that sound. Sophie hesitated half a beat, then took off after him.

"Sophie!" At least two voices called after her, but she was still outside herself, outside her normal restraints. Why come on a mission like this and stay in a safe zone?

And why in the world was her angel leading a charge down a hallway? Was there some demon moving things in the building? Was her angel—now all three of her angels—charging toward a confrontation? Sophie noted that it was only her and her three angels entering the wide hallway, past a dented door sagging on one hinge. She hadn't expected the other humans to take chase like Anthony did back home, but she might have anticipated another angel or two joining the charge. Where was the new warrior angel she had met?

Her swift steps popped and cracked on grit and fragments all along the filthy, tiled hallway. Those tiles were under a heavy coating of dust, but it wasn't as slippery as she feared. Sophie's angels had no fear of tripping or slipping, of course. Her biggest angel was way ahead of the rest. He was just barely within sight when he turned the first corner.

Over her breathing and the slapping of her running shoes on the hard floor, Sophie heard other sounds. Echoes? Not voices. Running. Other feet. She followed her angel around a second turn and heard those other feet more clearly. Then a voice.

"Here." The voice was high and breathless.

"Who is that?" Sophie's voice came out a little panicked, a fact that made her shake her head at herself. She slowed at a doorway where her first angel stood waiting. He folded his arms like a guard posted at the door.

"This is the only room that still has glass in all the windows, you moron." It was a harsh whisper. Probably a girl.

"Who's there?" Sophie skidded to a stop in the doorway. Her female angel was close at her left shoulder when Sophie paused to adjust to the room being lighter than the halls she had been running down. Now she heard someone jogging up behind her.

Scuffling sounds in the room betrayed whoever was hiding behind an overturned folding table. Someone swore. The sound hissed expansively and echoed off bare walls.

That echo was broken by Ross speaking just behind her. "Sophie, what are you doing?"

"Yeah. Why are you chasing us?" A teenage girl stood from behind the table.

Sophie jumped at the sound of each of those voices. She hadn't expected Ross to be so close behind, and she sure didn't expect that girl to stand up.

"I'm ... I'm sorry. I didn't mean to ... to scare you." It was a strange thing to say, given that Sophie was surrounded by her own fear. A cluster of little demons were spinning around her like flies. "Get out of here." She waved them away.

Ross looked like he would retreat, but seemed to reinterpret her gesture and stopped after backing off just one step.

"Uh, who are you guys? What are you doing in here?" Sophie managed to get her voice almost to its normal range.

"Well, we could ask you the same thing." The girl looked down as a boy about her age stood from behind the table.

"Oh." The thought that prompted that one syllable from Sophie was about teenage couples finding a place to be alone. Here she was in the role of the adult breaking that up. It was not a familiar role. She adjusted to answering the girl's question. "We came to do a sort of therapeutic visit for a woman we know. She suffered in this place and needed ... *closure* for that."

"Oh. Weird. That must have been the screaming we heard." The boy could have been the girl's twin from this distance. The gray light from the dust-covered windows showed two skinny kids wearing a combination of black and gray clothes. Unisex clothes. Similar short haircuts.

"Why are *you* here?" Sophie sensed they weren't just local teens looking for a place to be alone. It wasn't a great spot for a date.

"None of your business." The girl stopped abruptly, as if she had intended to say more. The *more* would not have been friendly or clean, Sophie assumed.

"This place isn't safe."

"We … we know what the risks are."

"I'm not just talking about broken glass and rotten floors." Sophie was feeling the floor beneath her feet flex as she shifted her weight.

"You mean the ghosts?" The boy wasn't as defiant as the girl.

"I don't know anything about ghosts, but I do believe in spirits. And there have been some very bad things done in this place over the decades."

"So?" The girl had not softened her defiance.

"We've felt something here." The boy looked at the girl, as if waiting for her to admit it.

"I don't believe in that stuff, but he has this cousin who says she talks to angels."

A chill ran up Sophie's spine. Of course that phrase struck home for her. But more startling than the girl's words was the nod from Sophie's female angel. A nod of recognition. Her angel apparently knew that girl. A girl who talked to actual angels?

"Really? Where does she live?"

"On the West Coast. Why do you want to know?" The boy sounded more suspicious now.

"Just curious." Right then, Sophie was distracted. A starving-looking specter was looming over the kids. "Are you two hungry? You look like you could use a meal."

"Is that supposed to be some kind of body shaming?" The girl crossed her arms over her chest.

But the boy turned to look at her. "Come on, Brandy. This is serious. We haven't eaten for days now. Those cookies don't count."

"I've gone without before." Her voice faltered. She turned toward the windows. "But it never hurt this bad."

"Hunger pain?" The words came automatically to Sophie. "This is a house of pain. I'm not surprised that applies to your hunger." She shifted her eyes invitingly toward the door, and the two consulted each other before following her out to the hall.

When the four younger folks reached the lobby, Sophie paused next to the crooked door twisting off its hinges. Bruce, Deborah, and Ivan were praying over Maris. She was weeping softly.

The teens shifted awkwardly and looked away from the little gathering.

When they finished, it was clear that Maris had found some peace. Sophie wanted to hear all about it, but not in the company of Brandy and the boy, who had introduced himself as Eddie.

Without hesitation, Bruce and Deborah had agreed to take the kids for an early lunch at one of the restaurants near the hotel. Sophie suspected Brandy would have refused if not for the added intensity of hunger imposed by the spirits in that house of torture. And perhaps she would have refused if not for Eddie.

Though they looked like siblings, they didn't introduce themselves that way. They didn't offer their last names. Maybe a couple or very close friends.

"Why did you go to that place for therapy? I mean, what could be creepier?" Brandy asked that after finishing her chicken sandwich and getting a good start on her order of fries. Perhaps she found some added boldness in her new gastronomic satisfaction.

"It's complicated." Sophie glanced at Deborah and then Maris, who had both turned toward her. They must have been wondering how much Sophie had already told the kids. Sophie asked Brandy a question. "Did you sense more in that place than just that it was creepy?"

"You mean spirits?" Eddie checked Bruce and Ivan, as if assessing how much he could say. "*Sense* is about right. There was something in there. We haven't slept well in that place."

"You were sleeping in there?" Deborah's voice hung up at the end, perhaps caught on a bit of her salad.

Brandy stabbed Eddie with her eyes and shook her head.

"They're not cops. They're not gonna do anything about it." He glared right back at the girl.

"How old are you two?" Bruce could easily pass for a cop.

"We don't have to tell you that." Brandy's voice wavered a bit, perhaps in the face of a father figure.

"Tell me about this girl who talks to angels." Sophie wasn't a cop, and she wasn't interested in pretending to be one.

My Cousin Talks to Angels

Eddie cleared his throat. He trusted the woman with the black hair and multiple ear-piercings. She seemed cool in all kinds of ways. And she acted like she really was open to his story about his cousin, Hope.

Brandy interrupted him before he even got started. "She's been in a mental institution about as much as she's been out." She was way past getting on his nerves. But now they had an audience, so Eddie ignored her.

"It started when she was, like, five years old. She's four years older than me, so I didn't see it back then. By the time I was hearing my parents talk about her 'problem,' she must have been eight or nine." He shook his head. "I think what freaked them out the most was how she went into all this detail about what they looked like. And probably her parents were worried that there were some really wicked things she was seeing. Not like she was just some little girl imagining sweet little cherubs and stuff."

"What kind of detail?" The young woman, Sophie, was totally zoomed in on this.

Eddie had to just ignore how attractive this Sophie chick was. Old, but cute. It gave him a buzz to have her full attention. "Well, like what color they were, and how long their hair was, and what they were wearing. Which, for a little girl, I guess, might be what she *would* talk about." He probably sounded sexist with that, but he was sitting far enough away from Brandy to not get elbowed. Brandy didn't like Hope anyway, so maybe she would let it pass.

"Really? Did you believe her?"

"Did I believe her? Well, I was just a kid. I kinda had to go with what the adults were saying. Like, I'd never heard of anyone actually seeing angels." He huffed a short laugh. "I'd never heard of hallucinations or whatever the doctors called it either. But no, I didn't think it was real."

"But now? Have you changed your mind now?"

Of course she was asking what he believed because he was telling Hope's story. But these people didn't seem very skeptical about this kind of stuff. Or at least they were too polite to make fun of him like Brandy did … all the time.

"She's one of the smartest people I know. I know that could be part of being crazy, of course. I've heard of people like that. But there's just this thing about her. She's … well, she's so confident. And it's the kind of confidence that doesn't even care if other people aren't gonna believe her."

"So, she's been hospitalized? Meds?"

"Sure. But she says none of them really stop her from seeing those things."

Sophie nodded. "I know." Then she glanced at Brandy like she was sorry she had said that part.

But Brandy didn't make fun of Sophie. "Do you … see stuff? You seem to know stuff."

Eddie was relieved to hear Brandy sounding like a dumb kid for a change instead of just him.

Nodding some more, Sophie looked at the woman next to her, Deborah. Eddie could tell these other people knew what Sophie was going to say. "I see stuff. And I have been known to talk to an angel or two." She took a deep breath. "Right now, I can see that the hungry spirit that was hovering over you guys in that place is still with you." She paused, then tightened her focus on Eddie. "And it has track marks on its arms." She glanced at Eddie's long sleeves.

He managed to not check that his arms were covered.

"What does that mean? We have, like, an addict angel following us?" Brandy still sounded skeptical.

"A fallen angel. What most people would call a demon."

"But not a *literal* demon. Just, like ... well, like an addiction?" Brandy seemed to be trying to get Sophie's words to make sense. Maybe she thought Sophie was as cool as he did. Sophie definitely had that same thing as Hope, that unbreakable sincerity. Confidence even though she was the weird one. The grown-ups with her didn't seem at all surprised by what she was saying. Having legit people like that believe you must help, even if you were a freak.

"You should talk to my cousin. I could give you her number and tell her you'll call." His voice came out weak. The high-calorie lunch was making him drowsy. Brandy's fidgeting next to him was distracting.

"I'd love to talk to her. I'd also like to get that thing to leave you two alone."

"The ... the demon thing?" His mouth was sort of numb. Brandy sometimes made him feel stupid, but Eddie could get there on his own well enough.

Brandy was acting stupid right now. Her feet were, like, running under the table, and she was shifting in her seat as if she were looking for an exit. She was buried in their booth though, and would have to fly over the table to get out. She looked like she might try.

The older guy, Ivan, said something. Eddie missed exactly what it was. He couldn't figure out who the guy was talking to. None of the other old people seemed really upset. But they were all locked in on Brandy and him. And their eyes were not, like, disappointed in them or thinking they were stupid. More like they really cared what happened to them. That was different.

More Than She Bargained For

It was a long lunch, and then they hung out for a while in the parking lot and the van before they took the two teens back to the institution.

"We'll wait here for you." Bruce was doing his reassuring dad routine very effectively. Sophie caught the faintest glimpse from him, a sign so subtle that she might have imagined it. He trusted her as much as he trusted Ross. That's what it felt like.

And the two youngest adults were again the ones who walked the kids down the halls of that haunted building. Sophie forced herself to ignore a sort of war going on between this building and the one to the west. She suspected the ruling warrior angel was giving their little group some cover.

"You don't have to come in with us. You could wait here. I can carry the stuff. We can carry it all." Brandy was talking to Eddie. She gestured to Ross and Sophie. It was the tenderest touch Sophie had seen from Brandy. But the girl hadn't said much since Ivan and Deborah cleared away that addiction spirit. Maybe this was the new Brandy.

"It's okay. I'm not worried. We have Sophie with us, and Ross, and all the angels they keep around." He laughed in a way that implied he was only half joking.

Sophie didn't challenge his characterization. She had never felt like she was keeping angels around, but she was keenly aware when they *were* around. And she was trusting their protection for one more trip into that torture chamber.

Maybe it was the afternoon slant of the sun, but the building seemed lighter inside. The air was still full of dust, and it was getting hotter as the day wore on, but Sophie felt less like she was running between battle lines. She wasn't, in fact, running at all on this trip.

Ross made a hissing sound a few times, like he was being startled by every little noise. But the walk to pick up two backpacks and two bedrolls was more uneventful than Ross's vigilance would imply.

By the end of that day, they had spent much longer ministering to Brandy and Eddie than to Maris. Several times during the evening, Sophie caught Maris showering the kids with a motherly smile. Surely that was only possible because of her newfound freedom.

Beyond the time they devoted, the group also donated money to buy bus tickets back to Minnesota where the teens had grown up together. And Sophie got the contact information for Hope Decker, who lived in California. She trusted Eddie would provide her an introduction.

It felt a bit rushed, putting the kids on an overnight bus north, but the momentum was undeniable, and no one resisted. Bruce, Deborah, and Sophie stood under the metal awning next to the departing buses, hordes of moths and midges flocking around the bright lights high above.

Sophie wondered how much difference it had made that she had been able to see the spirit that was oppressing Brandy and Eddie. She couldn't imagine the transformation she had witnessed this afternoon without that clear picture of the addiction spirit on them. The experience reminded her how much power a single spirit could have over more than one person when those people simply cooperated with it.

When they arrived back at the hotel, Sophie got a call from Anthony, timed perfectly for her solo walk toward her room.

"Hey, Anthony. How are you doing?"

"I'm doing good. Nothing to report here. But I was hopin' to get the latest from the front lines."

Sophie snickered at the aptness of his characterization. It felt like a vanquished battlefield she was treading toward to her room. "*Victorious* is the summary of the day. Though the fight was more than we bargained for. In some ways, that is. In other ways, not nearly as bad as I expected."

"Okay, you better unpack that for me. Good headlines, but I want more." He sounded like he was settled down for the night. It was past ten, according to the phone.

"You ever wonder how many of those dark spirits are out there? And how many of the good angels?" She pulled her key card from her back pocket.

"Uh, well, probably not as much as you have. But it is the kinda thing I could get into."

She sniffed a laugh, but she sobered at the memory of the crowd she had initially seen in the orphanage. "I guess an experience like this can distort that perception. I mean, we went to a place that was really overrun by enemy spirits, but I look around me here, and the air is mostly clear." She pried off one shoe and then the other just inside her room door.

"You say you went to a place. You mean a literal place?" His voice was clear and his responses sharp even if he sounded extra relaxed.

"Yes. A literal place. This institution that was first a boarding school for native kids taken away from their tribes. Then it was an orphanage that must have been run by some really sadistic people. House of torture is how I think of it."

"Oh, dang. Yeah. I wonder if there's a connection between those two uses of that building. But I suspect you've already worked that out."

"Well, I'm here with, like, these professional demon fighters. So yeah, we put some thought into that connection."

"Man. That all gives me the shivers."

"I saw some shivers a few times today. And felt 'em too."

"You saw the folks around you getting freaked, and even Sophie the angel queen got freaked?"

"Angel queen? Please."

"All right. Sorry about that. It's late."

"Busy day at work?"

"It's Sunday."

"Oh, right. Totally lost track. I remember wondering at the beginning of the day whether it was all right to visit a demon-filled building on a Sunday. I guess it worked out."

"The Lord is workin' every day. I'm pretty sure that's what Mama would say."

"Yes, I think you're right." Sophie sat on the corner of her bed. "Good thing I had my running shoes on today. I wonder why I wore them originally."

"What? Why are you talkin' about shoes?"

"Ha. Yeah. I was running after my angel in that freaky place today. Good thing I had my running shoes on."

"What the—? Why were you running? Why was an angel running? Again."

"Huh. Well, now that I look back on it, he was charging off to show us these two kids who were hiding in that haunted place. We thought the noises they made were ghosts or demons or something. Then my angel took off, and I knew I had to go with him. I was kinda out of my head by then."

"Why were you out of your head?"

Sophie ruminated for a couple seconds. "Really, the answer is God. Like the Spirit of God was filling me up and just made me feel kinda invincible, sort of."

"Invincible ... sort of?"

Sophie laughed. "Sounds so crazy I can barely stand hearing myself say this stuff."

"But it's true though, right? The Spirit, like I feel sometimes in church, can get on you and make you feel powerful. Like, there was that prophet in the Old Testament—I think it was Elijah or Elisha. One of those. He went running down a mountain because God got into him. I even seen a sister or two do that at church. Pretty crazy."

"You think those sisters were chasing angels?"

"Maybe. But maybe they're doing that without worrying about what they're chasing."

Sophie laughed some more as she lay back on her bed. Her sci-fi friend was so easy to convince of the craziest things. "Oh. And I got the phone number for a girl in California who talks to angels. She's been treated like a crazy person all her life, and maybe she is, but she just might be the same kind of crazy as me."

"Wow. That's weird. In a good way."

"Yes, it is."

A Change of Plans

When Sophie heard about Hope, she restrained her own hope that this girl really did see and talk to angels. Maybe the girl was only crazy like people said. But Eddie was one of those believable skeptics who seemed to have his own justifications for almost believing. Justifications Sophie might trust.

That Monday morning, she sat at the breakfast table with Bruce and Deborah, unable to eat much until she told them her news. "I'm thinking I should generally stick with the folks back home and work on doing ministry with them." She had formulated that line in her room before attempting it for real. There were things she could add, ways to explain, but she wanted to leave those out. She didn't want to risk putting herself on shaky terms with the Albright's.

"Is there a particular issue …?" Bruce fiddled with his fork, now idle next to his plate. He had finished his eggs, pancakes, and fruit. Lots more than Sophie had managed to eat.

"Not with you guys. No. I'm not, like, quitting in protest or something." She took a deep breath. "I knew this mission would be a stretch for me, but I wanted to learn. And I did learn. I learned from you and got to see some more of the world around us. The spirit world included."

"But you don't think you could learn anything more?" Bruce shrugged one shoulder.

"We really have appreciated your help, Sophie." Deborah's voice hovered between consoling and grateful.

"I'm sure I could learn more. And maybe we can hook up again another time. I just feel like this was a big dose. Big enough for a while. I don't wanna get burned out on this stuff. I'm really just starting out. So, I think it would be better to sort of ramp up gradually."

Bruce nodded slow and long. "That makes sense." He pursed his lips. "I knew you were just starting out, but the high level of your gift made me forget about that. Maybe a sort of willful forgetting."

"And I know I try to be tough, to not show stress. So I'm not blaming you at all. I don't feel abused or anything even remotely like that." Sophie stopped in the middle of all she felt like saying, realizing a more ardent defense wasn't necessary.

"So, no protest, no abuse." Deborah grinned with a little irony. "And we definitely benefited. So, we can try again later, huh?"

"I think so. My life is a little up in the air right now. I wanted to do this with you guys while I'm still looking for a good, permanent job." She hesitated to let them into her plans. "And now I feel like I'm supposed to meet this girl, Hope, out in California. While I have a little time off, I wanna go out there and see if I can help her in some way."

"Oh." Deborah sat up abruptly. "I just got a chill." She laughed. "I guess that's a confirmation of your plan. At least for me."

Bruce looked at his wife and bobbed his eyebrows. "I guess I can't argue with that." His whole face settled into a gently teasing smile aimed at Deborah. He turned that same grin toward Sophie. "I suppose that means I shouldn't tell you about our next mission."

Deborah reached over and gently slapped the back of his hand, where it rested on the table.

Sophie answered his tease with a mild laugh.

After breakfast, while the rest of the team met with Maris and Heather, Sophie purchased her plane ticket online. Then she looked back through the texts she had exchanged with Hope the night before. It hadn't been so late on the West Coast when Sophie had returned to her room.

"Eddie called me about you. I'd love to meet you. I really would. When can you come to California?"

"Actually, I could fly out there in the next couple days. I think I'm done with this gig and have some free time."

"OMG. That would be awesome."

The rest was about schedules and arrangements. Hope didn't seem to care a lot about details. Sophie focused on those Monday.

She did have lunch and dinner with the team. The others were still meeting with Maris and Heather that day, doing the sort of things Sophie imagined pastors and therapists did after she did her part. Both Heather and Maris were brighter and more engaging, though both seemed exhausted. Heather left before supper, but Maris stuck around. Ivan and Lee left Monday night. Sophie hugged them and thanked them. She had their phone numbers and pledges to keep in touch.

On the phone Tuesday morning, before Sophie left for the airport, Hope sounded pretty groggy. "Um, sure. I'm awake. Mostly. Huh. So, you're really gonna do it. You're really coming out here."

That Hope was still testing those facts after Sophie had already paid for a flight to LAX was a little frustrating. But she recalled that the young woman was probably on some kind of pharmaceuticals. Probably legal ones.

"Are you sure you want me to just show up out there?" Tightening the commitment wouldn't hurt.

"Oh, yeah. Totally. No problem at all. Really. I'm just waking up here."

Sophie checked the time and subtracted two. It was 8:00 a.m. on the coast. She wasn't surprised to discover that was early for Hope. Still, she was tapping the brakes a little to remind herself that she knew very little about this girl. Eddie seemed reliable and honest—for a runaway drug addict—but she wouldn't know much for sure until she met Hope.

"I'll call you when I land, and then I can get a cab to a rental spot near you. I need to look at it before I settle in there, but online it looked like it could work out."

"Hmm. I thought you could stay with me. I don't mind sleeping on the floor. I have this really good air mattress that Eddie used when he ... well, he ran away before and stayed with me for a bit."

"Oh. Well, maybe for one night. My flight makes one stop and arrives around 10:00 p.m., like I said."

"Yeah. You should definitely crash here. That's what I was thinking."

This girl was more than ten years younger than Sophie. The only younger people Sophie had spent much time with in recent years were rookie programmers. Hope seemed like even more of a next gen kid than the young guys and girls at Sophie's old job. Sophie was preparing to be the big sister in this relationship.

After finishing her conversation with Hope, Sophie said goodbye to Deborah and Bruce one last time. Their parting had not been as carefully arranged as the Albright's ministry generally was, but Sophie got more than one hug from Deborah because of the multiple goodbyes.

She said goodbye to Ross in front of the hotel as she waited for her ride to the airport.

"I could have taken you there, you know." He grinned shyly.

"No, it's fine. I'm covered." Arranging travel on her own was actually a big step. Sophie hadn't traveled this far by herself before. It had always been with her mother, like on their trip to see her *abuela* in Puerto Rico. This new independence wasn't just about growing into being a responsible adult, it was about learning to live within her gift even in a strange place and an unpredictable environment.

"Okay. Well, it was great to meet you and see you in action. Even chasing you down the halls of a haunted orphanage." He chuckled deep in his skinny chest.

Sophie absorbed the warmth from Ross's smile, a smile that reminded her of Anthony. She decided to call Anthony when she got to the airport.

"You have a new mission already?" She was a *little* curious.

Ross nodded for a second, squinting at her as if assessing what he could tell. "A local priest has been in touch with the owners of that property, where the old orphanage is. He wants us to work with his church to purge the place."

"Wow." Sophie was impressed and not the least interested in sticking around to see how that goes.

The ride to the airport was thankfully short. The driver had two grumpy imps sitting next to him. He only had a few things to say. All were complaints. Sophie wondered if the imps were there because the driver was so grumpy or if he was so grumpy because the imps were there.

As she dragged her carry-on luggage toward the security line, which wasn't too long this time on a Tuesday, she dialed Anthony and stood six feet behind a small family waiting in that line.

"Hey. You in the middle of another day of demon chasing?" He spoke low, reminding her that he was probably at work.

She let go of her case and adjusted her face mask. "No. The team is wrapping up and heading out. I'm actually at the airport catching a plane for California."

"The team is going out there to minister to somebody?"

"No, just me. I'm going to see that girl who talks to angels. I'm hoping I can help her out a bit."

"What? Wait. You're traveling on your own? Like a side mission?"

"Sort of. Maybe more personal than a mission." She laughed through her nose. "Part of it is just learning to travel on my own with no ... fear of what might happen." She sized up the four angels surrounding the small family in front of her. The angels idled, their glow set to dim. But they were there.

"Like you were afraid to travel before."

"Alone. I've never flown this far on my own before."

"To the West Coast?"

"Yep."

"LA?"

"Yeah. I'm gonna stay at least the first night with this girl, Hope."

"I wonder if she really sees angels."

"Talks to angels is the way I first heard about her. She's been treated in the way you would expect for a young woman who claims to talk to angels."

"Yeah, I get it. Hmm. Seems like a worthy mission for you." He hummed some more. "I mean, you could help her figure out what it is she's really seeing—if it really is something."

"Right. I think so too."

"So, you called to tell me about your change of plans?"

"I called you because I miss talking to you."

"Really? Yeah. Well, I miss seeing you too. Come home soon."

"Home? Sure. Yeah, I won't be long."

The Girl Who Talks to Angels

Hope Decker bounced her knee and stared out the sliding glass door to the dim light on her small balcony. She was tempted to call Eddie, but it might be too late for him back in Minnesota. And he would ask questions she didn't yet know how to answer. Probably by tomorrow she would have something more definite to tell him. Assuming this chick didn't kill her in her sleep.

Where did that thought come from? Hope leaned back in the squeaky desk chair and spun toward her computer screen. She had logged out of the customer service console, so that was good. She had at least been paying enough attention to do that right. She checked the clock on the computer. Nearly eleven. Sophie should be there any minute.

Taking another of those increasingly frequent deep breaths, she tried to remember if she'd taken her bedtime pill. She might forget it after Sophie arrived. Hope got up and bent over the blue crate she had set up as her nightstand next to her mattress. The pill bottle was there. She must have taken the dose when she put the bottle in place. Of course she did.

Hope jumped when the intercom honked like a police car trying to get her attention. "Oh. Uh." She gained her balance after wavering on her way to fully upright. She pushed past three unfamiliar angels on the way to the door. Did this chick bring her own? Of course she would. She was hardcore on this stuff.

"Hello. Come on up." She hit the open button for the door at the bottom of the stairs. With one last deep breath, she checked around the apartment. She tried to ignore the unfamiliar spirits. Then she opened her door calmly. But the thumping footsteps were still a couple stories down. Thump, thump, thump. Was this girl heavy? Did it matter?

Finally Sophie came into view when she rounded the last flight, a backpack over one shoulder, suitcase in her other hand. She wasn't heavy, she was lugging stuff. And maybe weary from her travels.

"Hey."

"Hey." Hope hurried several strides toward the top of the stairs. "Let me take one of those."

Sophie handed her the backpack. It looked like an automatic reaction. The backpack was heavy. A computer and some other stuff, no doubt.

Sophie's tense motions reminded Hope that this might be awkward and scary for her guest like it was for her. "This way." She led Sophie to her door and pushed it open for her. She pointed to the bedroom door. "This is you."

"But ..." Sophie gestured toward the mattress on the living room floor.

Hope shook her head. "No. The ... the bedroom is for you. Give you some privacy."

"You're giving me your bedroom?"

"I'm from the Midwest. My parents taught me to be polite."

Sophie laughed, as if she recognized the type. "Yeah. But I'd be fine on the air mattress."

Hope stepped into the bedroom, past Sophie, and walked to the corner of her bed, where she set the backpack. "Can I be honest?" She turned and faced Sophie.

Sophie parked her rolling case. "Sure. Of course."

"I just ... I feel ... I would feel safer out there. I mean, if someone else is here." She took a hasty breath. "It's people."

"What do you mean?"

"I ... I mean, I'm not afraid of the angels and such. But I'm afraid of people."

Sophie's dark eyebrows were lowered a bit. "So, you wanna be out there so you can escape easier?"

Hope nodded.

"What about me? Would I have to escape out the window?" Sophie grimaced toward the one window in the bedroom. Then she smiled.

Laughing a lot harder than she intended, Hope let out some sounds that were supposed to be words but hadn't grown up yet. Sophie seemed all right. At least better than Hope had feared. She seemed pretty normal, actually.

That was when Hope stopped laughing to take another look at the new angels. "Those three are yours. The big guy, the cute chick, and the tough one. Does that one use *they* pronouns?"

Sophie's jaw dropped. Then she laughed and clapped her hand over her mouth. She turned deep red and laughed until she was panting for breath. Was she crying? Trying not to cry?

Hope just stared. Waiting. The three angels crowded around Sophie. Interesting that they got to the apartment before she did. Maybe they were scoping the place for her. All three. Three was a lot.

Hope turned to her own girl spirit, the shy one that was always nearby. "That one's with me everywhere. I haven't tried traveling a lot though." She made a half wave toward her angel girl.

"Yeah, I haven't traveled much. This is really the longest trip by myself ... ever."

"So, you came all this way just to help me out?"

"Is that what Eddie told you?"

"He was all gushy about you. He said you could help me somehow. But I doubt he really knows what he's talking about." She stopped rambling. Sophie was checking out Hope's angel—the girl who kept her company. That's how she thought of her. "Astrid is the name I gave her. She hasn't objected yet. Sort of ignores it. I assume she would have to kill me if I ever learned her real name. Or something like that."

"I don't know about that." Sophie was shaking her head. "I don't get names from any of the good ones. How long have you known her?"

"Known? Well, I've seen her all my life, as far as I can remember. But she didn't start talking back to me until I was, like, six or seven. She warned me from the start that people would think I was crazy if I told them about her. So, I kept the secret."

"Until ..."

"Oh, you know. You get comfortable, alone in your bedroom, and you jibber on like you're talking to a friend, assuming no one is ever gonna pop open the door. A kid's naive assumptions, really."

"Who caught you?"

"My big brother. He said it was freaky. But he just treated her like my sort of invisible friend and let it go. Until one time we were fighting over the TV remote, and he said something. My mom was already suspecting something was up with me. I didn't really play with other kids unless I had to. I was nine by then, too old for an invisible friend, she said."

Hope finally woke to the fact that they were just standing at the foot of her bed. "Maybe we should talk out there."

"So you can escape?" Sophie grinned.

"Right. Gotta check for exits."

"Like some international spy."

"Or a crazy girl who talks to angels."

Sophie followed her into the living room. "How much did Eddie tell you about how we met him and what we did for him and ... Brandy?"

"Brandy. That girl's a mess. Pretty mean. But Eddie is devoted to her."

"So, he didn't tell you specifics?"

"He said you were with a group that could, like, tell the nasty ones to get lost. And they did. He said you bought him a bus ticket to go home. Him and Brandy. Of course I appreciate the bus ticket thing. But the thing about telling one of them to take off—I don't know about that."

"You've heard of exorcists, right?"

"In movies. Is that real?"

"Not like the movies, but there is a way to get free from ones like that guy over there." She nodded toward the dusty, rusty one that hovered in the corner most of the time. "Doesn't *she* tell you about getting rid of him?" Sophie nodded back toward Astrid, who was standing between them and the front door.

Sophie's angels were lined up between Sophie and that rusty guy. *Nasty Man* was what Hope called him sometimes. She wouldn't say that to Sophie.

"He's always around. Or almost always. I don't mind so much. I've seen worse."

"Do you talk to him?"

She shook her head. "I don't recommend it. He'll mess with your head." She hesitated. "He's pretty mean."

"So why do you let him hang around?"

"Is it really up to me?"

Sophie turned to Astrid. "Why haven't you explained this to her?"

Astrid responded. "I was waiting for you to get here, Sophie."

Hope and Sophie both swore. Then they simultaneously apologized.

A New Hope

Sophie had let Hope talk her into taking the bed. She was too tired to put up a fight about anything. But she believed the girl really would feel trapped in the bedroom with a stranger in the apartment. Hope seemed fragile. The meds were holding her together, perhaps, but only like masking tape, and not enough of it.

She slept solidly. The toll of the intense ministry in Iowa was compounded by the long flight and some bad nights. In the dim of the morning, Sophie lay on the overly soft mattress listening for signs of life from the living room or kitchen. She could sense at least two angels in the apartment that were not in the bedroom. Only her female angel was visibly with her. Should she ask for her name? It didn't seem right. Though Sophie was sure she wouldn't have to be sacrificed if she found out. Not like with Rumpelstiltskin, however that fairytale went. She had probably heard a sanitized version as a kid.

Maybe Hope was a sound sleeper. The meds could do that. It was only six in the morning, but that was eight back home. Sophie slid out of bed and jarred her knees when she found the floor closer than she remembered. She hurried to the bathroom as quietly as she could, dealing with one of the consequences of sleeping straight through the night.

A glimpse of one foot was all she saw of Hope, motionless on what did look like a good quality air mattress. Not that Sophie had much experience with those.

Sitting in the bathroom, she recalled the moment last night when Hope described Sophie's three angels. That was the first time she had met someone who saw them all so clearly. There had been a little girl at Detta's church who describe three shiny lights, but that wasn't the same. The comment about *they* pronouns was surely a joke, something Sophie had joked with herself about. She still hadn't settled the angel gender question. Probably gender was like everything else she saw in the spirit world. Mostly symbolic.

She shook her head as she washed her hands. Hope had drifted off to sleep around midnight. Probably drug induced. Sophie wondered what she was taking. Last night Sophie's head had been spinning, so she didn't learn much about Hope's situation. What was she expecting to learn? The girl definitely did see angels. That was really important to start with.

On tiptoes and with only small joint-cracking sounds, Sophie made it back to the bedroom. She was hungry, but she had a granola bar in her bag. More granola than bar by now.

She sat on the bed and opened her laptop, picking crumbs from the granola bar wrapper. There were a few emails she wanted to see on the computer instead of her phone. Priscilla had sent a picture from a baseball game she attended with that new guy, Curtis. Their smiles were both genuine. Was she in love? Sophie envied someone who had a clear answer to that question. Yes or no. *Definite* was something she aspired to. About love. About angels, she was definite enough for now.

That Astrid angel came through the door. Through the closed door. She tilted her head to one side as if studying Sophie.

"You have a message for me?"

"Just love. The Father loves you. He is glad you're bringing your strength to one who needs that same strength awakened in her."

Sophie stared at her. What kind of message was that? Not a lot of useful information. "Should I help get her free from that rusty guy?"

"That will come."

"But I shouldn't push it?"

"Not yet. It will come."

"So, like, just be her friend?"

"That will serve her very well." Then she turned and stepped back through that wooden door.

"Ooookaaay." Sophie shook her head and let the conversation seep into the cracks in her personal protective surface. Okay. Be friends. Take her time. She could do that.

She heard a grumbling from the living room. Maybe Hope was talking to herself. Then more talking. It sounded like a conversation. Sophie sat perfectly still, not exactly trying to hear what Hope was saying, but not *not* trying. She drew a big breath through her nose and chuckled. It just occurred to her that she had spoken aloud to Hope's angel. Her host might have heard something of that conversation. Not much, though. Sophie couldn't clearly hear through the door as Hope and her angel conversed.

She closed her laptop and slipped off the bed. Less of a jolt. This time she recalled that there was no bedframe, no space under the box springs. Was that purposeful? A defense against having things hiding under her bed? Did Hope realize spirits could actually hide inside the box springs? If Sophie pointed that out, would Hope get rid of that too? What about a mattress?

A big sigh enforced an end to that Ferris wheel of useless thoughts. Sophie pulled the hem of her long T-shirt down and walked through the bedroom door ... after opening it.

"Good morning. I guess it's not so early for you as it is for me." Hope's straw-blonde hair was all stabbing to one side, the bare side of her face creased pink from her pillow.

"Yeah. Sorry. Was it going to the bathroom or talking to your angel that woke you?"

"I don't know. I could sense movement. I didn't really identify what I was hearing until I opened my eyes to see that guy."

Sophie's big male angel was standing by the kitchen. Was he going to cook them breakfast? More likely he was standing there to block that surly dude who was hunkered in the corner by the kitchen counter. Good. Restrained. That was the way Sophie liked to see the bad guys, if she had to see them. Her guardian was good at subduing.

"He's guarding you from the nasty one like he guards me." She spoke to Hope while still monitoring the angels.

"So, you really think they guard us?"

"Don't you? Isn't Astrid your guardian angel?"

"I don't know. That all sounds too ... Hallmark for me. I mean, is that really a thing, even?"

Sophie had been through this with Kimmy once. There wasn't anything exactly that said *guardian angel* in the Bible, but the idea was there. Still, Sophie hesitated about what to tell Hope. Did the girl even care what the Bible said? Kimmy wasn't impressed.

"I don't think Hallmark invented the idea of guardian angels. It's a really old concept that the Greeks and Hebrews and other ancient cultures held." She snorted. "Here I am sounding like the History Channel."

"Will there be commercial breaks? I'm hungry."

"Me too. Do you wanna go out to eat?"

"It's not even six thirty. I don't know where the nearest all-night truck stop is."

Sophie laughed. "Okay. Right. Sorry. Still adjusting."

"No problem. I have cereal. The healthy kind."

"Not Cap'n Crunch?"

"Sorry. All out."

"Bummer. I could get my sugar high on early."

Hope paused. "Do you take meds?"

"To numb the angel sightings? Not for a long time. I got healed of my anxiety and stopped those meds too."

"Right. But healed?" Hope heaved herself up off the mattress, which was even lower than her regular bed. She was rail thin like Eddie, so it wasn't a tough trick for her.

Sophie answered her obvious skepticism about being healed. "Yeah. Back when I was totally freaking out and completely on my own, I met this church lady. Pentecostals and healing and all that. Those were the folks who believed me when I told them about the angels."

"Really? Pentecostals? Aren't they the ones that dance around with snakes and stuff?"

"Ha." Sophie followed Hope into her little kitchen. "My friend Detta would run and hide if she saw a snake. She's a strong lady, but she nearly passed out once when a toad hopped across her sidewalk." Slowing down, Sophie got back to Hope's question. "Not all Pentecostals are like that." She paused and looked at her big angel. "And I suppose not all of them are like Detta either. She's probably uniquely tolerant and wise. She's taught me lots. And none of it has ever proved to be a scam. I was afraid of that. I didn't trust church people before I met her."

"So, do you …?"

"Do I? Do I what?"

"Believe in God like Astrid does."

Sophie chuckled softly. She couldn't help herself. "Like Astrid does?" She backtracked again. "So have you ever tried going to church?"

"Oh, I grew up in church. It was, like, my parents' total social network. Business, parties, it all happened around the church. But those folks didn't think any sane person could claim to actually see angels."

"Okay. Well, there's lots of different kinds of churches and even more different kinds of church people." Sophie took a cereal bowl from Hope. "I mean, I found out that I actually had a big advantage. Like, most church people just *try* to believe in supernatural stuff. For me, it was easy. And what they believed about good and evil and angels and demons all fit right in with what I was seeing. I just had to find Christians who really believe in what I see."

"Really believe, huh?" Hope sounded about half interested, let alone half convinced. Maybe she would have to meet Detta to really trust her. Weren't there any Christians around here she could meet?

Sophie consulted her female angel. She wasn't talking.

"It's not like I don't favor Jesus. I mean, if Christians had any resemblance to him at all, I could get with them. But I just don't see it." Hope set the cereal box on the table.

"How close have you looked lately?"

Hope's face hardened.

Sophie shrugged. "I'm not trying to get you to sign up for anything. I just gotta be honest. This stuff makes lots of sense to me now because I *did* sign up with Jesus and with people who worship him."

"Okay. I won't make any Jesus jokes around you."

Sophie smiled her acceptance of the deal and poured some brown roughage into her bowl.

Hope retrieved the milk from the fridge. Almond milk.

Okay, Sophie was traveling. She would try most things at least once. And it turned out to be surprisingly good. Both the roughage and the milk that didn't come from a cow.

While Hope took a shower, Sophie sat in her desk chair and looked out the sliding glass door over the roofs of neighboring apartment buildings. The sun was up, and the mist of morning was thinning. They weren't that close to the ocean as far as Sophie knew, but maybe it still influenced the air up here in the hills. A flatlander, she started to calculate how it was that she could see over the top of a building that was at least as tall as the one Hope lived in. Steep hills. Exotic.

When Hope came out of the bathroom wearing only a towel, she stopped and studied Sophie. "Are you straight? I mean, it's okay with me if you're not. I just don't wanna cause any trouble with, like ..." She jogged her head and lifted both hands to indicate her meager attire.

"I'm straight. And not easily offended."

"Oh. That's good. Especially the last part." Hope looked like she wanted to say more, but just closed her mouth and proceeded to the bedroom.

Once they were both dressed, Hope suggested going for a walk. "There's this park along a river canal. And this time of day, it'll be really nice. You know, not too hot yet."

"Are you near the desert here?"

"Kind of. I mean, so much of California is dry, but we're not, like, *in* the desert proper."

Something about Hope saying *we're* made Sophie wonder who she included in that, who was part of her life. It was a diversion. Not important at the moment. But the girl seemed pretty isolated.

It was a nice walk. Palm trees reminded Sophie that she was far from home. In the warmth of summer, that distance wasn't so obvious as it surely would have been in the middle of winter.

"What do you do for work?" Sophie was taking in the scenery. The river was low but still running swiftly enough to see the ripples from a dozen yards above it. The water was green in spots, but the idea of running water was refreshing. She was congratulating herself for actually seeing the scenery and not just ogling the various angels. There was one big ugly demon hanging over a small walking bridge. She supposed Ivan and Lee would want to get to the bottom of what that guy was doing there.

Hope answered her question. "I'm a customer service associate for a smart thermostat company. I help people configure their devices. Hand-holding, mostly. Over the phone."

"Ah. So it helps that you can't see them or their angels." Sophie scoped that fat demon one more time.

"He's a beauty, isn't he?" Hope glared at him and shook her head sharply.

Sophie took a moment to relish the fact that someone was actually seeing the world the way she saw it. "You ever wonder what they're doing where they hang out?"

"I've been trying not to see them most of my life. I try not to think about any of it."

"How's that going?"

"I think I've given up on caring about most people most of the time. That makes it easier to not care what their angels or demons are about."

"Oh. That ... doesn't sound so good."

"What did you do?"

"Mostly I was angry all the time at everybody. People and angels both."

"Oh. Well, that sounds so much healthier." Hope snickered in a way that joggled her chest and shoulders.

"Yeah. Aren't you glad I came out here to help you?"

"Ha." Hope took a deep breath. "You think we *get* each other just because we've been seeing these things all our lives?" She gestured toward an angel jogging behind a middle-aged woman with a thick waist.

Sophie disciplined herself to not comment on that chubby jogger and her svelte angel. "I think it helps. Though I expect there are other folks who would get you if you gave 'em a chance. I find science fiction nerds are pretty easy to get along with."

Hope laughed so hard that she had to stop walking for a couple seconds. "Did you talk to Eddie about his theories on alien abductions?"

"Oh. No, we didn't get that far in our relationship."

"Relationship? He's pretty young for you."

"Yeah. I was thinking big sister."

"Sounds about right. Eddie could use one of those."

"I thought he and Brandy were brother and sister at first."

"They've been together since they were kids. Little kids. I always wondered if they got together because they look and act alike, or if they look and act alike because they've been together for so long. I wasn't around at the beginning."

"You lived in Minnesota?"

"Yeah. Our whole family is from there."

"Okay, so you came out here to … get away." Sophie avoided the word *escape,* though she wouldn't blame Hope if that's what it was.

They paused under a cluster of palm trees. "I always dreamed of living out here. And I thought I might find more people who could put up with me and what I see."

"Folks back home weren't into it?"

"Definitely not. Church people couldn't decide whether to commit me or cast the demons out of me."

"It wouldn't hurt to get rid of that nasty guy." Sophie couldn't see him now. Maybe he resided exclusively in the apartment.

"Yeah. You'll have to show me how that goes." Hope turned on the balls of her feet and started walking again, swatting at a fly or bee.

Sophie's female angel was walking ahead of them with Hope's wispy girl. They didn't exactly seem to be talking, but they gave the impression of a comfortable reunion. Sophie could only imagine. Angel relationships were among the advanced topics she hadn't explored.

"How long have you been out here?"

"Since I turned eighteen. What's that, four years? Really struggled at first. First real contact I made turned out to be a drug dealer. Got me hooked on heroin. Then I got arrested and sent to rehab."

"Arrested?"

"I was high. I assaulted this lady who was telling me I had to pay for the groceries I had in my cart. Can you imagine the rudeness of her telling me *that*?" She shrugged. "Rehab was way better than jail." She laughed. "Better drugs."

"Like methadone?"

"Yeah. Or ... I ... there was another one. I don't remember. Don't need to remember now. I'm clean. Found better friends. Or at least got rid of the bad ones."

That last comment reinforced Sophie's impression that Hope was pretty much on her own. What was Sophie supposed to do about that?

Bossing Demons

Hope made apologies to Sophie—she had a meeting with her supervisor that morning. But the rest of the morning was quiet. After their walk, Sophie had sat with her laptop doing something that looked fairly boring.

Hope made cream cheese and cucumber sandwiches for lunch. They sat on the little balcony to eat. A coolish breeze was coming from the west. She liked to imagine she could smell the ocean, whether that was possible from this far inland or not.

"So, you gonna show me how to get rid of that nasty guy?" She glanced over her shoulder. He went invisible as soon as she said that.

Sophie craned her neck and then closed her eyes. "I can actually see them with my eyes closed sometimes when they go invisible."

"Huh. I guess I've noticed that. Though, like I said, I generally try *not* to see them."

"Yeah. I know how that goes." Sophie looked at her with serious business in her eyes. "You want him to leave?"

"Yeah. Sure. He creeps me out."

"Okay. The only way I know how to do it is through the authority of Jesus."

"So, like, 'In the name of the Father and the Son and the Holy Ghost,' kinda thing?" Hope had seen that in a movie or two.

"Something like that."

"Sure. Fine. Don't let me hold you back."

Sophie took a deep breath and nodded for a couple seconds before closing her eyes again.

Hope looked over the rooftops toward the haze that represented what she could see of the ocean. Tried to relax.

"In the name of the Lord Jesus Christ, I command that nasty demon to leave this apartment and leave Hope right now. And don't come back, and don't harm anyone around here either." Sophie opened her eyes and sent a searching gaze around them. Maybe she was thinking about the neighbors. Or maybe there was some other thing she was looking for.

At a swift movement from over her shoulder, Hope swung around to just catch that nasty demon swooping up and away. She had never seen him do that before. Usually he just went invisible. After tracking his swoop, however, a flash of deep red froze her.

"You saw that?" Sophie's eyes were beaming into Hope's, her whole face in fighting mode.

"Uh, yeah. What was that?"

"Another one."

"Another one? Another creepy guy?"

"Another spirit. This one doesn't look like a guy." Sophie closed her eyes and then tensed as if a jolt of electricity had come through the deck chair. "Oh. She knows you. She's ... attached to you, like, in a deeper way." Sophie opened her eyes and turned her head slightly. "I think she was hiding behind the creepy guy."

"What? Really? They can do that?"

"They do it all the time."

Hope swore and then apologized, given that Sophie was a church lady—as unlikely a church lady as she was. "Uh, do I need to d-d-do ..." It felt like she was glitching over a remote video connection. Like even the connection with herself was bad. Then everything went red. That red she-devil or whatever was right in her face. "Get her off me." Her throat squeezed shut, and that plea turned to an embarrassing squelching sound.

From some distant place, some high up place, Sophie's voice called down. "You have to tell her you won't serve her anymore."

The words swirled inside Hope's head. "Serve her?" Then she could see the beast more clearly. She recognized it from when she used to hang with Marcus, her old boyfriend and drug dealer. The she-beast was still there, clearly, like some really rotten leftovers. Hope tried to laugh at the idea of demon leftovers but couldn't find the breath. "Help me." She might have said that part aloud. Maybe just a whisper.

Sophie was kneeling in front of her. She said something forceful, but the words got distorted and lost. Not lost on that red beast though. She was pissed. Really pissed. She was going to kill ... who? Sophie? Hope? Maybe both of them.

"Call the police." Hope might not have said that part aloud either. Her tongue seemed to be literally tied. Locked. Then she laughed. A belching, gasping, hysterical laugh. Where did that come from?

Suddenly Sophie was clear. Right in front of Hope. Staring. Maybe a bit worried. "Tell her you don't need her anymore."

"I don't … I—I don't … I don't need you anymore, you bit—" The curse got interrupted by another belch. How gross. *What the …?*

"I declare you free in the name of Jesus. Obsession spirit, I command you to stay away from Hope, and from this apartment, and to do no harm to anyone around here. Go where Jesus tells you to go." She was bossing.

Sophie was bossing that demon. Maybe all demons.

It was awesome.

Layers

Sophie got up from her knees and swept the sand or dirt off her bare legs. She checked the air around them. Only guardians. All four were visible. They were acting sort of free and easy. Not quite celebrating, maybe, but a fist pump wouldn't have been a total surprise. The big guy was smiling at Sophie with that "Proud of you, girl" look. She was pretty proud of herself, truth be told.

"How do you feel?"

Hope looked up at her like a kid needing a hug. Sophie was not a hugger. Not like that. But the hug dilemma flipped off screen with the arrival of four little fairy imps floating above Hope's head like bubbles from a bubble pipe.

"What are those?" Maybe that was a dumb question.

Hope looked up and laughed. "Ha. There you guys are. Where have you been?"

"What?" Sophie was trying to filter on two levels. She recalled times when sending one spirit away revealed another. She was also trying to figure out Hope's relationship to those little fairies. That little flock reminded her of someone. Of Crystal, probably.

"Oh. Well, I used to see these little ones when I was a kid. Maybe all the way up until I moved out here."

"Which was when you got involved in drugs."

"Oh, I was doing different stuff back home, but yeah, that was when I got with Marcus and started doing heroin."

"Maybe these ones are, like, subservient to the big red ... uh, bad girl that we just sent away."

"Bad girl? I suppose. I mean, I wonder if these ones are really bad, though. They kept me company back in the day." Hope glanced at her angel, who had her arms folded over her chest.

Sophie laughed at the obvious body language on a heavenly body. "Your angel agrees with me. We should send the little ones away."

"Really?" Hope turned from Sophie to her angel and back. "I don't know."

"What if we send them away and you see if you feel better? Maybe you won't miss them."

"Uh, well, I guess that's possible. I mean, it seems like just about anything is possible with you around."

"I would attribute that to God, actually."

"Whatever. I don't think I'm ready to argue with you either way."

"Okay. So, you agree that the little fairy ones should all get lost?"

"I do." She pronounced it solemnly and then snickered.

Sophie appreciated the humor but didn't want to take these cutesy ones too lightly. She gave the usual command for them to leave in the name of Jesus, and they gathered into a pitiful little huddle and looked pleadingly at Hope.

"I get the impression that they—" Sophie changed her mind about telling Hope the little spirits hung around her because they liked being with a person who could see them. She didn't want to complicate the already tangled emotions connected to them. "They're waiting for you to confirm you really want them to go away."

Shrugging, Hope stuck out her lower lip. "Let's do it. I haven't seen them for a while. I don't think I'll miss them these days."

With that, they all vanished. Sophie didn't have to go back over the command for them to leave.

Hope's angel was glowing brighter than Sophie had seen up to this point.

Looking a little spaced out, Hope's eyes meandering around the balcony, her head wavering slightly. She drew a long breath. "Wow. I don't even know how I feel." She lowered her head. "I kinda feel empty. Or lonely. Or something."

"Would you be open to asking God's Spirit to fill in that empty place? That's what Jesus offered to his followers."

"You mean, like, Pentecost? That was one weird story."

Sophie chuckled and let her offer lie where it had landed. Not exactly on receptive soil. She prayed instead. "Thank you, God, for setting Hope free. Please bless her and protect her and keep all unholy spirits away from her. Keep them from coming back and filling up that empty place." This was uncertain territory for Sophie. Most people she had dealt with were already Christians or pretty open to becoming one, especially once they saw their oppressors vanquished by the power of Jesus.

"You do this kinda thing all the time?" Hope wavered as she stood up. She gripped the back of the deck chair.

Sophie reached out to steady her and found a strange coldness on her skin. "Are you okay? Do you feel that cold?"

"I have this strange taste in my mouth. And I just thought about my sister for the first time in forever."

"Charity?"

Hope snapped her head toward Sophie. She nearly pitched into Sophie's arms. "How do you know about her?"

"I don't really know. I just had that name pop into my head. Though I guess it was a good guess she might be named Charity."

"She was my twin."

"Oh. *Was*. Oh, wow."

"Why wow?" Hope gripped the frame around the sliding glass door.

"I think that cold was something to do with a human spirit. I guess some would call it a ghost. I'm not sure what to call it."

"Like a real ghost?"

"I actually don't know much about those, if they even exist. I just felt this coldness around you, and you started talking about your ... deceased ... twin sister."

Hope shivered hard. "Oh." She swore. "Wow. Okay, wow. Now I'm saying wow." She looked at Sophie with a question in her eyes.

"I guess we tell it to go away. Whatever it is."

"Sure." Hope was hugging herself as if she were freezing in eighty-six degree weather.

"So, any spirit related to Sophie's sister, Charity, has to go where Jesus tells you to go. Go now and leave Hope once and for all." Sophie had one hand on Hope's shoulder, afraid she would face-plant on the balcony.

"Oh." Hope stared toward the coast across the terracotta rooftops. "Why is this happening?"

"What part?"

"The parts. The one after another."

"That's pretty typical of what I've seen. It's like there's a hierarchy among these things, and one has to stay quiet as long as another is in charge."

"Was the nasty guy in charge?"

"Hmm. I don't know. Another thing I've seen is the really powerful ones hide and throw the weaker ones under the bus. So to speak."

"Huh. And you're the bus?"

Sophie snuffled a laugh. "Not really." Then she thought of something. "But I do get to drive the bus sometimes."

Recovery

"Are we done yet?" Hope let herself grin even though she was still worried about the answer to her question. Even asking seemed risky.

Sophie sat on the couch with her legs folded to one side. "How do you feel?"

"Kinda unsettled. Stirred up."

"Yeah. Hey, is it okay if I call someone to get her and her prayer group praying for you?"

"You could have done that without asking me."

"Yeah, I could. But it's like it works better if you go along with it."

"Huh. This is so out there. I have no idea what I even want. It's like landing on another planet and being asked what part I wanna live on when I've never even heard of the place." She shook her head. "But hey, is this prayer lady gonna pray for me to, like, get converted?"

"What if she does? It's still always gonna be up to you to choose."

Clucking a laugh, Hope rocked back in her desk chair. Despite its utilitarian purpose, it was her favorite seat. The easy tipping back was the best part. She often tipped way back when she was on a support call. One guy accused her of lying in bed while talking to him. He was probably flirting.

What was the question? "Really, I'm just spinning. Like my head, I think, is literally spinning. Or maybe just my brain inside it." Once Hope got her mouth going, it was hard to stop. At least harder than usual. She was distracted now by the four angels posted around the room. One in each corner. "It's like a peripheral defense or something. Is that what they call it?"

Sophie shrugged. Then she looked from one angel to another. "Sure. Looks like it." She turned back toward Hope. "Okay for me to call her? Detta, my friend?"

"Uh, sure. Go ahead."

Sophie got up and went out to the balcony. She left the door open a few inches but closed the screen. There weren't many flying bugs around, but Hope still remembered summer in Minnesota and her mom yelling at her for not closing the screen door as fast as possible. Her mom had mosquitos in mind, of course. Maybe Sophie did too.

Hope used to picture her mom keeping the angels outside—at least until they asked nicely to come in. One of the apparently good ones that hung around her mother was likely to do that. She seemed not to feel welcome in the house. Hope had grown familiar with that feeling herself.

Wow. Such a brain drift. It was like trying to take a fast corner on a snow-packed Minnesota road. That thought triggered a memory. Her dad driving the family car, a van. The big kind. And the thing sliding around a turn. He was saying words Hope had never heard her dad say before. She was, like, six years old. And she saw angels hovering over the vehicle but sort of watching powerlessly. Her angel lady was one of them. Just watching, then reaching impotently as the van flipped onto its side and crashed roof first into a big willow tree. Hope knew it was a willow tree because her dad always included that in his telling of the story. None of them had been seriously hurt. Seatbelts and car seats really worked.

But Hope hadn't forgotten the impotent angels. It wasn't that they didn't care. They were hovering over her as she and her brother and dad flew out of control toward some dangerous end. The angels got no credit for the save. That went to the car company and federal safety laws.

Why think of that now? It was like Sophie's magic was stirring up all kinds of stuff. Hope forced herself to focus on the computer screen for a few minutes. She checked for important messages from work. Nothing urgent there. She deleted some nonurgent stuff.

Sophie slid the screen door open, then wedged in through the heavy glass door. "You want this shut?"

"Yeah."

She slid both doors shut. "My friend Detta is gonna be praying." She hesitated like she was trying to decide how much to say. Then a text message interrupted her. She read it, then glanced at Hope. "Detta says to tell you something. I don't know if it will make sense to you."

Hope shrugged.

"Well, she said to tell you that 'angels are only as powerless as our prayers.' Which, to me, sounds kinda harsh. I don't think people at my church would say it that way, but …" She stopped when Hope raised her hand.

Why she was raising her hand, Hope wasn't even going to try to explain. "You don't have to go on and on apologizing. What she said makes perfect sense to me."

"Really?"

Hope laughed at the stunned look on Sophie's face. Then she debated telling her why that little saying or whatever it was seemed to fit right in. What would it mean if she admitted that this distant church lady had, like, read her mind? Whatever.

"I was just remembering the time my dad crashed our van. And I was flopping around like a rag doll, seeing these angels lined up above the car just watching it slide and flip and slide some more. They were, like, powerless to do anything about it." She raised her eyebrows at Sophie. "I mean, they were powerless. And we generally didn't pray about stuff. We just did a memorized prayer at supper and bedtime. And not even that every day. So it was like that lady was saying …" She didn't know what else to say, but at least she was being honest with Sophie.

"Wow. Okay. I guess I should stop doubting Detta sometime soon, huh?"

Hope shrugged again. She was reserving the right to go on doubting. But maybe Sophie didn't have an excuse by now. The question was whether that was where Hope wanted to be. Right where Sophie was. With her faith.

The traumatic shock of all that had hatched out of her and then flown away was more than Hope had expected today. Or any day. She just wanted to zone out now and let it slide. Or at least let it coast for a while. Sliding out of control was no fun. She looked at Sophie and tried not to sound too pitiful. "Okay if I just listen to music and catch up on my social media stuff?"

Sophie nodded and smiled. It was a knowing, big sister smile. A permissive smile. Just what Hope needed. Maybe later she would need a big sister butt kicking.

What Next?

Detta returned from lunch with Roddy. Roderick. "Roderick, if you like." She quoted him aloud. "If I like? If I like what?" She settled her purse in the middle of the kitchen table, assuring herself she would move it as soon as she settled down. What was spinning around inside her? What had he really said that was so wrong? She was mostly rewinding polite and friendly words from him. Was the pleasantness of those words so suspicious?

"You know men just want one thing."

"Ha. Who says? That's not right." She shook her head briskly. "What's gotten into you, Detta?"

That was when her phone rang.

She took in a purging breath before answering. "Sophie. How are you doing? How's California?"

"So, Anthony told you about it?"

"Sure. We're a team when it comes to keeping up on your comings and goings."

"Well, that's good. It's nice to have a team on my side."

Detta could imagine early days in Sophie's life when there was a team of doctors and psychiatrists who claimed to be on her side. She pushed past that distraction. "So, you met that girl, the one who talks to angels?"

"I'm staying with her. She sees things pretty much the same way I do as far as I can tell."

"Yeah. It would be hard to really compare, I guess. But she sees and talks to them?"

"And they talk to her. Although maybe not much more than what I'm hearing these days."

"That all sounds good. Did you get to help her with the whole thing?" Detta had only caught a refracted version of the girl's issues through Anthony. He had been much more focused on his anxiety about when Sophie was coming home.

"I actually did some deliverance for her. She had a few layers of spirits hanging around her."

"Oh, well, praise the Lord for that." Detta felt a surge of motherly pride. "So, how is she doing?"

"We've both been pretty quiet since I sent those things away. She's just chilling and maybe checking on work stuff online. I was wondering what I should be doing for her."

"You're wondering about the aftercare?"

"Exactly. I forgot what you called it, but yeah. What am I supposed to do after?"

"Well, that really depends on the state of the person you're ministering to. I mean, the ministry isn't over just because you see the spirits leave. The person needs to be filled up with God's Spirit in their place."

"But what if she's not ready for that? I told her that. I mean, I can't think of what else she could need or how to really help her apart from that."

"That's right. Your head's in the right place, Sophie. And your heart, of course."

"I wonder if she would be willing to talk to you."

"Really? Long-distance aftercare?" Detta hummed. The lingering haze from her time with Roderick—yes she did like calling him that—smothered her confidence about what she had to offer. "I ... sure. I'd be glad to talk to her if she wants."

Sophie hesitated. Maybe she was hearing the pause in Detta's answer. "I'll ask her. Maybe later. You have prayer meeting tonight?"

"No, that was last night. The summer break is over. We're back to our regular Tuesdays."

"Oh. I guess my prayer request is too late. Can you still get the word out to the prayer circle about where this all stands?"

"Sure. We were just waiting to get an update. I'll pass it along." She paused. "I'm still wondering if I should tell the ladies about this new man I'm seeing."

"A new man? You ... you went out with someone?"

"In fact, I did. We had lunch together. A lunch date, I suppose."

"What's his name?"

"Well, I think I'll call him Roderick. Others call him Roddy, but he's a dignified gentleman, and I like Roderick better. He said I could call him that." She hummed again. "It was kinda flirty, like I could use that name as a special thing between us." She realized she was using the same voice she used to talk to herself. "But I don't wanna bother you with all that."

"Why not? I wanna be bothered. Where did you meet this man?"

"Ha. Okay, you're not gonna let me off that easy, huh?" Detta sat in a kitchen chair and kicked off her sensible low heels next to the table. Her post-lunch fog included forgetting to take off her shoes.

"Is he from church?"

"Not my church. He goes to the church my sister Loretta attends. He was part of a group from there that went to pray for her memory loss. I met him at her house. That was just the first, uh, meeting." Why was she having a hard time talking about this? Was she ashamed of having a date with an old man? Ashamed of being an old lady that did that kind of thing?

"So, he called you later and let you know he was interested?"

"Interested? I suppose it was pretty obvious from the first text message."

"He started by texting you? Detta, you are now officially part of the modern world." Sophie snickered. She and Anthony were united in the fun they got over Detta's technical challenges.

She laughed. "I guess it is official, then."

"So, how was the date?"

Detta tried to figure out the answer to that question in the span of one big breath. "Well, he was very polite. Very ... friendly. I mean, in a gentlemanly way."

"Is he a ... widower?"

"Yes. His wife died about five or six years ago. Roderick and I didn't talk about that though. And he didn't ask for details about my James either."

"That's, like, the third or fourth time I've heard you say his name—your ... husband's name. And it's only been lately."

"I know. I usually don't talk about him. It's been such a long time. Our life together. His life." She grunted a harsh breath. "See how I get? No good comes of talking about him."

"You just sound sad. I think that's pretty normal, isn't it?"

"So, here you are practicing your aftercare on me?" It was a joke, but maybe also changing the topic.

"Oh. Yeah. I care about you all the time, Detta. Always glad to help." Her voice was light and playful.

Detta got back to Sophie's request. "So, you'll let me know if your friend wants to talk to me? Send me a text. Someday you can TikTok me or Inst ... whatever that is."

"That's not ... Oh, well ... sure, I'll let you know. Thanks, Detta."

"You're quite welcome. We'll keep prayin'."

"Her name is Hope."

"Oh, fine. That's a fine name. We'll be prayin' for Hope."

They ended the call.

Detta would wait for a text or a call. She drifted to wondering what was next for her and Roderick. He would call her, he said. He sounded sincere. If he did call, she would know she hadn't been too cold or distracted during their nice little lunch.

That table in the restaurant sure was small. They looked like a couple of giants hovering over that little white wrought-iron disk. At least she didn't spill anything or knock anything onto the sidewalk. Roderick would probably call.

Would Hope call?

Detta got an idea of something to tell that girl. She picked up her phone to send Sophie a text.

Prayer and Desperation

That evening, Sophie followed Hope out the front door of the apartment building. The front sidewalk was elevated, a sort of bridge to the small parking lot.

"We can walk from here. It's just three blocks." Hope waved a hand to the right. "Actually, there are about four good taco places within a few blocks of me. That makes this prime real estate as far as I'm concerned."

"Yeah, I'm with you on that. I have to drive a couple miles to get to the nearest good taco place. The one close to me makes me nervous. I really can't recognize the meat they use, and the veggie tacos are still greasy somehow. Anyway ..." She didn't want this evening to be spent complaining about tacos. That probably wasn't effective aftercare.

"I'm hoping my comfort food will settle me down. Or maybe fill me up." Hope shook her head and made a sort of freaked out face.

"You still feeling that emptiness?"

Hope nodded.

"I remember missing the slumpy guys that used to follow me everywhere when they first disappeared. But it was kind of like missing a cut that took a long time to heal. You know? Not like missing something I really enjoyed. Just something I was used to."

"That makes sense. So, you had some of those ugly ones hanging with you ... before?"

"Before I started following Jesus more seriously. Yeah. For me, getting rid of them was just the next step. It was all part of the process."

"But what if I don't sign up? What if I just decide to chill for a while and see what that's like?"

In a way, that made sense to Sophie. How did Hope even know who she was or what she wanted until she tested life without those spirits? Sophie decided not to push anymore, including about Hope calling Detta.

As they waited in line at the little taco place, Sophie texted Detta to let her know not to expect a call. Not to worry. Though Sophie doubted Detta was really worried. Still, she might get concerned now that she knew Hope wasn't willing to talk. But Sophie decided against trying to explain the whole situation in a text.

Chicken tacos for Sophie. Fish for Hope. They sat at a table under a slightly tattered red umbrella on the patio. It overlooked the river that trickled past less than a block farther down the hill.

"This is the quintessential California experience." Hope grinned at Sophie. She seemed freer, more childlike. But that could just be her getting more comfortable with Sophie.

"Fish tacos on the patio?"

"Right. I mean, I figured when I moved here that if I was gonna be poor and maybe even homeless, then I'd rather do it in eighty-degree weather than eighteen below like back home."

"Were you ever homeless?"

"Yes. But I usually found somewhere to sleep indoors with someone I knew. And it didn't last long. That was the depths of ... what, despair? The pit of despair, like in that funny movie."

"*The Princess Bride?*"

"Yeah, that one."

Sophie chuckled and took a big bite of a soft-shelled taco.

Hope stared down the hill, a grin ready to take over her face. She didn't seem very stressed about anything just now. Her ferocious focus on the tacos was compelling. It probably enhanced Sophie's own enjoyment of the food and the setting. They *were* pretty good tacos. Spiced just right. Still warm and very tender.

"Okay, I agree. These tacos are good enough reason to move to California." Sophie sipped her fruit-flavored water through a paper straw.

"You could live with me. We could take turns on the air mattress."

"Or get a bigger place." Sophie tipped her head, thinking Hope should dream bigger.

"You make a good living at coding?"

"I generally have more than I need. Even the contract stuff pays well enough. And living in the city where I do isn't cheap."

"Nice. I thought about getting into programming, but I was afraid of staying focused."

"You don't have to be focused on support calls?"

"It's easy to stay tuned in when someone is, like, grousing in your ear. Staying focused on a project with no one in my ear seems risky. I would probably get in trouble with that."

"You could get a job working in an office."

"Wow, there's a weird idea." She snorted a laugh at her own joke.

"What happens if you don't have someone in your ear?"

"I get, like, distracted by the … you know." Hope glanced over her shoulder, maybe at her angel or Sophie's.

Sophie also checked the floating and flying things around the folks at the next table. A chatty little family with three hyper kids, their angels were intently watching them.

"The good ones or the bad ones?"

Hope squinted one eye. "I mean, I didn't really think of them like that. The church people thought they were all bad, and the palm reader I met here said they were all good. I figure the truth is somewhere in between. Like, the angels are all just folks doin' their jobs, sort of."

"But what if part of their job—at least the bad ones—was to distract you so you couldn't get better work? Or to make it so you would freak people out?"

Hope scrunched her brow. "What happened to you? You said something earlier about getting caught talking to an angel."

"Yeah. That was my big guy. I was getting carried away at work—in the office before we started working remotely. I think my boss was already jumpy about things changing and having people working where she couldn't see them. But yeah, she caught me talking to that guy over there." Sophie lifted her straw to her lips as she nodded to her biggest angel.

"I kinda wondered if they would go away." Hope looked at her own angel and sighed. "Or maybe I would stop seeing them after today. I mean, earlier, I was thinking that." Hope shifted in her seat.

Seeing her new friend squirming worried Sophie a little. Maybe she was just worried that Hope wasn't really grown up yet. She didn't just need Detta to talk to her, she probably needed someone like Detta to mother her. Sophie offered up a silent prayer for whatever it was Hope needed.

"What was that?"

"What?" Sophie craned her neck to see what Hope was seeing.

"Something just, like, flew up from you."

"Really? Flew up from me? What kind of thing?"

"It was small. Like a ... like a bird, only mostly transparent."

"A ..." Sophie checked the surroundings. "A spirit?" No one reacted to her saying that aloud. A breeze from the west was huffing at her ears, limiting the range of her voice, perhaps.

Twisting her mouth, Hope shook her head as she reached for her diet soda. "I don't think so. But then, I haven't been, like, carefully categorizing these things like you have."

"Uh, well, I wouldn't say ..." Probably it wouldn't do to deny that description of Sophie's angel interests. Relative to Hope's blind careen through her life with angels, Sophie had been more careful, at least lately. "I guess I'm not worried about whatever it was you saw. My crew looks pretty satisfied."

"Yeah. They seem like they have nothing to worry about." Hope turned to her angel, who seemed to be perpetually asking a question. But maybe that only started after their session this afternoon. What was the question?

"So, you saw something go up from me?" Sophie weighed how much to admit. "Uh, right when you said that, I was praying."

"What? Like, *praying* praying?"

"Sure. I do it all the time. And right before you said you saw that thing, I was praying for you to get the support you need out here."

"Huh. You ever seen that before?"

Sophie scowled and shook her head once. "Not exactly. I see the good ones sort of get active when people pray." She lowered her voice on that last word. Some teens sitting behind Hope were laughing and grabbing their paper products hastily off the table, but that probably wasn't about what Sophie was saying.

"So, that thing I saw might have been, like, a messenger carrying your prayer?" For someone who claimed to have no faith, Hope seemed pretty willing to entertain some faith-filled explanations.

"Do you ever pray?"

Shaking her head and crumpling her trash into a ball, Hope nodded to Sophie's garbage.

Sophie nodded acceptance of the mute offer.

"I don't. Well … maybe when I get desperate. It's kind of a habit from when I was a little kid." Hope snorted. "I think I used to pray more when I was doing the heavy drugs. When I was coming down off a high. Like, desperate, you know?" She had all their garbage now.

"Yeah. I know desperate."

Hope stood up. "Glad I'm not desperate now. Don't wanna ever go there again."

Sophie sent up another prayer about that.

What's Gotten into You?

"Hey, Mama. How are you this morning?" Anthony liked to call his mother on the way to work. It gave him someone to talk to on the train. He had done it several times even when he was working from home.

"Very well, thank you. How did you sleep?"

"Pretty good. Though I had that dream again where I'm chasing Sophie through the city, and she's just ignoring me 'cause she's, like, on the heels of this angel." He noticed the guy standing closest to him on the platform raise his head as if he'd heard that last part.

"Well, you can take that as a reminder to pray for her. Maybe if you were praying for her more, you wouldn't need your dreams to remind you."

"Whoa. Really? I mean, that sounds a bit … judgmental."

He could hear her inhale a big breath. "Sorry, dear. That *was* pretty harsh, I agree. I'm … I'm a little out of sorts, I guess. I was gonna blame it on Sophie, but she seems to have a good grasp on things."

"You talked to her yesterday?"

"Yes. She called from California. Things are going well with her friend. She was asking me about deliverance aftercare."

"Oh, so she did that for that girl out there?"

"She did some deliverance ministry. She's done that before, as you know, but not so much of the follow-up stuff we do with folks."

"That makes sense. She's more like part of the commando team, not the ... the social workers that have to help folks after the trauma." Probably not his best analogy.

"She is very versatile."

He snickered at his mother, as well as his own awkwardness. Then he sobered. "Are you sure she's coming back?"

"Coming back? Of course. Why wouldn't she be? Did she say something to you?"

"No. She didn't say anything. I just wonder how much there is to keep her here."

"There's her mother and her friends and her church. I think that's plenty."

"Uh, yeah. It sounds good when *you* say it."

"But you're thinkin' she won't be coming back to *you*?"

"Huh. Don't hold back, Mama." He laughed as a train slowed to a stop in front of him, the screeching brakes drowning his voice.

"I'd say your train arrived at your platform. Unless you're fixin' to slaughter a hog or three."

He laughed harder. "Is that what you did back home in Mississippi?"

"My daddy would come home with a hog once in a while. I don't think I know how often or why he got 'em. I suspect some folks paid him for his handyman work with things other than cash."

"You think they were cheating him?" Anthony settled into a seat before the train started to roll again.

"Oh, I don't know. Wasn't just white folks payin' him that way, I think. And even they might have told him up front that all they'd pay with was chickens or corn or pork."

"Pork on the hoof."

"That's right."

He tried to imagine life in the rural south sixty years ago. Only scenes from movies came to mind. "Wait. Did you say you were feeling poorly or something?" He was rewinding during the pause.

"Hmm. Out of sorts I think is what I said. I been considering somethin' and haven't decided what I think about it." Her voice was low, more muted than usual.

"Okay. Are you gonna let me know what it is?"

"Well, I guess part of it is, I'm worried what you'll think when I tell you."

"Okay, now you got me worried. What is it? Are you okay, Mama?" Anthony noted that same guy glance his way. He had his phone up but wasn't wearing earbuds. Anthony decided to turn down his volume. If he could contain himself.

"Okay. Well, you were bound to find out sometime." His mother told him about meeting a man from his Aunt Loretta's church and going out to lunch with him.

"Wait. Are you just worried what I'll think 'cause you went out to lunch with this man?"

"Well, first it's lunch, then it's dinner and a movie. Dessert might be involved before long." His mother gave a husky laugh. Maybe a relieved laugh.

"Huh. Very funny." He thought about it a second. "Is this the first time you've dated someone since Daddy died?"

A long pause followed. "Well, there was a man when you were just a little guy. He and I got interested in each other, but I called it off. It was only a few years after ..."

"Wow. I didn't know anything about that. Was there anyone else?"

"I think you're gettin' a little too nosy there, my boy."

"Okay. I guess I am." He settled his voice into a calmer range. "I really don't have anything to say to stop you. I mean, I don't think there's anything wrong with you goin' out with gentleman callers." He snickered at himself.

"Ha ha. Well, Roderick is a gentleman. And I expect he will be calling."

"Do you want him to call? How do you feel about him?"

"I'm interested. I like him. But I think I'm kinda tangled up about the whole thing. There's ... I guess there's still some guilt about ... about betraying your father."

"How is that possible? He's been dead over thirty years." He turned his head toward the sign on the platform for the next stop.

"Well, like I said, there was that other man, Earl Fowler. Yes, that was his name. I haven't said that name in maybe twenty-five years. Mm-hmm. That was too soon, me and him. I wasn't ready when I went out with Earl. I think that's really what I'm dealin' with here."

"Huh. I guess I can understand that. But that's old news too, of course."

"That's how it is sometimes. The old wounds are the deepest and the hardest to recover from."

"Wounds? Really? Did that guy hurt you?"

"No. Not like that. I think it's just my own guilt, my self-doubt that left a mark."

"Okay. I'll trust you on that. I'm probably just lucky I never had anything like that happen to me."

"Well, you lost your father before you even got to know him. That certainly left a mark."

"How do you know?"

"Remember the spirit that looked like a soldier that Sophie said she saw hanging around you? Didn't you think of your father when she said that?"

"That was a long time ago. I'm not sure what I thought about it then." He lowered his voice again. "I guess I was just freaked out that something in an army uniform was stalking me. I didn't think about where it came from."

"I guess we didn't do the proper aftercare for you."

"We?"

"Me and Sophie."

He snorted a laugh through his nose. The train was slowing again, approaching the next stop.

The Angels Look Concerned

Their second full day together, the feminine angel that followed Sophie around was watching Hope with unmistakable concern on her face. What do you do when the angels are worried? Hope didn't seem to notice. Should Sophie point it out? Hope's own angel was looking sad and tired. More proof that what Sophie saw was symbolic. She was sure angels never got tired.

"You're going home tomorrow, then?" Hope stood up from her computer chair after checking in with work. She had said she needed to get some hours in. Tomorrow she planned to put in a full shift. She'd just done a couple hours that Thursday.

"Yeah. I got a good price on a one-way flight. Considering it's short notice."

"You could stick around longer, but I really have to work soon."

"No problem. Really, it was a good deal. And I think folks at home are starting to worry that I'm not coming back." Probably only Anthony really fit squarely in that category, but maybe Crystal or Kimmy would too if she stayed much longer.

"You have a guy friend?" Hope was filling a tall glass with water. She glanced at her angel even as she spoke to Sophie. That angel looked like she was ready to help Hope do the dishes or something.

"I have friends who are guys. And there *is* one particular guy. I can tell he's getting sorta anxious about our relationship. Like wanting to make it more."

"More? Like more sexy?"

"Oh, I don't know about that part. He's a church guy. I think he's just looking for a commitment. Some definition."

"Ah, yeah ..." Hope drifted into the living room, her voice fading as if her head was only loosely following her feet.

"What about you?"

"Uh, well, I'm a girl on my own. A girl apart." She took a deep breath. "A girl destined to disappoint just about everybody."

"That's pretty cruel."

"My mom told me that when I had my first crush. Seventh grade."

Sophie swore and made no apology. "Some people have no right to raise children."

Hope bugged her eyes and recoiled. "Now look who's being cruel."

"There's a difference between dissing somebody because of the way they were born and dissing somebody who should know better and just plain doesn't." That probably wasn't what Sophie was supposed to say. Certainly not all she wanted to say. She was clearly messing up this aftercare stuff.

"Thanks, Sophie. Bad language and all, I appreciate the support." Hope scooched back on the couch to sit up a little straighter. "It's nice to have someone on my side. Someone who knows what it's like."

"We're staying in touch after this, right? I mean close."

"Pen pals?"

"Way better than that."

"Text pals?"

Sophie snickered in a weaselly way that was embarrassing, but maybe she and Hope could be the kind of friends that never had to be embarrassed. That reminded her. "Have you noticed the angels all looking kinda concerned? I noticed it before you started working."

Expanding her narrow chest with a big breath, Hope surveyed the crowd in her little apartment. There were a couple of new lingerers. Dark. Unfamiliar. Unclear. "You think the others are worried about those guys?" She nodded toward what looked like a dense ball of smoke in the corner of the living room.

"I don't expect they ever worry like we worry, but I think they care what happens to us. I think I can see something about how God views a situation by the look on their faces. Concern, not worry. For me, worry means you can't do anything about what's happening."

"Not sure I see the distinction."

"I don't know if I can explain it. Maybe I don't see it so clearly either." Sophie was building some concern that the little cloud near the ceiling was sticking around. "Do you know what that is?"

"I have no idea. Like I said, I try not to know stuff like that. The lady that tried to get me to make friends with the spooks was way too bizarre for me to wanna be all obsessed like her."

"That one doesn't even look like a creature or being or whatever. More like a weather front."

"Atmosphere?"

"Yeah. Like an atmospheric disturbance."

"A disturbance in the force."

Sophie chuckled for one second. The similarity to what Anthony would have said distracted her, but this was probably serious. "You know, a cloud is ... well, it blocks a clear view. It's the opposite of clear. I wonder if that cloud spirit or those spirits are about where you go next. I mean, like, how you relate to these spirits from here on. You can't ignore them, obviously."

"I know." Hope tipped a sideways grin. "I stopped taking my meds this morning. I've been clear all day. Maybe I don't see them any more clearly, but at least I'm not pretending I can ignore them or that they can be drugged out of my head. Still, I know what you mean. Maybe I have to decide."

"Take a side."

"Yeah. Maybe."

"That's what happened to me. I realized I needed to take a side. I could see how bad the bad ones were and started to believe how good the good ones were. So ... I decided."

Squinting one eye and shaking her head again, Hope just stared at that cloud. After a couple seconds, she said, "I think that's just one. Like a cloud spirit."

"The spirit of fogginess."

"Must be from San Francisco."

Again, Sophie couldn't help laughing. She actually didn't try hard to resist. She was getting tired of worrying and tired of trying to bend Hope away from the things that worried her.

"Hey, cloud spirit. Leave here ... in the name of Jesus." Hope sounded serious, though her voice cracked a little.

Sophie agreed with the sentiment and suspected her agreement helped. The cloud disappeared.

She checked the angels. Hope's seemed to glow a bit brighter. She looked tougher, more confident. But not exactly happy. No angel high five in the offing.

"Are you gonna make friends with her? Maybe that would be enough for starters." Sophie turned from the slender angel to the slender girl.

Hope watched that girl angel smile at her. "I thought we already *were* friends." She furrowed her brow a bit. "Though maybe not the best of friends."

Smiling at the younger woman, Sophie was thinking *she* could be Hope's best friend. But that might not work long distance. And it only seemed possible because Hope was so isolated from everyone else. That left Sophie clouding over like the angels.

But *not* like that cloudy demon.

Heading Home

Sophie lay in bed listening for waking sounds from Hope. It was way too early again. They had tried a compromise schedule between Sophie's bedtime back home and Hope's bedtime on the coast. That probably didn't add up to Hope being awake at six in the morning.

Flying out after noon, Sophie would leave Hope on her own. That's what it felt like. The big sister feeling was real. Abandonment was a real problem.

Sophie had been a big sister once. She had a little brother who did not survive long enough to have his own apartment that Sophie could visit and eventually leave. She looked at Hector's name tattooed on her wrist. Was Hope at all like Hector? Hector had died recklessly. Was Hope reckless? Her solitude seemed cautious, but her refusal to commit to a relationship with Jesus felt reckless. Maybe it felt safe to Hope. Safer to be on her own and not dependent on anyone else—especially a religious figure. Church leaders had failed her in the past. Had Sophie failed her?

"You can only offer the invitation, Sophie. It's up to her to accept or not. Don't let accusation interrupt the rest of your visit." The feminine angel's voice rang like bells echoing across hills, though she only stood at the foot of the bed.

Nodding, Sophie thanked her messenger silently and prayed to the one who sent that message. "*Let God be God.*

I'm just a girl who gets advice from angels." She smirked as her angel faded to invisible.

"How did you sleep?" A couple hours later, Hope was seated at her kitchen table stirring a cup of tea.

Sophie had dozed off again after the message from the angel, a testament to the soothing effect of those instructions. "I got more sleep than I usually do. I guess I needed it."

"Am I tiring you out?"

Breathing a laugh and shaking her head, Sophie padded silently into the kitchen. "Not likely. Watching movies on laptops last night wasn't very tiring. More like it was your cousin and all the folks around that whole Iowa adventure."

"Ah. Sure. They got to you before I did." Hope set her spoon on the table and raised her head to make eye contact with Sophie, who was just two steps away. "You ever wonder whether it was, like, some kind of fate that you met Eddie there in Iowa, so you and I could …" She shrugged and diverted her eyes.

Sophie patted her on the shoulder. "I think God is good at making the best of any situation. It seemed pretty good for Eddie and Brandy that we found them. But I did think it was cool that the scruffy kid in the haunted orphanage had a cousin who talks to angels." She pulled a clean bowl toward the edge of the table and reached for the box of cereal.

"I'll have to check in with Eddie on how it's going back in Minnesota. He may need to come out here for some real recovery."

"You think his family won't be good for his recovery?"

"Oh, I don't know. They were religious like *my* family. At least that's how it seemed to me. They had those priest angels hanging around them. You know, the ones with the hats and robes and all that."

"Ah. Religious spirits. They always look like cartoons of actual priests to me. I've known a couple really cool priests. And even the not cool ones never looked like those costume religious guys."

"I don't know about that. Our church leaders were called pastors. All guys. The religious ones, like you call 'em, always look male. For me, that's significant."

"Male priests? Yeah. It is part of the history of the church." As much as Sophie had followed her gift into understanding angels and demons, she hadn't pursued all the religious and political implications of what she saw. It was usually enough to know which spirits were helpful and which should be shown the door.

"Who knows if Eddie won't fit in at his parents' church now. You say he converted, so maybe he won't mind people telling him what to say and what to like and how to think." Hope stared toward the balcony.

"I doubt that. I don't know anyone who wants all that."

"You sure?"

Maybe Sophie hung around with a different crowd. She could only *imagine* people who lacked the ability to think for themselves and needed someone to tell them how to feel. Maybe those were just characters in movies Hope had seen, but they seemed to be dominating her perception of Christians.

Sophie screwed the cap back on the almond milk carton. "I don't know. It just doesn't fit the people I know. But I haven't been in the church you're talking about."

"I haven't been to church in a long time. Maybe they've upgraded things. I mean, the women pastors are an improvement for me."

Sophie thought of Detta and Ellen as women leaders, though she wasn't aware of either of them having a title other than Sister. There were a few women leaders in her own church, but she had only met one of them, and that very briefly. Sophie was supposed to start attending a group that met in a house once a week, and that had a woman leader. Maybe she should be more deliberate at initiating such relationships, but initiating relationships wasn't her strongest gift.

"What are you worrying about?" Hope swallowed some cereal and reached for her tea.

"How do you know I'm worrying?" Sophie checked for her angels in the room. The big guardian was standing casually next to the fridge. Maybe she should ask him to put the almond milk back. "Does my angel look worried?"

Hope turned toward him. "I wasn't even seeing him until you just said that. No, girl, I can tell by your *face*. I don't need angels to tell me everything."

Sophie smiled at the teasing tone in Hope's still-scratchy morning voice. Maybe that scratch was the reason for the tea. "You feeling okay?"

"Yeah. Nothing serious. I didn't sleep much last night."

"Probably my fault for making you go to bed early."

"Ha, well, there you go. It's not always about you. This time it was more likely about me not taking the drugs. And probably about the angels."

"What angels?"

"Or whatever you call 'em. I don't think they were the good guys."

"Who? Which ones?"

"The people next door had some visitors. And those visitors kept coming and going through my wall. I told 'em to stay out, but they didn't seem to hear me. My girl stood at the bottom of the mattress like she was protecting me, but it was like all the coming and going was happening without me."

"You wonder what the neighbors were doing?"

"I don't wanna think about that even if their demons use my walls as doorways or whatever. I'm very careful not to see them once they pass to the other side of the wall."

"Yeah. I can see them through walls if I want to, but I know what you mean. I'm not looking for trouble or for some kind of inside info on the neighbors."

"You live in an apartment?"

"Yeah."

"Wouldn't it be cool to live in a house and not have to deal with the cross traffic?"

Sophie stirred her cereal to coat it with milk. "I don't know. I'm not sure that's a good solution. I mean, these things don't have to care about walls and property lines. Especially if no one sets spiritual boundaries."

"Spiritual boundaries?"

"It can come with ownership, I guess. But I bet most people don't even think about it. Even in a place they own. So they have cross traffic, as you say, and know nothing about controlling it."

"*That* I know is true. The part about most people being clueless."

"What I can't figure out is how much it matters. Do those creeps affect anything by passing through? I mean, I get freaked out by things passing through. But if I was like everyone else, would it matter that demons take a shortcut through my place?"

"Well, not *everyone* else."

Sophie breathed a laugh through her nose and had to adjust her swallow to keep from choking on a mouthful of cereal. Actually, that tea was looking good.

Hope didn't have a car, so there was no dispute later that morning about her driving Sophie to the airport. But she did offer to pay for the taxi.

"No. You don't have to do that. I came here on my own. I talked you into it, remember." Sophie stood her rolling suitcase next to the front door. She was giving herself two and a half hours before her flight.

"It wasn't hard to talk me into it though."

"No. I could tell that." Sophie stopped short of sharing how much it worried her that Hope was so alone that she would accept a stranger into her home from halfway across the country. Meeting her had salved some of that worry, but not all of it. Hope was certainly isolated. Probably lonely.

"Video calls are what I would like." Hope said it like she was answering a question. It was probably a question that had formed in both their minds, not yet spoken.

"That sounds good to me." Sophie tipped her head to the side. "Hey, have you ever seen any kind of angel over a video call?"

Hope wrinkled her nose and faded her eyes toward the ceiling above the front door. "I don't think so, but maybe that's because I'm ignoring them. Usually I'm working when I'm on a video call." She focused on Sophie. "Why? Are you planning to show me your latest angel or something?"

"Ha. Not really. I was just curious. Just comparing notes."

"Right. We need to do that." Hope hesitated. "You know, you never told me if you've met anyone else who can see like we do."

"Not that I know of. I've met folks of all kinds who see hints or are just sort of intuitively aware of angels, but they're not really seeing them like us." She offered a crooked grin. "So far, you and I are members of a very small club."

"Looking for new members."

"Yeah. Maybe you'll meet a guy who sees like you do. That would be a match made in heaven." Sophie suspected her concept of heaven was different than Hope's, but she said it anyway.

A text arrived on Sophie's phone.

"The cab is a couple blocks away. I should get down there."

For the first time, Hope looked like she was going to cry. Then she stood up stiff and straight. "Well, I need to get in a full shift today, so that's good." Then she slumped and let out a sob.

This time Sophie released her inner hugger. She grabbed Hope tight. "We'll stay close, girl. Not just staying in touch. We are close. And you can come visit me. And I'll come back out to see you. No worries." She could feel something like fear sweating off Hope. A glance around them revealed no new spirits Sophie could see. She shoved past the distraction and pulled out of the hug.

Hope sniffled hard. "I know. I trust you. I know you're not just saying all that." She forced a smile. "Call me before you get on your plane, will you?"

"I will. Thanks for letting me stay here. I really had a good time. Next time I get the air mattress."

"Okay. Right. Next time." Was there some small skepticism wrapped around that last sentence?

Sophie had no doubts about what she had promised. And she was determined to disprove as many of Hope's doubts as possible.

Home Again

The plane ride home was more stressful than the westward flight had been. The woman next to Sophie had a tussling trio of demons. They repeatedly bumped her, though maybe it was just the rotund woman's arm that touched Sophie. She kept up a steady stream of prayers, wondering what she could say to the grumpy and talkative woman.

"I don't think my sister wants me to come for this visit, but I have to make sure she's not taking stuff from our mother. I think she's skimming stuff. Maybe not money, but some of the dishes and valuable things like decorations and art."

Even subtracting her awareness of the grimy gremlins ensconced in that woman, Sophie didn't know what to say. At one point, she caught an eye roll from the man seated on the woman's other side. He generally stuck to pretending to sleep or to staring out the window like he was watching a rivet on the wing gradually work its way loose. But the plane didn't crash, and those gremlins remained with their hostess through to the end of the ordeal.

Sophie called Hope again when she landed. Their conversation when she was at LAX had been awkward and dissatisfying. She wanted better. "Hope. I'm back home. Well, at least at the airport." She had to leave a message. Hope was probably on a support call, unable to pick up right away.

In the cab from the airport, Sophie called Anthony. "How's work?"

He hummed and cleared his throat. "Oh, not bad. Still dealing with problems with remote users even after all this time."

"Well, it can be complicated."

"Mostly it's the people who are complicated. But how was your visit? Are you really taking a cab from the airport?"

"Yeah. I maybe went a little overboard on doing all this on my own. Wouldn't have been a bad idea, really, to have a friend meet me."

"Mm-hmm. There are lots of us who would be glad to do it." He paused for two beats. "But did you make a new friend out on the coast?"

"I did. I really did. Or maybe I adopted a little sister." Sophie paused. "I wonder what she would think of my mother."

"Huh? Ah, well, that would be interesting. But she's too old to be adopted, obviously."

"Not obviously. But probably. I mean, of course she's too old. I wasn't being literal." She shook her head sharply. "But you knew that, I suppose. I'm a bit crabby."

"Yeah. Get some sleep and beat that jet lag."

"You mean you don't wanna go out and get a drink or something?"

"Really? You're up for that? It's, like, almost nine o'clock."

"Oh yeah. I don't think my brain clock is adjusted back to central time." She allowed a big sigh.

"Yeah. But this weekend we should go out. I could buy you dinner even, not just a drink."

"That would be nice. I need to talk to someone I know. In person. I'm tired of being on the road even if it wasn't really that long."

"You're a home girl, I know."

"I *am* a home girl." She gave a smaller sigh, this one more restful. She was at home with Anthony in a way. What were the limits on that? There had to be some. Her stomach groaned. The sandwich at LAX was biting back now. The snack on the plane was probably worse, seasoned by the bitter woman seated next to her. "I do need to rest. To recover."

"What was the hardest part?"

"I think it was the flight home. I sat next to this woman who wouldn't stop complaining about her family. And I think the cranky critters wrapped up inside her kept her from noticing that I really didn't wanna hear any of it."

"Really? *That* was the hardest part?"

"Well, the hardest part of today. Except saying goodbye to Hope, I guess." Sophie smacked her lips at herself. Her feelings were certainly clearer than the mixed-up muddle of words coming out. Of course she was going to miss Hope. It was hard to leave her alone.

Her phone buzzed with an incoming call. "I should take this. It's Hope. I left her a message when I was at the airport."

"Okay. Welcome back. See you tomorrow or Sunday. I'll text a plan."

"Great. Do that. G'night, Anthony."

The cabbie glanced at her in the mirror as she took Hope's call.

"Hey, girl. How was work?"

"The usual. Except I was trying to see if I could tell something about the ... the angels at the other end of the calls. Like, not seeing them 'cause they were audio calls, but trying to sense things like the mood or whatever."

"How did that go?"

"Didn't go, really. But it kept me from being bored with giving the same damn instructions over and over."

"Huh. Right. I can understand that."

"So, are you at your place yet? We should do a video call from there sometime so I can see where you live."

"Not there yet. We could do that. Probably tomorrow. I think I'll just collapse and sleep on the doormat tonight."

"Uh, well, I guess it is later there. How was the flight?"

"Not great. Woman next to me was a nightmare."

"She wasn't alone?"

Sophie surprised herself with a laugh. "Yes. In fact, she was not alone. I kept feeling like the ones with her were bumping into me, but it was probably just her doing it."

"Have you ever had that? Where you can feel 'em touch you?"

"A few times."

"Me too." That seemed to take Hope somewhere far away from the conversation. Perhaps lost in her memory of those angel touches. Or were they demons?

Sophie shivered and caught the driver checking her in the mirror again. She didn't like talking on the phone in a cab. Now she remembered how much she didn't like it.

While she and the driver exchanged that reflected eye contact, a large object flashed across the windshield. Sophie jumped before figuring out it wasn't a physical object.

The driver slammed on his brakes before Sophie saw the next large obstacle. A delivery truck backed out of an alley just yards in front of them. They lurched to a stop two feet from one of the large truck tires. The cabbie shouted something in a language Sophie didn't recognize. She didn't regret her ignorance this once.

The replay that ran in Sophie's head raised a question. What was the first thing that crossed the windshield? And another question. Did the driver hit the brakes because Sophie jumped, and thus avoided the truck because of an angel sighting? Of course she would never know.

"Sophie! What happened?" Hope was still on the phone.

"Oh, I don't know for sure. I mean, this truck pulled in front of us suddenly, but before that, I saw something that made me jump." She left the driver out of her account. He was spending as much time looking at her as the road now, which was not reassuring.

"Wow. Wait. So you saw something, like maybe a spirit, cross in front of you, then you almost hit a truck?"

"The cab almost hit it. Yeah." She wanted it clear that she wasn't driving. Not this time, anyway. She hoped the cabbie would get back to it, concentrate on it even.

"Oh, wow. Do you think it was a warning from a good guy? Or maybe an accident demon?"

"Ha. You ask good questions." Sophie snorted. "I wish I had good answers."

"Okay. Well, I'm glad you didn't get hurt anyway."

"Yeah. Just scared. I'm more awake now than I was."

"That's probably not good."

"No. Not this late."

"Okay. I'll let you go." It sounded like resignation, but maybe a healthy kind.

Part of Sophie was afraid of how tightly Hope would cling to her. Another part of her was afraid of losing touch with her new friend. "Good night."

"Good night, Sophie."

Hijacking a Dinner Date

Detta greeted Sophie at the back door. "You don't mind me hijacking your dinner date?"

"Was it really gonna be a date?" Anthony was behind his mother, sampling raisin oatmeal cookies.

Sophie only glanced at Anthony. Detta guessed the girl didn't want to answer that question about a date directly. At least not in front of her. Or maybe it was Anthony she didn't want to hear her answer. Detta extracted herself from such speculations as she extracted herself from Sophie's hug. None of her business, strictly speaking.

"It's so good to see you. It feels like it's been ages." Sophie slipped out of her clogs, still looking at Detta.

"Oh, a couple weeks, I guess. How's your mother?"

"She's good. We went shopping for a dress for her today. Speaking of dates, she's going on a date tonight."

"Really? Is that something new?"

"It is new, though maybe it's just about her business. She's going out with one of the investors in her cleaning business. He's an old family friend."

"Well, that sounds a bit complicated."

"Probably not as complicated as I'm making it sound."

Anthony might have mumbled something. Detta couldn't tell. He had his mouth full. The raisin oatmeal cookies were his favorite these days.

"At least she can think about dating now that she finally stopped worrying about me." Sophie drifted toward those cookies.

Anthony handed her one.

"I expect there is some of that. It just might be." Detta sidetracked to wondering how much to say about Roderick after their third date. She would decide on that later when the kids were well fed.

When they were seated at the table, done with prayers, and Sophie was dishing her food, she asked Detta a question. "Is there anything I can do if I'm seated next to someone with some annoying demons on them? I can't really cast them out or anything, can I? Not for a stranger?"

"Hmm. Well, being a stranger isn't the most important part. I think they have to want it in some way. I recall a story about the apostle Paul and one o' his friends in a town where this fortune-teller girl was following them around shouting things. They were true things, as I recall the story, but it was getting annoying. So, the apostle cast out the spirit that gave the girl her fortune-teller powers."

"Okay. That sounds a little familiar. I must have read that part." Sophie was done dishing. She started to poke into her salad.

Detta continued. "And the folks who basically owned the girl were all upset the apostle cast it out, but I notice there's nothing in there about the girl being upset." She checked to make sure Anthony had his food. Detta picked a piece of french bread off the plate in the center of her kitchen table. "In fact, it seems to me the girl *wanted* to be set free, which is why she was following around the man most likely to do that for her."

"There's also that story where the severely demonized man comes running out of the tombs and falls in front of Jesus." Sophie crunched on a forkful of greens.

"That's right. That's another example. It's hard to believe that fella didn't want to be set free. Why else would he go running right up to Jesus?"

"But this woman on the plane and my cab driver in Iowa—neither of them came to me, really. I just got planted with them and had to ignore what was hanging around or even jammed up inside 'em."

"Oh." Detta didn't envy Sophie's gift at times like this. "Right. I guess you could try binding the spirits. You could certainly forbid them from bothering you. That's within your authority."

"My authority. Hmm. I guess I'm still working on that part. For most of this, it's been about my skills, not so much my authority. I mostly rely on others for that. Bruce and Jonathan, you and Ellen."

"But it's on you too, Sophie. You know that now, right?"

Anthony stepped in. "She helped that girl in California. There wasn't anyone else there that time. And that Chinese girl in the alley."

Sophie turned toward him, maybe a little surprise in her eyes. "I know that's true." She let her gaze fade toward the dining room. "I just worry that I didn't do enough for Hope."

"Like get her all the way into the kingdom of God?" Detta didn't look directly at Sophie. She knew what her friend was talking about.

"Yeah, like that."

"It doesn't take your spiritual authority for that. You can get her free, but she has to decide for herself about following Jesus."

"Yeah. That's what one of my angels told me."

Detta and Anthony stopped chewing and stared at Sophie. Hearing from her angels was new.

"So, how often do they ... talk to you now?" Anthony found a question before Detta.

"Oh, not often. They don't seem real chatty." Sophie bobbled her head. "I mean, I always knew they were serious and not just there to be my invisible playmates."

"So, do they answer your questions now?" Detta used a slice of bread to help scoop some rotini with red sauce.

"Generally, no. It's like they have their own agendas, I think. If I happen to ask a question they were, like, hoping I would ask, then they answer."

"Sounds kinda tight." Anthony peppered his voice with disapproval.

Detta tipped her head toward her son without looking directly at him. "Well, the Lord doesn't have to do anything in ways that make sense to us, I'm certain. But I guess that can be a bit frustrating."

"Not nearly as frustrating as the woman on the plane. I prayed a lot on that flight. Maybe that was a good side effect. But part of the frustration was seeing but not being able to do anything about it. Hope and I were talking about that sort of thing."

"Hope? That girl wants to cast spirits off the people around her?" Anthony was talking with his mouth full, but Detta knew not to say anything. It was too late to train him now.

"No. Maybe she was just listening to *me* wondering about that part. I mean, we both see things coming and going from our neighbors. She says she can ignore them once they get through the walls, which I believe, but I have a hard time imagining not wanting to shoo them away even if they belong to the neighbors."

"Belong? Attached, I suppose." Detta did correct Sophie, at least a little.

"Yeah. That's what I meant." Sophie showed no sign of offense. But she was showing genuine appreciation for the pasta and sausage.

Anthony might have had more to say himself, except for how much he loved her marinara sauce with sausage.

Detta decided to take advantage of their satisfied silence. "I had another date with Roderick last night."

Sophie chewed and nodded, "Was that, like, your second date?"

"Third, if I'm counting." She chuckled and cut a piece of sausage with her fork. The oregano and sage rode toward her on a thin spiral of steam.

"So, how's it going?" Anthony asked that in a neutral tone, like he was checking on her progress at cleaning out the garage. Which was not going so well.

She suspected her son's nonchalant attitude was counterfeit. "We get along fine. I enjoy talking to him, and he tells a story very well. Very entertaining."

"So, he's an entertainer?" That sounded a bit more hostile, more like what she expected from Anthony. Or maybe feared from him.

Detta noted Sophie staring at Anthony. "I said he was entertaining, not an entertainer. He was a salesman at a car lot before he finally retired. And it probably didn't hurt that he had the gift of gab in that job."

Anthony had stopped eating. His brows were hunkered together over his nose.

Sophie was still staring at him. Maybe at something else too.

"What is it, Sophie? What are you seeing?"

"I thought we got rid of that soldier guy." She kept her eyes on Anthony even as she answered Detta's question.

"Wha—?" Anthony had that look on his face that Detta learned to discern when he was about six. Guilty. But what would he be guilty about now?

"That spirit was related to Anthony missing his father." Detta regretted talking about her son like he wasn't there, but some part of him seemed to have left the room.

"You've been missing your father?" Surely Sophie knew something about that feeling from personal experience, though Detta didn't know how much the two young folks talked about their fathers.

"Huh?" Anthony had apparently returned to the kitchen. He looked pretty normal except for a bit of sauce visible at one corner of his mouth.

Sophie pointed at that sauce.

Anthony got the nonverbal message and lifted a paper napkin to take a few swipes. He cleared it eventually. "I don't think I've been *missing* him really, just curious about him. Or ..." He wandered away again.

"Maybe we can talk about this after we eat." Detta didn't want a perfectly good meal to go to waste.

The young folks both nodded and retreated into their focused feeding frenzy. Detta thought of a school of fish she had watched on a TV documentary. Well, there were just two of these feeders, and they looked more preoccupied than frenzied. What did it mean that Sophie was seeing that military-looking spirit around Anthony again? He *was* acting strange. As if he was in a mood or something. Detta filled her mind with prayers as she finished her pasta. She left half a piece of bread and some salad. Her appetite had dulled with her fretting.

It only took a few minutes for Sophie and Anthony to finish. Detta didn't offer the peach pie for dessert. They could come back for that. The kids had eaten cookies anyway.

What did it mean that she was so content to think about food arrangements when her boy was apparently under some kind of spiritual attack? Her calm probably had to do with those skills Sophie had mentioned. And Detta's conviction of her own authority. The only question was what Anthony wanted.

"Let's go to the living room." She scooted her chair out and looked at Sophie. She was mute but compliant. Anthony, on the other hand, made a grumbling sound and didn't move.

"Anthony. Let's go sit in the living room." Sophie stood and reached for Anthony's shoulder.

He glared at her, took a big breath, and then surrendered. He scooted his chair and followed the women out of the kitchen. Maybe he was thinking the same thing Detta was—that this was all familiar. The three of them, the living room, a spiritual battle on the horizon. It had happened at least twice before, including once when Anthony gave up a few stalkers—ones he didn't seem to recognize or understand at the time.

Detta suspected he knew something about the one lingering this evening. "You wanna tell us what's goin' on?"

His eyes were hard and glassy. He did not look like someone who wanted to tell them anything. Not Sophie, not his own mother. Anthony was still standing. He blinked slowly at the front windows. Detta had opened two of them to let a breeze through.

"I think I know what this is about." He didn't sound glad about that realization.

Detta was glad. It was better than thrashing around in the weeds without even knowing what they were looking for. "Tell us as much as you feel comfortable saying." She had some hope that his comfort level would rise above telling them nothing.

Anthony turned from the window to look at Sophie for a few seconds. Then he dropped to the couch. "It's kind of embarrassing."

"We won't judge you. You know that." Sophie's bright encouragement sounded like she was convinced it was true. Anthony's darting eyes didn't look so sure.

"Well, I don't mind telling you I was thinkin' about my dad. And sorta mad at him for not bein' around to tell me what to do. I mean, to give me advice."

Detta started to ask what he wanted advice about, but something told her she didn't need to know that part. This was really about Anthony's dad and some well of resentment against him, apparently.

"How long have you been angry at your father for not being around?" Sophie sounded as uninformed about this new concern as Detta.

"I don't know. Recently. I was just wishing he was around. I don't know if I blame him." He stopped abruptly and rubbed his stomach. "I don't feel very good."

Detta commanded whatever was disturbing his stomach to stop it and not bother them. She assumed it wasn't the sausage.

Relaxing a bit, Anthony let his hand drop to the cushion next to him. His chest rose and fell with a few purging breaths. "I wasn't really *blaming* him, just wishing he was here to talk to. It ... it sort of occurred to me that he would know what to do."

Again, Detta resisted the urge to ask about what. As counter as it was to her motherly instincts, that bit of detail seemed irrelevant. "I wonder where you got that idea though. I mean, have I told you things that made you think he would know what you should do about your life?" She didn't talk about James like that with Anthony. At least she didn't think he could interpret anything she had said about his father that way.

"Oh. You said—" He turned his head left and right as if he'd forgotten where he'd put something. "Well, I don't know what it was you said. But I just had this thought that if only my dad were here, I would know what to do."

"That's kind of a strange thought, though. After all these years." Sophie was scowling. Maybe she was reflecting Detta's doubt. Detta hadn't hidden any of it.

Anthony's voice turned apologetic. "I mean, maybe I don't really know what he would say. And I guess I don't know how good his advice would be, but ..." Again, he drifted away. At least his eyes did. "Actually, I guess it is kinda odd for me to think that. I wonder where I got the idea."

"Not every thought that comes into our heads is just from ourselves." Detta knew that from experience, and she thought Anthony did too.

"You mean ... you mean one of those ... *spirits* planted the idea?" He rubbed his chin where a shadow of whiskers could be seen even in the low light of the living room.

Detta reached for the lamp next to her chair and switched it on. "I think we should just pray and ask for direction and then send that thing away as soon as we get clear about it."

Sophie nodded gently and kept her eyes on Anthony. "I know you don't need this spirit. He's not gonna give you good advice. And he really doesn't know what your father would be like either. He can't know that."

"How ... how can you be so sure about that?" Anthony squinted one eye at Sophie.

"Maybe it isn't exactly knowing. It just feels to me like this guy doesn't have much to offer. He looks confused. It's like his clothes are on backward, like he doesn't even know which way is which. I think he's a spirit trying to confuse you."

"That's weird." Anthony recoiled before he could say more. Then he looked at Sophie. "Yeah. Let's get this thing off."

As soon as he said that, Sophie sat up straight, then tilted her head to one side and looked at the nearest window. "There he goes."

"What? Already? Out the window?" Anthony did that squeaky, doubtful voice his mother knew well.

"Were you wanting to wrestle with him for a while first?" Sophie grinned at him with her eyebrows raised.

"But what was the point?"

"Confusion. That there was no point was the point." Detta checked internally for some inkling that her explanation was too simple.

"So, this thing was the same one that was around last time we did this?" He looked at Sophie.

"At first I thought so, but I think that was part of the confusion. It wasn't really about your father. It was about something else." She faded as if she didn't want to say more.

"Confusion. I guess it makes sense now. As much sense as confusion could make." He quirked his mouth playfully.

They all laughed.

It was good to laugh together, but Detta knew there was still an issue Anthony needed to deal with. She suspected Sophie was part of that solution. Just what part, she forced herself not to speculate. It was hard, but it *was* possible to mind her own business.

"Pie, anyone?"

"Yes." A unanimous decision. No confusion at all.

While You Were Away ...

Kimmy called Sophie on Sunday evening. "Do you have some time to talk about what's going on with Crystal?"

"What do you know about Crystal?" Sophie was good friends with both Kimmy and Crystal, but they weren't really close with each other. As far as Sophie knew, those two never got together without her.

"Well, that's just it. She called me all in a mess the other night. I was up late with Betsy. Her schedule is out of whack, so I was sort of awake. But it was weird to have Crystal call *me*. I guess she couldn't reach you. It was when you were gone to Iowa or wherever."

"In a mess, how?"

"Well, that part wasn't clear to me then. Now I think I know what it was." She breathed hard into the phone, maybe a laugh. "I mean, I thought she was doing drugs. She was acting like some people I know from the old days." She said that with obvious irony. She and Sophie had met at drug rehab. "But I don't think it was *that* kind of paranoia. I think maybe there might have been some actual people trying to recruit her into a cult or something."

"Oh." Sophie let that word fall hard. The weight of it came from the believability of Kimmy's speculation. "Okay, I'll call her. I saw some missed calls and a text, but I couldn't tell how urgent it was. She didn't say much on the message she left." Sophie wasn't sure about that last part. There was one voice mail from Crystal that sounded muffled or blank. Like a butt dial. She had been so preoccupied with Hope in California that she hadn't tried to figure it out.

After hanging up with Kimmy, Sophie found that voice mail again. She had to crank up her phone volume to full.

Crystal was whispering. "Sophie, I was really hoping you would pick up. Oh, it's probably too late. But I need some help. I mean right away. I have these people in my apartment and they won't leave. Oh, wait. I gotta go." And that was it. That was two days ago.

Sophie called Crystal's number. No answer. She left a message. "Call back ASAP."

She received no return call on Sunday. Sophie got back to work with her coding client but took a break midmorning Monday. Still no word from Crystal.

That afternoon, she decided to go to Crystal's apartment to see if she was there, maybe having phone trouble or something. Standing in front of Crystal's building, she texted again. For several seconds, it looked like Crystal was replying. The little ellipsis became animated on Sophie's phone, but nothing arrived. This was getting stranger. Sophie resorted to praying. "Probably should have thought of that sooner, shouldn't I?" She checked with her big guardian. He had remained visible for the past twenty-four hours. That had reinforced the feeling of a crisis in progress.

Sophie strained her neck to check Crystal's windows. All the shades were down. None of the windows were open. It was warm but breezy, maybe a day for opening windows. But with Crystal not answering her phone, what were the chances she was at home? Dragging her backpack off her shoulder, Sophie found her key ring. She located what she thought was

Crystal's spare key. They had exchanged keys years ago. Sophie had only used Crystal's once, to water plants when her friend went on a cruise.

In the entryway, Sophie pressed Crystal's buzzer. No need to storm in there if her friend was able to answer the door.

Nothing. Probably she wasn't at home. Sophie fumbled with keys and tested a couple until she found the one that opened the stairway door. Sophie started the climb, trying to recall the last time she had been up these stairs. She and Crystal had met either at Sophie's place or at restaurants lately. The last time they met was in a bar. That dinner had been completely focused on a postmortem regarding a guy who had broken up with Crystal. Was the current crisis more guy trouble?

Sophie knocked. Then she spoke loudly with her lips near the door. "Crystal, it's me, Sophie. Are you in there?"

Not a sound. She actually heard a distant cricket. Probably from outside.

Again, Sophie had to search through the keys, rebuking herself for not keeping track of which one had opened the entryway door. She isolated three keys that looked alike. As she fumbled, her feminine angel passed through the door. She could have done that invisibly, but apparently she wanted Sophie to see her go in. Probably that meant going in was a good idea.

Once she unlocked the door, Sophie called again. "Crystal, are you home?" She let the door close behind her. The place smelled normal, like her friend had been around recently, though it was a bit stuffy with the windows all shut. Sophie passed through the entryway and checked around for signs of foul play. Whatever that would look like.

The feminine angel was standing next to the far kitchen counter looking down at something. Sophie took the hint. She joined the angel by the counter. There, on the butcherblock, was a notepad. Something was scrawled on it. Crystal's writing. She had written it quickly, not taking time to go back and straighten or fill in missing parts of letters.

"Crystal is at this address?" Sophie asked the angel.

The angel nodded and then disappeared.

Clearly Sophie should go there. That part of the angel's nonverbals was clear enough. But she didn't want to go any further by herself. She texted Anthony. **"Are you available tonight? I think Crystal is in some kind of trouble."**

"Sure. I can get off at 4:30."

Her phone said it was just past four. That would work. **"Meet me at Crystal's place?"** She switched to her contacts list and copied Crystal's address to send to him.

Waiting in Crystal's apartment felt very parental. Sophie sat on the couch as if expecting her girl to come home from a date. She texted Detta a simple prayer request and waited some more.

Anthony texted her when he arrived in front of her building. **"Nothing available. Illegally parked in front."**

He was sitting in his new electric car, idling silently. No revving engine to go with the feeling of crisis Sophie was carrying.

"What's up with Crystal?"

Sophie slipped her backpack onto the floor and settled in the passenger seat. "I wish I knew. She won't answer my calls or texts, and she made a few desperate attempts to reach out while I was out of town. I feel awful that I didn't investigate sooner. I hope she's okay."

"What kind of desperate?"

"The kind where you have to whisper when you leave a phone message and then get cut short."

Hissing through his teeth, the way he might when seeing someone bang their head on a cupboard door, Anthony put the car in gear. "Where to?"

"Can you help me figure out what this says?" She handed him the sheet from the kitchen notepad.

"Your eyesight going bad?"

"No, Crystal's handwriting."

"That's Downy Road, but this number isn't really clear. Forty-seven eighteen? Or forty-one thirteen? Or forty-one seventy-three."

She had hoped Anthony would narrow the choices, but his ability to read Crystal's scrawling was no better than Sophie's. "We can look those up on the GPS and see which one's a legit address."

"How do you know this has anything to do with where Crystal is?"

"My girl angel was looking at it. Clearly it's significant."

Anthony had punched in the first possible interpretation of the address already. No match. The third one yielded an actual location. "Okay, that should be it. Baker's is on the way. We can stop and get a burger or Italian sausage."

Sophie checked with the angels in the back seat. They didn't react to Anthony's idea in any obvious way. Probably it was okay. Sophie could eat something. Maybe they would make better decisions with food in their stomachs. "You haven't had enough Italian sausage lately?"

Anthony smiled as he carefully pulled away from the fire hydrant he'd been blocking.

"What are you grinning at?"

"Nothing." He kept his eyes forward.

"Not nothing. It was clearly something."

"I was just thinking it was nice to have you ask about that. Nice that you knew I'd just eaten Italian sausage, and you were looking out for me."

Sophie stared at him as he drove. Finally he looked at her, his eyebrows raised in question.

She spoke evenly. "I just decided not to make fun of you for what you said."

"Thank you." He kept his grin on. He made the first turn prescribed by the GPS. "How is Crystal doing, generally? I mean, did she seem okay when you saw her last?"

"She was okay, but I did recently have to get her free from some spirit she picked up at this healer guy's place. She thought he was Christian, but it didn't sound like the kind of Christian stuff I've heard of. And this wizard spirit showed up."

He recoiled from the neck up. "You think this trouble now has to do with more of that?"

"She knew better than to go back to that guy. The creepy being he left on her was pretty convincing."

"Hmm. But what are the chances she would get into a totally different kind of trouble? I mean, even for Crystal?"

"Hey. Go easy. She's one of my best friends."

"I know. But you have to admit ..."

"I know, I know." Sophie breathed hard through her nose. "I guess she said something to Kimmy that made her think a cult was trying to recruit her."

"Oh. Well ..." He didn't bother finishing that *I told you so*.

At Baker's, they both ordered burgers and fries. Anthony got root beer, Sophie a sugar-free iced tea. Anthony wolfed half his meal at a picnic table near his car. "We can go now. I'm good to travel."

"You think a few minutes will make a difference?" Sophie asked without skepticism in her voice, not sure what the right answer was.

"It's a rescue mission, isn't it?"

Sophie noted all three of her angels standing around the car along with one of Anthony's. Whether he had more than one had not yet been firmly established in her mind. "The angels are acting like it might be a sort of rescue mission."

Half of them went invisible when she said that.

Back on the road, Anthony started twisting his hands on the steering wheel like he was trying to wear ridges for his fingers. The GPS said to turn right at the next intersection. Still, he almost missed the corner.

"You okay?" Sophie spoke with french fries in her mouth.

"Sure. I do this sorta thing all the time." He glanced at her before focusing back on the road. Then he swore and slammed on the brakes.

Sophie just stopped herself from cursing too when she saw Crystal walking on the edge of the road. There were no sidewalks in this part of town.

Crystal slowed her pace and raised a hand to shield her eyes from the sun, which was directly behind Sophie and Anthony.

Sophie checked behind them and swung her car door open.

Jumping as if she would bolt for cover, Crystal only stopped when Sophie called her name. "Oh, Sophie!" She staggered and then ran into Sophie's arms.

"Where have you been? What happened to you?"

"Oh, Sophie. It's such a weird and embarrassing story. I … Hey, could you guys help me get my car? My phone is in my car."

"Where is your car?"

"Parked back by the house where I was being … well, not exactly detained. But … well, take me back there, and I'll tell you about it on the way." She was wearing a stretched T-shirt that hung off one shoulder and cutoff jeans. Not her usual attire for a social call.

During a one-mile drive, Crystal described being lured to some house under the pretense that someone from her twelve-step group, which Sophie didn't even know she was attending, needed a ride. When she arrived at the farm, Crystal didn't find Debbie, the girl she was there to transport. Instead, she found that healer guy who had messed her up a couple weeks ago, along with some of his followers.

"Who *are* these people? What kind of religion is it?"

"They say things that sound like they're Christian sometimes, but also some of the new-agey stuff I used to be into. It's like they invented their own thing, I think." Crystal sounded weary.

"And you had to escape without your car?" Anthony slowed as Crystal pointed to a driveway that tunneled through some dense trees.

"I have my keys, but they parked my car in, so I couldn't get out. They kept saying they would move their cars, but then it wouldn't happen. Meanwhile, they were telling me about their revelations and their calling to convert the dying world. Stuff like that."

"So, they were recruiting you?" Anthony was driving slowly, as if waiting for further directions.

"I guess. I just couldn't figure out how forcefully they were, like, doing it."

"So just drive right up this path? Am I gonna get trapped?" He flicked a hand toward the windshield.

"Oh. Hey—let's do this. Pull in a little farther and then turn around. I think there's a flat place past these trees. That way, if we have to make a break for it, your car will be ready."

"Really?" Sophie's voice squawked girlishly.

"Just in case. It was never clear that I was actually free to go. They made me leave my phone in my car. But at least they didn't take it away. And they left me with my keys." Crystal jangled her key ring, which she held up to demonstrate.

"So they didn't detain you exactly." Anthony slowed when they cleared the initial tunnel of trees. He made a looping left turn and adjusted a couple times so his car was just off the drive, pointed toward the road.

"Will your car be okay?" Sophie was feeling bad for Anthony having to use his new car as a rescue vehicle. It wasn't designed for off-road driving.

"I guess." He set it to park and turned to look at Crystal behind him. "Should I stay here with the engine running?"

Crystal shook her head. "You should come with us. It might be easier to get them to cooperate if we have numbers. You two guys look way tougher than me."

Sophie didn't resent that comment and suspected it wouldn't hurt Anthony's feelings either. Crystal was pale, thin, and nervous. Not very tough looking.

"Okay. I have remote start, so we can, like, hit the ignition as we run down the lane." He held up his key fob.

It wasn't clear to Sophie whether Anthony was serious, but maybe he didn't know any more than she did. Crystal might be overreacting, but she had gotten involved with some pretty strange people over the years. Who knew how crazy this batch was?

September rapidly approaching, the shadows of the trees along the edge of the driveway were a tangle of darkness at this time of early evening. Maybe Sophie was overly suspicious of those shadows. The angels looked like they were simply out for a stroll in the country. And, technically, they probably were walking outside city limits. But Sophie was scuffing, not strolling.

"Are you dragging your feet?" Anthony bumped her, shoulder to shoulder.

"I can't see very well. Is this level ground here?"

"I think it is. I didn't have any trouble walking out this way." Crystal was wearing old canvas sneakers and no socks.

"Did you make a run for it, or sneak out?" Sophie lowered her voice as she finally caught sight of a building.

"I snuck away during a break. They had a kind of church service and were doing this sort of Reiki healing, I think. Or something like that. The ceremony had most people's attention." She sped up and skipped ahead a little, pointing under some skinny trees. "My car is over there. Only one car blocking it in now."

"Unless we wanna try driving it through those bushes and over that field." Anthony was clearly not serious about that, but he was still holding his key fob in his hand.

"At least I can get my phone out now. I was too panicked to try on my way out. I thought they would expect that and would be watching my car."

Sophie glanced at Anthony to see his reaction to this window into Crystal's state of alarm, but the shadows were cutting across his face just then, and she couldn't read his mood. She could easily see the angels, however. They were walking in a formation that surrounded the three of them now, Crystal's angel in the lead. Where had that angel been when Crystal was being lured here under false pretenses? Or having to sneak away without her car?

Turning to look at the house again after Crystal retrieved her phone from her car, Sophie realized the lights she had been noticing were not all natural. There were a few outdoor lamps that must have been triggered by the early woodland twilight, but there was also a scattering of angels around the large barn-like house. They seemed focused inside, but perhaps unable to enter the building. Was that right?

Drilling through the walls and windows, Sophie got an impression of a crowd of demons churning among a group of people. She couldn't count the spirits in the flowing mass of humans. She couldn't see people through walls. That was not her superpower. She glanced at Anthony before realizing she had only thought that thing about superpowers and hadn't said it aloud. Catching herself assuming he was reading her mind recalled his comment in the car about her looking after him. She shooed that thought away for now.

As they approached the house, Sophie prayed aloud. "Lord, please lead us to a person who will help us get Crystal's car out. Thank you."

When she said "Amen," her biggest guardian turned slightly to his left, and the other angels adjusted their direction. Naturally, Sophie followed them. Which meant bumping into Anthony and having to grab Crystal's arm. "This way."

"Angel directions?" Crystal was pressed close to Sophie's shoulder, whispering.

They emerged from the trees to a yard that was light compared to the cave of trees. The smell of a campfire hung in the air, though Sophie couldn't see the source. Two young guys, probably around twenty, were pushing each other and laughing. The guy with the longest hair stumbled into Anthony. "Oh, sorry, dude."

"No problem. Hey, can you help us? We're looking for the person who owns the orange Prius down there by the driveway. It has our friend's car parked in."

"Oh. Bummer." The guy, wearing shorts and a ragged T-shirt, whipped his head toward his friend. "Orange Prius? Is that the hybrid-type car Jazzy drives?"

The other guy looked at Anthony and Sophie but seemed not to see Crystal. "Uh, I think so." He turned toward the house. A half dozen people were milling on the porch. "Jazzy, can you move your car? You got these people parked in."

While that was going on, Sophie watched her angels and Crystal's doing a blocking maneuver against a witchy-looking spirit. The guardians looked like security at a concert protecting the pop star. Crystal was that pop star, apparently. The witchy spirit was stretching a claw-like hand toward

Crystal. Was that how Crystal was lured here in the first place?

A middle-aged woman spun her attention toward them, responding to that young guy. "Oh, sorry. I'll get my keys."

"I haven't met *any* of these people. I suppose she really didn't know my car was trapped." Crystal snorted, still speaking in an outdoor whisper. "I wish I'd known it would be this easy."

Sophie faced away from the two strangers and spoke into Crystal's ear. "I think it's easy because it's an answer to my prayer. My angel led us to these guys."

"Hey, you do angels?" The first scruffy guy was obviously too close for Sophie to conceal those last few words.

"No. Uh, God does angels. But I get to see what he's doing with 'em sometimes." That answer, half smart-mouthing and half sincere, just popped out.

"Oh. That's cool."

Sophie muttered under her breath, "Yes, it *is* pretty cool." She followed Crystal and Anthony, who were now tagging along with the woman named Jazzy. Their angels were still holding back several reachers and graspers.

No problem for them.

Job Interview Turns Strange

On Wednesday, Sophie checked in on Crystal while getting dressed for a job interview. "Have you recovered from whatever that was at the farm?"

"Yeah. Including recovering from my gross embarrassment over the whole thing. I mean, part of it was not knowing what was allowed. I might not have understood what they were doing. And maybe I just wasn't talking to the right people about getting my car out."

"Maybe." Sophie set her high heels on the corner of her bed. Her dark gray suit was her go-to for interviews. Part of her costume in the business world. "There were some pretty aggressive spirits there, like I told you. They might have been influencing your perception of things more than you realize." She grunted slightly as she knocked one of those shoes to the floor.

"Yeah. I get that. Hey, what are you doing?" Voices in the background implied that Crystal was at work. Maybe the distraction in Sophie's voice inspired the question about what she was up to.

"I'm getting ready for an interview. A financial services company that has all these calculators and things on their website. They want to upgrade them and start selling some of the tools they designed. I would be part of the upgrade process."

"How does that feel? Being upgrade material?"

"Oh, I wouldn't put it on my résumé that way. I think they used some packaged programs and just contracted for custom work in the past. The real upgrade is probably having a small team in-house."

"How small?"

"Not clear yet. I'm guessing two or three people."

"That doesn't sound very promising."

"Yeah. I know what you mean. But maybe in a smaller office they won't mind if I consult an angel or two during the day."

"Maybe you can look for a monastery that sells bread and jam and stuff and do their web programming instead."

Sophie laughed at a mental picture of herself working with robed monks who designed illuminated web pages in gold ink on parchment. "Okay. Well, I was just checking to make sure you recovered. Are things back to normal?"

"Yeah. I go back to my twelve-step group tonight. I'll have to decide whether to say anything to Debbie. I mean, did she know those people? Why did they use her name to get me to drive out there?"

"Oooo. You think that twelve-step group is safe?"

"I think the cult people just somehow connected me with her. I doubt she actually had anything to do with them. But I should probably find out."

"Uck. It grosses me out to think of you getting trapped out there. Even if you did get to escape."

Crystal sighed. "I gotta get my ... *stuff* together and not be such a sucker for those kinda people."

"Sounds good. I'll be glad to help. No more trips to other states. At least for a while."

"Good. You'll have to tell me how that was. I gotta go now."

"Okay. Me too. Love you, Crystal."

"Love you too, Sophie."

A chest-expanding breath and a hard drop of her shoulders relaxed Sophie a little, but she wasn't as nervous about this interview as some. Maybe she didn't want it so badly. It did seem like the team would be too small.

Finally dressed, she stepped down the front stairs, reviewing a mental checklist on the way. Résumé, keys, phone, address for interview, breath mints. Seemed like it was all there, including her train pass, which would be in her wallet. Wallet? She stopped at the last landing and confirmed the wallet in her briefcase.

The firm was located high in a massive office building downtown. Sophie paused to crane her neck upward at the steel and glass architecture. But, of course, she saw more than architecture. The array of creatures flying in and out of the building induced a shudder and an internal rebuke for thinking she could look without being bothered by what she saw. She snorted at herself as she walked through the automatic rotating door into the air-conditioned lobby. That brisk AC alerted her to the amount of perspiration she had produced during her commute.

Sophie walked toward the elevators with her arms raised slightly at her sides, getting some airflow without looking too obvious about it. She wore a sleeveless blouse under the jacket. She debated with herself on the way up in the elevator but kept the jacket on. As she rode, a series of spirits blasted up and across the elevator shaft. That distracted her from making a wardrobe adjustment.

When she stepped off the elevator, she located a metallic sign that said Hansen Equities. It was behind a glass wall to her right, above a reception desk. Several other companies apparently shared the floor. Sophie noted one burly spirit clasping the handle of an office door as if preventing someone from leaving. She closed her eyes and prayed for focus. This building seemed particularly crowded with otherworldly denizens.

Willing a large, hooded beast to fade from view between her and the Hansen door, Sophie focused on the receptionist—a human receptionist seated beneath that silver lettering. "I'm Sophie Ramos, here to interview with Maeve Tiggler." Sophie shifted her slim briefcase to her left hand in preparation for a handshake or fist bump, but the receptionist just turned to the phone and hit a button. Sophie glanced around the dramatically lighted reception area.

The young woman behind the desk relayed news of her arrival. She looked at Sophie when she was done. "Maeve will be with you in just a moment." She gestured toward a small enclave filled with cushioned chairs arranged in a close square.

"Thanks." Sophie blinked away an image of a gaunt figure towering over the receptionist. She said another silent prayer. Was it just her own nerves, or was this place tense with spiritual conflict? Sophie pulled out of that introspective nosedive when she heard her name called just before she sat on a low couch in the corner.

"Sophie?"

She straightened her legs and turned to greet a squeaky-clean woman with straight dark hair and a slender, dark suit. Sophie did a double take, however, at the sight of a gruesome spirit that seemed to have a hook through the well-appointed woman. "Uh, Maeve?" Sophie tried not to look at the demon. Or the hook piercing the tall woman's shoulder.

Maeve was staring suspiciously at her. "Yes. So good to meet you?" She didn't sound like it was really so good, her tone puzzled. Probably she was questioning Sophie's shifting gaze and poorly restrained wincing.

That hook seemed to strain upward, as if it stretched the woman to her full height. Sophie wanted to ask Maeve if she wanted help getting off that metal torture device. Only, of course, it wasn't made of metal. And, of course, Sophie was blowing this interview with these distractions. *"Help me, Lord."* She managed to keep that plea internal.

Maeve led her to a conference room, withholding further comment. No small talk. But the interviewer might have been preoccupied with what she was hearing from another spirit that hovered just above and whispered in her ear. Sophie was glad to not know what it was whispering.

Sophie checked for her angels. Around her on all sides were angels of all kinds. Holy ones and unholy ones. Her usual three were slipping through the traffic, clearly unfazed. But not unaffected. The big guardian had his eyes fixed on Sophie as if he could prop her up with his gaze. No hook required. The feminine angel was closest. She held out a hand that Sophie was tempted to try to grasp. Holding hands with her angel—she hadn't tried that yet.

Physically, this office with its dark carpeted hall, wood-paneled conference room, and wide windows overlooking the city reminded Sophie of other businesses she had visited over the years. But spiritually, it reminded her of the intimidating infestation at that orphanage in Iowa. What were these people into?

Once Sophie was seated and had declined a glass of water, Maeve told her what the company was into. But the professional, lingo-laden description of investments in emerging markets and of their niche funding tools balled and knotted inside Sophie's head.

A glance at the stout warrior angel that was her third escort diffused some of her confusion. That angel nodded knowingly. Sophie understood the gesture to imply that the tangled business model was connected to the spiritual overcrowding. The angel's knowing nod seemed to say, "*It is as it appears.*"

The milling spectral crowd included a few unfamiliar holy angels, but they seemed to be relegated to the corners and even outside the plate-glass windows. A couple of them seemed to be trying to get someone's attention. Not Sophie's, but someone else entangled in the mix of rebellious spirits, perhaps.

Sophie did not want to work in this office. Not even connected to it remotely. But she didn't feel free to bolt out the door. She thought of Crystal's dilemma the other day. And she considered what the job recruiter would think if she heard Sophie ran away from the interview.

After a description of the programming position, Maeve offered the opportunity Sophie was waiting for. "So, do you have any questions for me so far?"

"Well, would you say that what you do here is controversial? Are there potentially some people in these emerging markets who might consider your work ... uh, exploitative?" She was sort of quoting her friend Baily, who worked with an aid agency concerned with economic development in Latin America. But then, Baily would probably have already figured out what this company was about.

"Oh, it's hard to work across borders without offending someone at least a little, so I'm sure you could find someone who considers our investment strategies controversial."

Another question popped into Sophie's head, this one probably not from the voice of her friend Baily lingering in her head. "How did this position come to be open?" In fact, Sophie didn't know whether she was applying for an existing position.

"Oh, he moved on to another company."

"Did that have anything to do with the nature of this company's practices overseas?"

"Well, we had our differences ..." Her voice deepened suddenly. "I see you already have reservations about working here. Were you sent to us by someone?" Maeve's suddenly vigilant tone corresponded with a tightening of that hook in her shoulder. She sat up even straighter.

Again, Sophie suppressed a wince. "Uh, the employment agency sent me, but I get a vibe here that I don't think fits with my ... lifestyle."

"Oh. And what lifestyle is that?"

"I'm a Christian. And I believe in treating all people fairly and avoiding exploiting poor people and poor countries wherever possible." Baily would approve, even if Sophie didn't know all the implications of what she had just said. The challenging tone of the interviewer had pushed her past a simple, rational answer. But Sophie looked at her feminine angel and knew that Maeve's hard response was, in part, provoked by the ruling spirits in this office. They didn't want her to work here any more than Sophie did.

Maeve was speechless for a second. That gave Sophie another opening.

"I don't want to waste any more of your time. Thanks for seeing me. I hope you find the right person for the job." She stood and reached a hand toward the interviewer.

But Maeve didn't seem to have control of her own hand. She raised it barely two inches before freezing half in and half out of her chair.

"Okay. I'll just see myself out, then." Short of starting deliverance ministry in the conference room, Sophie couldn't think of anything to do for the woman.

"Wait." Maeve suddenly stood next to Sophie at the conference room door.

Sophie worried that one of those big spirits was going to prevent her from opening the door.

"I can walk you out. I … I understand why some … people wouldn't want to work here." Just a foot away, Maeve's eyes were dark and pleading, her pupils large and liquid.

A wave of sympathy warmed Sophie as they made brief eye contact. She put a hand on Maeve's arm. "It's not too late to get out."

But the sympathetic moment Sophie thought they were sharing evaporated instantly. Maeve's brow tightened. "I don't want to get out." That whispering spirit was hovering over the tall woman again. "I like it here." Her tone had turned more robotic.

Sophie grabbed the door handle and pulled too hard. There was no one, demon or human, holding the door shut.

She just missed bashing Maeve with her elbow. "Sorry. I need to get ... to get going." Breathing was becoming harder.

Sophie uttered a mostly silent prayer, maybe muttering some of it as she pounded her heels over the dark carpet toward the reception area. She was glad for her suit jacket now. The place seemed to be getting colder, and naked arms would have felt too vulnerable. She glanced at the feminine angel at her elbow and wondered if she would explain these feelings. But Sophie didn't actually need a lot of explanation. She didn't need to know everything. She just wanted out.

Next to the office's glass door, she found Maeve right behind her. "Okay. So sorry it didn't work out. Have a good day." Maeve said those lines like she was in a play. Then she lowered her voice as she opened the front door for Sophie. "Pray for me, if that's something you do."

Stunned again, Sophie stood in the doorway. She thought of people in her church who would have grabbed the opportunity to lay hands on this woman right here in front of the reception desk. But Sophie wasn't one of those people yet. And she assumed Maeve wouldn't welcome that obvious breach of office protocol.

"Uh, sure. Of course I'll do that. Uh, have a ... blessed day." Sophie tried more eye contact, but Maeve was looking over her head. Sophie nodded to no one in particular and strode toward the elevators. She glanced over her shoulder and saw Maeve staring after her. Behind Maeve, the receptionist was doing the same. A silly urge to wave at them came and went. Instead, Sophie faced the elevator bank and waited for her escape pod to arrive. Then she remembered to push the button.

"Okay, Sophie. Get a grip." As she muttered that little encouragement to herself, she applied the blinders she had developed early in her life. She didn't want to see any more of those corporate demons.

But she did pray for Maeve Tiggler all the way down to the first floor. At least she could do that much.

A Good Talk with Her Mother

"What are you going to do? You aren't planning to avoid all employers who have spirits active around them, are you?"

Sophie paused to appreciate how far she and her mother had come for those questions to make perfect sense between them. Sophie had the same questions, of course.

"Maybe I could work for a Christian organization."

"You've seen bad spirits working in churches and other places where people believe in God. That won't be a guarantee."

More evidence of their progress, even if what her mother described was frustratingly true.

"Maybe Bruce and Deborah need some computer programming. They keep *their* group pretty clean." She grinned sheepishly at her mother. Sophie was just trying to imagine a Christian organization that paid attention to spiritual warfare. The Albrights were the most obvious example. She supposed her church, or Detta's church, would be good at that.

"You don't really think that's true, do you? That you have to only work for Christians?"

"No. And I really don't need to work for a place where there's no enemy activity. I mean, even my old company wasn't so holy, but it was possible to work there without going crazy over all the spirits coming and going."

"You don't have to worry about being crazy anymore, Sophia." Her mother stood from the kitchen table and removed their plates from the golden place mats. They had finished eating several minutes ago.

"I know, Mama. I don't mean literally crazy. I just mean there are clearly places that are more livable. They don't have to be perfect. That place downtown yesterday was way out of control though. You should have seen the look on that woman's face."

Her mother contemplated for a few seconds. "Do you wonder if you were sent there to help them out of their troubles?"

Ugh. That was the sort of question Sophie didn't want to hear from anyone. Even her mother. The weight of the whole fallen world seemed to settle on her with the notion that she should go to dark places to help people get free. Dark places that didn't invite her. An invitation meant everything to her.

"I ..." She took a deep breath and relaxed the nerve her mother had pinched. "I did think about that. I do think about things like that a lot. It's a real question for me." She watched her mother rinsing dishes and putting them in the dishwasher. "How much can I help in a place that isn't interested in my help? Not even acknowledging that they *need* help." She stood and joined her mother at the sink.

"That woman asked you to pray for her."

"Yeah. That really caught me by surprise." Here was a weakness Sophie was well aware of—her tunnel vision. Most of her life, she had strained to narrow her scope. That was probably one reason she wasn't very flexible when something unexpected came across her screen.

Her mama slipped an arm around Sophie's waist. "Don't fret, Sophie. I'm not pressuring you to do or be anything right now. We all have room to grow. Including me.

Including you. I certainly don't know better than you how to use your gifts." She leaned back a little. "I hope you don't mind me asking you questions."

"Of course you can ask, Mama." She wrapped both arms around her mother's shoulders. Her mother had recognized her discomfort at these particular questions. But the only reason they were even discussing them was because they were both hard and important questions. And it was Sophie who had brought them to dinner with her.

"I need to find programming work. I don't want to do the demon chasing stuff full time. I'm sure of that now. Who pays for that kind of work, anyway? But I need to find work that leaves me room to do ministry and maybe even travel."

"I understand. And I will continue to pray for those things. They are good things for you to want, I believe. Surely God wants them too."

As she looked in her mother's dark eyes, a speculation tripped out of Sophie's mouth. One that had spun around in Sophie's head during early mornings spent trying to get back to sleep. "You ever wonder what might have happened if I knew what to do when Daddy was still here?" Anthony's struggle with his missing father had helped feed this new fantasy.

"What?"

Sophie immediately regretted saying it. Too speculative. Unsuited for outside viewing. Outside her head, that was. "It's just a sort of wild fantasy I have."

"About your father?" Her mother rested a hand on the edge of the sink as if to prop herself.

Nodding, Sophie stepped away and leaned her backside on the cabinets. "I know I was just a kid, but God gives gifts to kids for a reason too. It wasn't a mistake that I could see things even then."

"What ... what did you see around your father?"

"You know, I don't really remember seeing anything particularly around him. I just remember, like, pieces of him. I remember his eyes looking at me when he was clear and sober. I remember his jokes and his laugh. I don't have a clear picture of what was haunting him. I know now there must have been some enemy at work on him. So, I just wonder what would have been possible if I knew what to look for back then."

"You were a little girl. You weren't responsible for saving anyone."

"I know. I guess it's a silly thing. Just thoughts I have when I'm lying in bed having a hard time sleeping."

"Those kinds of thoughts will not help you sleep."

"No, that's for sure. They don't help me sleep."

"Hmm. What do your angels say about it?"

"Oh, I haven't asked. I'm not sure they would answer questions like that. I do pray though. I ask God for peace about it. But I don't think even God wants to answer my 'what-if' questions."

"Peace is good. God would surely tell you not to worry. You'll find what it is you should be doing with your gift. And you'll find it in the future, not in the past." Her mother grimaced briefly. She reached around with one arm but gave up. "I've been having pain right in the middle of my back. I think I injured it when I lifted a floor buffer with Connie at work." She hunched her shoulders forward, leaning her head toward Sophie.

Sophie didn't pass up the opportunity. She set a hand on her mother's upper back and took a pause to see if she'd get some specific direction for how to pray. She stifled a shout, however, when a dark little creature poked its head over her mother's shoulder.

"You get out of here. Get off my mother. You have no right to be here. Leave her in the name of Jesus."

Her mother lurched forward and turned to stare at Sophie wide-eyed. "What—" She froze with her mouth half open. "Wait. I just felt something loosen back here." She reached back again, this time with greater ease. She said a very rapid prayer in Spanish.

Sophie giggled. "I didn't expect that. I thought you just strained your back at work."

"I did. I mean, I thought that too. That was the thing I could remember when I first noticed it." Her eyes drifted toward the cabinets. "Though I really didn't feel like I hurt myself at the time. I was just thinking later that must have been when it started."

"But maybe it wasn't. Maybe that explanation was a trick. Maybe it really started when that little goblin jumped on your back."

"Gob-lin?" Her mother pronounced it with the care of someone unfamiliar with the term.

Sophie couldn't blame her. It wasn't a technical term. Not a word her mother's priest would use.

"Is it gone now?" Her mother stopped stretching and focused more tightly on Sophie.

"How does it feel?"

"It feels fine, but it was fine most of the time before. The pain just came and went away each day."

"I suppose it could have started when you hurt yourself. Maybe that thing jumped on you when you lifted the buffer."

Her mother frowned. "I don't want to think about that. I don't want to picture spirits jumping on my back when I'm at work."

"I'll pray protection for you. I don't think I've been praying that for you enough."

"Okay. You should. You should pray for your mama's protection." She smiled warmly at Sophie.

And Sophie prayed right there in the kitchen. She left out some specifics, however, to not scare her mother. She could pray those prayers later.

Her mother spoke up as soon as Sophie finished. "I wonder if Connie's angry at me. I docked her pay because she left early several times last month. You think she might have done something?"

That started Sophie praying against any curses from her mother's employees. In a sense, it relieved some of Sophie's concern. At least it would make sense that an employee would curse her mother, intentionally or otherwise. That felt better than worrying that random critters were jumping on her mother whenever she turned her back.

"Should I say something to her?" Her mother's brow was fisted, her eyes searching Sophie when the second round of prayers was finished.

"I wouldn't. Even if she did curse you, she may not have been aware. Not all curses are intentional, not necessarily spells spoken by witches or stuff like that."

"You know this?"

"This, *Madrecita*, is something I know."

Her mother nodded. She patted Sophie's cheek. "Good."

Is Hope Lost?

Sophie laughed at Anthony's joke but stopped short when her phone buzzed. She debated checking who it was. Something told her to look. That prompt might have just come out of anxiety accumulated from finding a critter clinging to her mother's back and from missing Crystal's pleas for help when Sophie was in California. She apologized to Anthony and checked.

The message was from Hope. **"I have to talk with you soon."**

Hope and Sophie had done an audio call that afternoon. It had been interrupted by a work call for Hope, but they hadn't been discussing anything urgent. What had changed since?

"Trouble?" Anthony grimaced sympathetically with one side of his face, his head tipped slightly. He set his fork by his plate and glanced at a passing waitress.

"Sorry. Yeah. Hope is having a crisis or something."

"You have to call her?" He looked like he was done with his curry.

"Later. When I get home."

"You been talking to her a lot?"

"Yeah. We've kept close since I got home. I was hoping we could, but I'm not real comfortable that it's close enough right now. She seemed okay earlier today, but she did go off her meds while I was there. I'm still not sure that was a good idea."

"Is she, like, stable? I mean, isn't it kinda normal for her to have a good day and then a bad day?"

"I guess that's normal for most of us."

He nodded. "Probably all of us."

"So, what gives *you* a bad day?" Sophie sipped her water and considered whether she could eat any more of the chicken curry. It was good, but she would probably regret overeating if she didn't stop now.

Anthony played with a bit of flat bread, then dropped it on his plate. "Since you asked, I worry about us. I just wonder when we can, you know, decide what we wanna be for each other."

Sophie's first reaction was, *Didn't we just talk about this?* But she knew it had been a while. Anthony had mostly let her put the conversation on hold. For a moment, she appreciated the fact that he felt free to bring up a hard topic. But then she had to decide how to actually answer his concern, and the joy dribbled away. One deep breath, and she started to answer.

But he interrupted. "No. Don't worry about it. This isn't the time. I'm glad you're gonna be around for a while. We can talk. You don't have to answer now. I'm not in crisis or anything. It was just you asking what gives me a bad day as if you didn't already know. That tripped me up."

"Sorry. Insensitive of me." That was what she was supposed to say. Truly she didn't know whether Anthony was in crisis about their relationship. He joked about normal things and even not-so-normal things all the time. Was he in more pain than she could see?

"Ha. I'm just being a drama queen, and you know it." He raised a hand to catch their waiter's attention.

"Drama queen? Isn't it drama king?"

"Me? I ain't the king of anything."

"Well …"

"Okay, I'm not the queen of anything either." He laughed.

That laugh smoothed some friction between them. If he couldn't laugh at hearing himself say absurd things, then they *were* in crisis.

"You still wanna get that frozen yogurt?" Sophie nodded in the direction of the shop just two stores down from the Indian restaurant.

"You still have room for it?"

"It's frozen yogurt. It'll just melt and seep right into the empty spaces."

"Is that how it works?"

"Obviously."

At home an hour later, Sophie kicked off her thin sandals. She sauntered to her couch as she pulled up Hope's number. It rang about ten times with no answer. She might still be on a support call, though it would be after seven in California. Hope didn't usually work that late.

Sophie sifted through her email, hunched over her phone for a few minutes. Then an angel appeared near the front door. Had she knocked? Shaking off that odd thought, Sophie focused on the gleaming feminine figure. It was Hope's guardian.

"Call her again. She needs you." Her voice was humming and sweet, but also firm and authoritative.

Calling again, Sophie waited through a half dozen rings, beginning to wonder if the angel knew what she was talking about.

Then Hope answered. "Uh, yeah. I don't know what happened."

"You want a video call?" Sophie had sent the offer already, waiting for Hope to confirm.

"I don't know. Maybe not. I'm a ... a bit of a mess right now."

"What happened? What's going on?" Sophie glanced at the visiting angel, who nodded and then disappeared.

"Uh, well, my ... my ex contacted me. He said he needed to apologize. Ha." She muttered something Sophie didn't understand.

"Wait. Are you high right now?"

"Am I? Well, I guess I am. Though I really, really didn't see it coming. I mean, I thought it was, like, really nice of me to meet him and let him apologize. You know, make amends and all that. And, well, I guess I should have known it was ... just a ... scam." She swore. Then she swore again, a bitter insult.

"Who are you talking to?"

"Creepy ... ugly ... nasty ... uh, you know. One of those things."

"What did you take?"

"Oxy. Just some oxy."

"How much?"

"A couple few pills is all."

"You don't sound good."

"I know. That's why I called. I'm freaking out. And I can't ... I can't stay, like, focused on even ... you know ... like, regretting I did it. There's, like, this ... I mean, more than one ... of those creepy things like I used to see with ... with my ex." She swore. "I can't even remember his name right now. How messed up is that?"

"Well, I don't care what the guy's name is. I'm just worried about you."

"Yeah. I'm worried too. And not just 'cause I forget his **** name."

"How long ago did you take the pills?"

"Couple hours. Just after ... or, I mean, just before I texted you. I did text you, didn't I?"

"Yes. You did." Sophie was glad to hear this was not an overdose situation. Hours after taking those pills, Hope would be out cold if she overdosed. Sophie had taken oxycodone in her dark past. Come to think of it, she couldn't remember *her* drug dealer's name just now either.

The night scrolled on and on. Sophie stayed on the phone with Hope until she started to come down. Early on, Sophie got on her computer and looked up overdose symptoms to confirm that Hope would survive. At least physically.

By the time Hope finally fell asleep, Sophie was recognizing the girl she had stayed with in California a couple weeks ago. Hope moaned and cried a lot on her way down from the high. Much of that was about self-loathing. Sophie had to keep talking her out of condemning herself. And Hope leveled out toward the end.

Sophie's last thought before she fell asleep was literally "*What now?*"

For the next two days, Hope didn't respond to Sophie's texts or calls. Sophie finally called Eddie to see if he had heard anything.

"She said she met with her ex-boyfriend and made a huge mistake. That's as much as I could understand between all the crying."

Sophie hadn't heard Hope cry before that long nighttime phone call. "Crying? You think that means she's still taking pills?"

"No. I don't think so. She told me she was off it. But she was really mad at herself. Ashamed of herself. Like that."

"Maybe I should go out there and see her."

"Fly all the way to California again? Maybe you should call her first."

"I've been calling and texting. She's not answering."

"Sure. Well, she probably thinks you'll be mad. Or you'll judge her or something."

"I told her I wasn't mad. I texted that I wasn't judging her. More than once. I knew that's what she'd be thinking."

"Oh. Well, I don't know if she'd believe you."

"Did she sound like she's still seeing spirits in her apartment?"

"Probably. I mean, she sounded miserable. As miserable as I've ever heard. I mean, she kept talking about how she was a screwup and her mother was right to hate her. It was pretty bad stuff."

"Does she have a group or a sponsor she can contact?"

"I don't know. I suppose. But I couldn't tell you anything about them. I think she was going to meetings when I was staying with her. At least that's what she said she was doing."

After Eddie, Sophie called Detta. "Should I go out there?"

Detta's voice ramped with incredulity. "What would you do? The girl needs some real change, Sophie. You gonna live with her and watch over her?"

"Maybe. I ... I don't know. I'm just worried that she's opened herself up to worse spirits than the ones I cast out of her."

"Oh. Well, Jesus said that could happen. She needs to get filled up with him."

"I don't know if she's ready for that. I mean, she should be responding to my messages if she was ready for that, right?"

"Well, dear, a crisis brings in all kindsa new possibilities for people. Maybe this will make her ready. But maybe she hasn't gotten there yet."

"I don't wanna wait for her to hit bottom."

"But you know that's what it takes sometimes. You know that, right?"

Sophie drew a long, exasperated breath. "I should fly out there and see her. I'm going nuts here wondering what's happening to her."

"I'll pray for her. And I'll pray for your wisdom. I'll get the group on it. I know you'll make the best choice."

Sophie wasn't so sure on that last point. She also felt a slight churn in her gut when she looked at her bank account. She could do it. She could buy a two-way ticket. But she would lose more work hours and maybe lose the assignment. And what then?

For the first time in a long time, Sophie literally got on her knees next to her bed to pray.

Heading West Again

"I could come with you." Anthony was leaning on the doorframe.

"Come on in. I can't believe you came over here so late."

"You sounded desperate."

"I am. You know I am. But just because I'm willing to fly out there again doesn't mean I've totally lost it."

"No, I know. I remember when Jimmy was taking another deep dive into the hard stuff. It was tough not to go down with him. I know how it is when you wanna help but you don't know if anything you do is gonna make a difference. But you, Sophie, you have a better chance than most of us to actually make a difference. If she trusts you and wants to get clean, then you can help her. You and your angels."

"And you want to see that?"

"Yeah." He grinned wearily. "See you chasing angels through the streets of LA. Ha. City of Angels."

"She lives in the suburbs."

"Okay. Well, whatever. I'd like to go with you."

"It could be rough. You'd probably have to sleep on the floor."

"Been there, done that."

Though she tried to talk him out of it for another five minutes, she really wanted him to go with her. She just wanted to make sure Anthony was sure.

After sixteen more hours of silence, when Sophie was on the airline website deciding whether to buy the tickets, Hope finally texted back one word. **"Help."**

Sophie cried. Then she called Anthony and told him.

He was silent for a long time, though he probably wasn't crying.

"What does it mean, exactly?" Sophie asked Anthony even though she knew it was an impossible question.

"We can be there tomorrow. We'll find out. Keep praying for her, Sophie. That's all we can do now."

Tempted to ask if Anthony was with his mother just then, Sophie didn't resist his encouragement. It was obvious. It wasn't simple, but it was obvious that she should pray. All she *could* do for now was pray.

Sophie finished her part of the web project she was working on. As much as she could do until others looked it over and added or subtracted. Or sent it back to her to be fixed. She hoped they wouldn't send it back until she had seen Hope and knew what to do with her.

"I'm waiting for boarding." She was speaking to Crystal the next day, sitting with Anthony, who seemed to be talking to his mom.

"You think she's, like, under the drugs, or is it spirits she needs help with?"

"Maybe both."

Hope had appeared to start a text to Sophie that morning, a reply to Sophie's final warning that they were on their way. But no words arrived on the screen following that bubble with the moving dots.

After saying goodbye to Crystal, Sophie saw an alert for an incoming text.

"See you soon. So glad you're coming!!!!"

Sophie showed the message to Anthony.

"From Hope?" He squinted at the small screen. Then his squint morphed to a scowl.

Nodding, Sophie let him finish the phone call she had interrupted. She shook her head and prayed some more. She should be encouraged that Hope had answered, but the enthusiasm of that new text was so odd after the long silence.

"See you in a few hours." Sophie hovered her thumbs over the keyboard for several seconds and decided to just send that much. It was her response to a single text message, not a response to Hope's drug trip, her plea for help, and then the maddening silence.

They settled into their seats after wedging their carry-on bags into the overhead bin. Sophie was strong, but Anthony was stronger. That was handy for bag wedging. It could be nice to travel with someone. Anthony in particular. But could he keep up with Sophie when it came to chasing angels and bringing deliverance?

"Do you check the wings to make sure the angels are on duty?" he whispered to her before leaning back toward his window. He had a pretty good view of one wing.

She snickered. "You make it sound like I fly all the time. I've only flown a few times since I stopped trying not to see any kind of … angel activity." She lowered her voice at the end, not wanting to alert the other passengers that crazy people were onboard.

The mention of angels on the wings, however, started Sophie thinking. And seeing. She noted a small huddle of spirits by the divider between coach and first class. They looked like troublemakers. Or maybe just mischief makers. Then her attention was drawn away by a small crustacean-like thing peering over the seat in front of her. She whispered a command for that one, and all other spirits on that plane, to leave her and Anthony alone. When she finished, she found Anthony staring at her.

But he didn't ask. He probably didn't want to know. He didn't want to know about everything she saw. She was certain of that.

She smirked at him. "I'll tell you if I see one sawing off one of the wings."

"Great. What good will that do me?"

"You don't have a parachute?"

"No. I thought you were bringing those. Isn't that why your suitcase was so heavy?"

She shook her head. "Shoes. Don't you know? A girl has to pack dozens of pairs of shoes."

Anthony scowled and glanced toward her feet before he apparently realized she was kidding. He rolled his eyes and shook his head, resuming his vigil over the left wing.

The flight was uneventful. They watched a movie together on the little tablets mounted on the seats in front of them. It wasn't a bad film, but a brief escape from their real-life drama was a pretty low bar. A two-hour distraction was worth at least three stars.

Anthony was standing next to her in the airport staring at the dense pedestrian traffic. "Did she say she was coming to pick us up?"

"She doesn't have a car."

"I thought everyone in California had a car. Isn't it required for statehood or whatever?"

"Statehood?"

"Whatever." He returned to gawking at the inhabitants of LAX while Sophie ordered a cab on her phone.

As she waited for an answer, Sophie wondered if the stretching sensation she got while traveling was only her imagination. Even a drive to the west side of the city required pressing through a bit of invisible resistance, like she was pushing through an elastic barrier. Was she sensing the spiritual atmosphere on a broader scale? A regional atmosphere? Was it sensing, or just imagining?

The South Asian cab driver could have been working back home. Only the passing palm trees distinguished the ride. The driver glanced at them in the mirror repeatedly, reminding Sophie to watch her words. But there was little to edit. Anthony had only been to the coast once before, and he was enjoying it like a kid on vacation.

"Hey, how far are we gonna be from Disney World?"

Sophie laughed. "You hoping we can go there, or are you just wondering if you'll see Mickey Mouse on the street after he gets off work?"

Anthony laughed with her.

When they arrived at Hope's apartment building, a knot tightened in Sophie's stomach. A text she'd sent from the airport got no reply. She called Hope's cell when the cabbie pulled away from the curb, leaving her and Anthony looking up at the front of the sunbaked four-story building.

Hope appeared to pick up, but the call was ended immediately. An accident, or some manifestation of a new level of intoxication?

They found her door button, and Anthony pushed that. The late afternoon temperature was nearing a hundred degrees. Back home it was only in the eighties.

Sophie could see sweat starting to bead on Anthony's forehead. "I hope she has air conditioning."

"You're confident we're gonna get inside? What's plan B if she's not home or not answering?"

Sophie waited a few more seconds. "Let's go around back and see if we see any signs of life on her balcony. She likes to hang out back there."

When she visited Hope before, Sophie didn't explore the rear of the building from ground level. She and Anthony ran into a gate, but there was no lock on the rusted gray wrought iron. Anthony pushed through, dragging his small suitcase behind him. The racket of their two cases rolling on broken concrete would make sneaking up on someone impossible, but that wasn't the mission.

At the back of the building, Sophie discovered it wasn't so easy to get a good look at Hope's fourth-floor balcony. She backed up against the tall iron fence between buildings and shaded her eyes. Her index finger caught a drop from her own sweaty forehead.

"Which one is it?"

"Actually, I don't think I really know which one." Sophie turned to try and figure it out by the view behind them, but she couldn't see much of that view from down there. She pulled out her phone and called again. This time it went to voice mail. "Hope, it's Sophie. Anthony and I are here. We tried your buzzer out front. Now we're behind the building. I don't know which balcony is yours. I was hoping to figure out if you're home." She sighed. "Okay. Call me when you get this, please."

Shaking her head, Sophie turned to Anthony. "I don't really have a plan B. I guess we can look for a motel or something. I found a house with a room to rent last time, but I never used it."

A scream from above them stopped Anthony's response. "Sophie! Help! Help me!" Hope's head and shoulders appeared over the edge of one of the small balconies. For just a second, it looked like she was being pushed against that edge. Then she was gone.

"I guess that one's hers." Anthony was staring skyward with his mouth open.

Sophie only glanced at him. There was no fire escape ladder as there might be back home. What was the fire plan in this building? That wasn't a helpful problem to solve just then. "C'mon, let's see if we can get in the front." She turned and dashed back toward the gate, Anthony and his case rumbling along behind.

At the front door, Anthony started punching buttons for other apartments, hoping one would buzz them in. It took six tries. When the electric lock buzzed, Anthony pulled the door open, and Sophie barged through. Half her brain was telling her that Hope was just being overly dramatic. The girl was high and out of control. The other half of her brain was in first-responder mode. Running toward real danger.

Reaching the fourth floor, regretting how little exercise she had done lately, Sophie panted heavily. Anthony seemed to be in about the same shape. She could see the sweat coursing down his face now. He was right there with her, headed for trouble.

Halfway down the hall, Sophie tried to recall if she was headed to the right door. Then she heard a voice inside the nearest apartment.

"Leave me ... leave me alo—" A pounding on the inside of the door might have been a body crashing against it.

"Hope! Hope! Are you okay? Hope! Open up!"

Breaking Down the Door

Anthony stared wide-eyed. "Should I break down the door?" He wondered why he even bothered to ask. He had never busted in a door, ever. He had been a crawl-in-an-unlocked-window type of kid, if he got locked out.

"Hope! Open up! We're here to help!" Sophie was leaning her head on the door.

One of the neighbors opened his door a few inches. A ruddy middle-aged man glared at them. "She's been acting crazy all week. Get her to a hospital."

"Okay, sir. Thanks. We'll try." Anthony nodded once at the man, who closed his door immediately.

He looked at Sophie. "Break it down?"

"I don't think so. I can feel her leaning against it." Sophie lifted her head from the door, but she left both hands on the white-painted surface.

Anthony swore, then apologized. He tested the doorknob. It wasn't locked, but the deadbolt seemed to be set. That meant kicking the door in would be a big mess. He knew that from the movies he'd seen. He wished one of his heavier friends were here. Ervin, maybe.

He took a deep breath and pulled his keys out of his pocket. His car key was an electronic fob, but it had a manual key folded inside. He pulled it out. It had reminded him of a tool someone in a movie would use to pick a lock when he first got it, but it was too thick to fit in the keyhole for the bolt.

"What are you doing?" Sophie scowled hard at him.

He didn't like the scoffing eyes she was aiming at him, but he had to admit it looked like he was trying to remote start his car from halfway across the continent. "Desperate. Don't know what to do." His mind thrashed at the problem. "Can an angel unlock a door?"

"Let's pray." That was Sophie's answer. Maybe she thought she should pray that Anthony would miraculously become more helpful.

He wished his mama were here for this prayer, but Sophie did okay. She asked for divine help in getting the door open and getting Hope free from whatever was wrestling with her. That Sophie assumed some spirit was wrestling with Hope was more than Anthony knew for sure, but it didn't sound like a physical attacker, really. Just one small body knocking around in there.

"Hope, unlock the door. We can't get in. Please unlock the door."

A scramble and then silence. Then a hard thump, like a shoulder slamming into the door.

"Turn the lock. Open the lock. The bolt is locked." Anthony's voice cracked two or three times. Did he really need to explain this?

Again, a momentary silence. Then a girl grunting. That turned into roaring mixed with a loud click.

Anthony grabbed the handle, turned, and pushed. He didn't fling it open for fear that Hope was on the floor just inside. He was right about that, but with the door open just a few inches, he was able to slide his basketball shoe into the gap to prevent Hope or her assailant from locking it again.

Sophie spoke more calmly now. "Hope, are you okay? Can you let us in the door? We can help you ..." Whether she was going to say more or not, her appeals gave way to a shout.

The door swung free, and Anthony saw something just past Sophie. A pair of legs dragging along the floor and around a corner. He gulped, swallowing a curse.

Sophie shouted, "Let her go! In the name of Jesus, I command you to let Hope go." She was inside the apartment ahead of Anthony.

He tripped on Sophie's suitcase and booted it through the doorway. The door closed on Anthony's case, leaving an easy escape route. It was a strangely calm thought, given that his entire body was shaking.

"Pray, Anthony. Something has her."

He shook himself out of paralyzing shock and started to pray silently, still standing in the entryway. That silent petition seemed to lack impact, so he started saying the words aloud. "Lord, we need your help. Send ... send support. Send help. Help Hope get free ... get free from ... to get free from whatever ... whatever this is." He stopped to take a breath. "Gotta get a grip."

As he continued to pray, he could hear Sophie commanding something to let Hope go. He could just see the bottom of one shoe where Sophie was apparently on her knees in a little hall that probably led to a bedroom or bathroom. He closed his eyes and prayed silently again, having found it hard to form words with his mouth. One of his prayers was for his mother to know that she should be praying. Had

Sophie kept his mama updated? Was her prayer group on the case?

Then he thought to call. "Mama, we need you to pray. Something is fighting with Hope."

His mother made a low grunt that was unfamiliar. "Okay, Anthony. You stay with 'em no matter what. You support Sophie, son. She needs you. I'll get the folks prayin' over here."

"Thanks, Mama."

"Love you, Anthony. You can do this."

"Love you, Mama." He ended the call and stepped around the corner.

Sophie was sitting on her heels now. She was in a doorway to a bedroom with her arms around a girl who was paler and skinnier than she was. Anthony had heard someone's hair described as a mop before, but this girl's hair was exactly the length and texture of an old cotton mop his mother had when he was a kid. He smelled something too. It was probably her. The girl was crying.

Sophie was talking. "I command all enemy spirits to back down and stay off of Hope. Leave this place, and do not come back."

But that only seemed to rile whatever was in this apartment. Hope's hands snapped free from her embrace with Sophie. The girl crashed to the carpet and writhed on the floor like she was in a frantic fight with something bigger than her.

Sophie lunged onto her hands and knees, reaching into that fray.

In a moment of sudden clarity, Anthony knew these two women were wrestling with something they could both see. To them, this was not a crazy girl writhing around on the floor. This was a girl fighting for her life against some person or beast that was clearly stronger than her, but maybe not more desperate. Anthony had his hand clasped over his mouth. That hand was shaking. Was he stopping himself from screaming?

"Pray, Anthony. Keep praying. Pray loud, in the name of Jesus."

So he did. It took a few seconds, but before long he sounded like one of those prayer warriors at his mother's church. He was calling for help, claiming the blood, and praising the Lord. Loud. He fought off a worry about what the neighbors would think. And he kept praying.

Though he couldn't see that other fighter, he seemed to see the effects of his prayers. Or maybe his mother's prayers. Or the prayer ladies' prayers. Hope seemed to be prevailing. Sophie was down on the floor with her, but she was not wrestling demons. She was grasping Hope. It looked like she was keeping the girl on the floor, keeping her from being dragged out of the room, perhaps back out onto the balcony.

The balcony door was open. Anthony stepped across the living room and slid the glass door closed. He latched it. He had to wrench his brain free of a vision of Hope getting thrown off that balcony.

Anthony started praying again as he returned to the bedroom. Calmer now, but the same words. The same claims and commands and praises. It was rhythmic now, familiar at least from having said it a few minutes before. Familiar from his mother and her friends. The prayer fighters. He could recall doing something like this down that alley in the city. He was so glad his mother had shown him how to fight, even if he'd assumed he'd never have to do it like this.

Now Sophie and Hope were both sitting on the floor, their arms wrapped around each other. It was a survivors' embrace, survivors of a collision at sea, waiting for the ship to finally sink.

As he looked on, still muttering prayers, Anthony saw more clearly that this was what it would mean for him to be with Sophie. To support her chasing angels.

Not Flesh and Blood

Sophie forced her breathing to slow. She was soaked in sweat though the apartment was much cooler than outside. Hope was quivering in her arms. She smelled like a neglected laundry basket. Sophie ignored that smell and clung right back. The strength of that embrace was about resistance. Resistance to her own fear as much as the enemy grappling with Hope. Seeing her physically wrestling that insect-like beast was terrifying.

"I can't breathe." Hope's voice was muffled.

Perhaps a spirit had her around the throat. Sophie had seen that before. But, as Hope slowly pulled free, Sophie could see nothing grasping her neck or throat.

Then Sophie recognized the plea of a kid tired of being hugged too hard. Hope was not the victim of a constricting demon this time.

After releasing her grip, Sophie noticed how tense her muscles were. As if she were at the gym on one of the weight machines. Hope didn't weigh much. Even less now than when Sophie had seen her last. How much did that demon weigh? Raising her head to look at the four angels arrayed against the bedroom wall, Sophie scowled at them. "Why aren't you guys fighting this thing instead of me?"

Her guardian bowed his head in a sympathetic way. The warrior angel nodded very subtly. But Sophie's feminine angel answered in her motherly voice. "You have fought bravely, but it will not result in her freedom until she lets go of the resentment."

Hope was wiping her hair away from her forehead. "I know, I know, I know. I just—" Then she growled and suddenly tipped backward again.

Sophie reached impotently toward her, but Anthony caught one of Hope's hands as it flailed through the air. He probably helped break her fall at least a little. Her sweaty arm slipped through his hand, and Hope thumped to the floor again.

That dark and glossy demon was on top of her again, but Sophie accepted that it wouldn't help for her to get back into the wrestling match. She tried to keep her voice calm. "You know about the resentment, Hope? What resentment? You need to renounce whatever resentment it is, right?"

Hope writhed less violently. She moaned. Maybe that was the start of an answer, but it didn't hatch into real words.

"Jesus, help us, please. Please give Hope courage and strength. Show her the freedom you offer. Help her to want it enough to make it happen." That prayer wasn't textbook, but it also wasn't frantically desperate.

Anthony added an amen.

Hope's growl turned to a groan, then a sustained grunting. Like someone trying to lift an impossibly heavy weight.

"You just have to say you want to. You don't have to have it all figured out or all settled. You just have to say you want it." Sophie was on her knees again. She was as close to Hope's ear as she could be without getting hit by the demon or by Hope, who was still wrestling hand-to-hand.

"*Uuuuuhhhhh.*" That was Hope's reply.

Somehow it raised a bit of belief in Sophie. "You can do it. Ask Jesus to help you. He's glad to help you even if you're not sure yet what you believe."

Hope's voice deepened, and she cursed Jesus. Harsh. Stark and offensive. How offended would Jesus be at having his name attached to such a profane word?

Sophie looked at the angels again. Her feminine guardian had a knowing sort of squint to her eyes. A hint?

Oh. Hope's resentment was against Jesus.

"Jesus loves you, Hope. Jesus would never bring you harm. I break the curse put on you by people who pretended to be working on his behalf while violating his true Spirit. I break their lies. I declare healing for the wounds inflicted by a fake Jesus. In the name of the true Lord Jesus Christ, I declare Hope free from the power of the lies."

That all came in a rush, but it sounded okay as it echoed in Sophie's head. She breathed a bit of gratitude for the time she'd spent with Bruce Albright and his team. Sophie had probably learned more from them than she had paused to catalog.

Hope lay still. "You think he still loves me?" Her voice was small and childish.

Anthony blurted an answer. "I know he does. Of course he does. You are totally lovable as far as he's concerned. And I can see that."

Sophie turned and looked at him. She had to stop herself from chuckling. His answer was a little weird, but helpfully enthusiastic.

Prying her eyes open as the glossy demon disappeared again, Hope looked at Sophie and then Anthony. "My mother." She groaned and began to weep.

Praying silently for some clarity about what was happening now and what to do next, Sophie stiffened at the sight of a woman approaching. When the specter reached Hope's side, she began to twist into some kind of creature. The bony arms became knotted branches. It leaned toward Hope as if bowed with the prevailing winds. What had started as a woman who could have been Hope's mother was now a tangle of vines around a rotting core. A missing core, perhaps. Sophie had to break herself away from staring at the intruder.

Anthony was still muttering prayers. Then he jerked as if someone had smacked him on top of the head. A swooping spirit had bounced off him. Fortunately, it ricocheted as if Anthony wore a helmet. His prayers intensified.

Reaching to touch his leg, Sophie prayed for peace and protection for her friend.

He glanced down at her and smiled, batting his eyes and shaking his head subtly.

Hope wasn't watching. She was curled into a fetal position, grunting as if something were being driven through her stomach. The creature leaning over her had sent vines toward her, perhaps into her.

"You need to forgive your mother even if you don't feel it. Say you forgive her and ask Jesus to help you forgive her."

Hope started saying something, but the words were garbled. Her speech degenerated to a whispering hiss, her lips curling and contorting.

"Release her mouth in the name of Jesus. Let go of her speech right now." Sophie bent over Hope, trying to block the twisty vine spirit. Even as she focused on Hope, she could sense two of the angels muscling in front of that spirit.

Looking up again, Sophie said, "I bless the holy angels and welcome their work in this place right now. Let the will of heaven be done here right now."

An invisible concussion in the air forced Sophie to blink and recoil. The shock wave seemed to come from everywhere at once. She made an involuntary sound, and Hope started to laugh hysterically.

Anthony muttered some confused question.

Sophie didn't ask him to repeat it. "Hope? Hope, what's going on?"

Hope fell silent. Then a low humming came from deep in her throat. "Hey. Get off me." She didn't shout this time, but a small animalistic figure rose from her chest and disappeared.

Sophie had seen no sign of that thing until now. She looked at the treelike thing still leaning over Hope. It seemed withered. Weakened. Had it been hiding that little animal thing? And where was the original demon? The one with the shiny shell?

"This is the one that remains." The apparent spokesperson among the angels indicated the viny thing still standing there. Sophie could see brittle vines running from the base of that withered tree right into Hope. Hope showed no awareness of it. No sign of discomfort. In the physical world, those vines would make lying on the floor very uncomfortable even if they weren't tangled with her insides.

"What do I need to do?" Sophie consulted that angel.

In response, she received one decisive nod toward Hope.

Hope's face was contorted. A gasping sob followed the twist of her mouth. Her eyes were shut tight.

Consolation. That was the word that entered Sophie's head.

Anthony stepped past Hope and walked right through that viny spirit. He sat cross-legged on the floor and put a hand on Hope's near shoulder. He muttered prayers. He was still on the job.

"Lord, bring your consolation to Hope. Open her heart where she's been afraid to open it before." Sophie knew this was a prayer people had prayed over her. Her mother had perhaps prayed something like it for years before Sophie's conversion. There with Hope, accompanied by Anthony, Sophie spoke simple, consoling words. Single words. "Peace. Joy. Release. Rest."

Hope opened her eyes. She looked up at that withered tree above her head. "You can go now. I don't want you here anymore. I don't need you at all."

And that spirit disappeared with a slight gasp and a swirl of vapor.

Struggling for Freedom

That freaky tree thing disappearing was awesome, but not even close to as amazing as Sophie showing up at her apartment. Hope closed her eyes and savored the goodness she felt in her chest, like a warm salve during a winter cold. A Minnesota winter cold.

And then Hope was back there. Back in her bedroom as a small girl. Six years old. That shy, shiny woman was there in the corner. She seemed shy to Hope because she kept her distance and seldom spoke. But she glowed sometimes. And that glow seemed to reveal what sort of person she was. The sort of person she would be if Hope got to know her.

Little Hope coughed. Her congested chest seemed to be the whole of her. Her entire self was full of sickness. And that golden figure looked sad that she couldn't come closer or bring something to help the little girl in the bed.

Hope's mother entered the memory. She entered the room carrying a thermometer in one hand and her cell phone in the other. "She's fine. Just the flu, I'm sure. She'll get over it. I wish everything was that easy."

Looking back now, where she lay on the carpet instead of her childhood bed, Hope understood what her mother had meant by that last comment. Her daughter had something wrong with her that was much worse than that cough or even the flu.

Vines. Her mother's anger was like thin, hard vines that pierced Hope's body. They dug deep. They touched things inside the little girl that she didn't understand, things she couldn't see. Hope could always see the shiny people. She could see the monsters. But she couldn't see inside herself. Until now. Now, as an adult who was free from those vines, she knew she was free from the dying tree that was her mother's love for her.

"Love." It should be in quotation marks. She knew that now. Those vines provided life or death depending on how Hope behaved. That "love" was about control. Emotional control.

A huge sigh. Hope decided to forgive her mother for that even if she had no idea how that would work. Sophie had said something like that, hadn't she?

"I wonder how many people who think they hate Jesus are really hating that fake one." Until she said it, Hope hadn't been aware of wondering that. Maybe she had been saving it through the wrestling match on the floor. She worried that it was a distraction right now. Shouldn't she be thinking about something else?

Sophie grasped her hand and helped her sit up.

Anthony, whom she had never met before, grabbed a tissue box and brought it to her.

That was when Hope discovered her face was sticky with ... stuff. Who knew what all? Ugh.

Her phone rang where it sat on the kitchen counter.

Anthony raised his eyebrows in question.

Hope nodded and held her hand out toward the kitchen. She knew who it was because that guy had just shown up.

Not Anthony. That other guy. The stern one in the suit that visited whenever her mom called. Talk about caller ID.

"I don't know if I want to talk to her yet." She said it before her phone reached her hand.

"Who?"

"My mom."

Anthony furrowed his brow. "How did you know it was her?" The ringtone was generic.

Hope nodded toward the suit guy. *The church guy* was how she thought of him.

Anthony furrowed his brow more deeply.

Sophie nodded slowly. "He shows up when your mom calls?" She jabbed a thumb toward the new arrival.

Relaxing his quizzical expression a little, Anthony let out a breath. He must have been used to this kind of thing with Sophie. They'd done stuff like this together before, hadn't they?

Hope addressed their stack of questions as she saw her mom's call go to voice mail. "I sorta think she sends him over here to make contact. Maybe even to get me to answer. To get me to comply. But it doesn't work."

"Interesting how often these spirits are counterproductive." Sophie sounded like she was talking about a computer application flaw.

Anthony slumped against the door frame. "I don't get it. Your mom has an angel that comes to get you to answer her calls?"

"We should sit in chairs like grown-ups, I guess." Hope struggled to her feet.

Sophie gripped her upper arm with one strong hand.

Hope answered Anthony's last question. "It's not what I think of as an angel. More like one of those counterproductive ones. And I doubt my mom is sending him on purpose. Or knows about it."

Sophie nodded. "I think Anthony's mom would call it a religious spirit."

"Oh." Anthony followed them to the living room. "Should I open the door?" He stood by the sliding glass door.

He was probably reacting to the smell. Hope was just becoming aware of it. She was pretty sure she hadn't washed in a few days. She couldn't remember how long it had been. She waved a hand toward the door and nodded, too embarrassed to make eye contact with the elephant in the room. Though she hoped she didn't actually smell as bad as she imagined an elephant would.

Bringing the conversation back around, Sophie sat on the couch and lasered her eyes into Hope's. "That religious guy is gone now."

Hope offered half a shrug. "Yeah. My mom knows nothing about it, I'm sure. I mean, she doesn't really believe in this stuff. She thinks religion is just about membership and rules and giving the right answers. I think that's how she plans on getting into heaven—having the right answers to a list of questions God is gonna ask her on judgment day."

Sophie looked at Anthony. "The religious spirits I've seen aren't scary looking. At least at first. You let them hang around, and they make themselves as pleasant as possible. But you cross them, and they show their fangs. Even if her mom could see that thing, she probably wouldn't be offended by him. I think it's symbolic of what the religious spirits do."

"Plenty of reason to stay away from that church ... and my mother." Hope was sinking deep into the couch.

A twist of her eyes implied Sophie was bothered by something. "Is there something else?" Obviously she thought so.

"Another one?" Hope shuddered. "Dang. I'm surprised any of those things stick around when you're in the house." A tendril loosened from the middle of her back, as if her spine had been entangled with some hidden parasite. A pretty big parasite.

"Go. Don't come back." Sophie sounded like someone telling the neighbor's dog to stop peeing on her lawn. No mention of the name of Jesus.

It instantly felt like a space had opened right at Hope's core. She sighed noisily. "You think you could just boss them around without having to use all the church language and stuff?" Even as she asked, Hope regretted reviving the issue. It really was the last thing she wanted to talk about even with that religious guy gone.

"That's how it works for me and everyone else I know who does this kinda stuff."

"You're getting to know lots of them, aren't you?"

"Yes. And I'm getting to know other people who are like *me*." Sophie smiled gently. She was looking straight at Hope.

"You think I'm like you?" Hope couldn't keep the childish hunger out of her voice.

Sophie nodded for a few seconds. "I don't know what's gonna happen to you, Hope. Not exactly. But I'm pretty sure you have to take sides. It doesn't work to just be a neutral observer. The fact that you can see so much makes you a particular target, I think. You need support."

"But does it have to be a church?"

"There are hundreds of different kinds of churches. I could hook you up with a church affiliated with the one I go to." Her voice faded a little at the end. Maybe she could hear herself starting to beg. Recruiting.

"I don't know. I need to get cleaned up and get some real sleep right now. Maybe then I can make a better decision." This was life lesson stuff she knew Sophie wouldn't resist.

"Yeah, that's probably a good idea." Sophie let her voice coast at the end, implying a waiting question.

"You guys can stay here if you want. I just need a shower and some sleep. Actually, I'd really ... I'd rather you *did* stay. To ... help me get settled. Ya know?"

"Yes. I do know. No problem." Sophie looked at Anthony, who nodded and smiled very gently.

Trouble Back Home

Sophie read the text from Hope as she waited for Priscilla to pick them up at the airport.

"Found a meeting that's in a church basement near me. Not my mom's kinda church." [Relief emoji]

Anthony was on his phone too. "My mama's really getting into this old Roderick guy."

"Is he really older than her or something?"

"Uh, I have no idea." He gestured toward Priscilla's car, which was maneuvering around a minivan loading passengers and luggage. "I guess it's kinda redundant to call him old *and* Roderick."

"You don't know any young dudes named Roderick?" Sophie couldn't think of any herself. She waved at Priscilla. She could tell her friend had spotted them already. Priscilla's bright smile was the perfect welcome home.

Priscilla paused to check before bursting out of the driver's door. "Hey, girl. How was it?"

Sophie hugged her with one arm. "It was as good as I expected. Maybe not as good as I hoped."

"That sounds like a preacher talkin'." Priscilla led the way to the trunk of her compact sedan. "Hey, Anthony." Her grin in his direction was less welcoming and more … well, flirting.

Sophie told herself that Priscilla only flirted with Anthony on Sophie's behalf. It was an odd arrangement, but probably true. She addressed Priscilla's comment. "Probably my answer is a cross between Pastor Julius and Anthony's mother."

"You better not let him catch you callin' him 'Pastor Julius.'" Priscilla shook her curls once and bugged her eyes.

That little bit of home, that reminder of reality as Sophie knew it, stirred a feeling of being away too much. It was more than flying around the country. The various kinds of spirits she encountered during her missions left her feeling even more disconnected from her sense of home than plane tickets and cab rides.

In the car, Sophie texted encouragement back to Hope. Going to a twelve-step group was definitely a good start. That it was in a church building didn't necessarily mean she was considering giving the real Jesus a chance, but Sophie would check later whether Hope had visited one of the area churches she'd recommended.

"So, Anthony, did I hear a rumor that your mama is dating some old guy?"

Anthony laughed, probably recognizing his own redundant comment from before. "Yeah. I guess the gossip girls are having a field day with that."

"You know that's a sexist comment, right?" Priscilla looked at him in the rearview mirror.

"Oh? So, what *guy* told you about Mama dating?" There was a humorous lift to Anthony's voice. Humorous and confident.

Priscilla sighed and rolled her eyes.

Sophie laughed at them. For just a few heartbeats, she wondered if they would be happy together. Would that bother Sophie? Those two as a couple? Asking that question, even just internally, set something stirring. It was probably a helpful thought experiment. Anthony getting with Priscilla would probably be good for both of them. It would be good for Sophie too. None of that couples' tension between *his* friends and *her* friends. And no more having to decide about defining her relationship with Anthony. It almost sounded good enough for Sophie to suggest it. But saying all that aloud wasn't really possible. It wasn't her style, at least.

Priscilla might have been reading Sophie's mind, however. She dropped Sophie off at home first and waited while Anthony climbed out of the back seat.

Sophie paused to note two angels glowing in the back now. They seemed content back there. She was too tired to even be curious about the significance of that angel glow. The idea of Anthony and Priscilla was too new and vulnerable with her still.

"Thanks, both of you." Sophie patted Anthony on the back and waved to Priscilla before heading up the sidewalk to her apartment building.

Anthony had hesitated before that back pat. Was he expecting a hug? More expressive thanks? Sophie was tired. She'd probably botched her exit. "Oh, well. Your will be done, Lord."

Her phone buzzed. A text from ... Detta. Not from God. But the timing was worth a grin and a headshake.

"Are you home?"

Sophie waited until she got in her front door to confirm. **"I'm home. Priscilla is driving Anthony to his place now."**

"Priscilla? Okay. I guess that's nice." Her response might have included a thought about the two of them as a couple, but that prospect was more likely confined to Sophie's jumbled head.

Sophie boosted the conversation. **"How are you doing?"**

"I'm well, but I think I need your help with something."

"Somebody else in trouble?"

"Maybe. Was hopping you could help me figure it."

Sophie smiled at the typo. "Hopping." She could actually picture Detta hopping. She had been in enough of those kinds of prayer meetings to know what that looked like.

A thought materialized in her head. **"Does it have to do with Roderick."** She hoped her texting app was right about the spelling of his name. Wondering about that made her forget the question mark.

Detta knew a question when she saw one. **"How did you know?"**

Sophie knew an obsession when *she* saw one.

Being the kindly mother she was, Detta suggested they talk the next day after Sophie got some rest.

Sophie would call while it was still early, knowing her friend to be an early riser and not wanting to keep her waiting long. She did talk to her own mother that evening, filling her in on the basics of her second West Coast visit. She spared her mother the gory details, as usual. But she was glad to get her mama praying for Hope. The girl needed all the prayer she could get.

Sitting at her breakfast table the next morning, Sophie texted Detta to see if it would be a good time to talk on the phone. Detta slept a little later on Saturdays, but still not as late as Sophie.

"Yes, please."

It wasn't new to have Detta asking her for help like this, but something in that two-word text felt odd. Maybe a little anxious?

"Have you heard from Hope since you got back?" If Detta was anxious, she was hiding it well. At least for now.

Sophie filled her in on some details, glad to get another prayer warrior up to speed. But she knew something else was weighing on Detta. "So, what did you need help with?"

"It's about Roderick, as you guessed."

A soft laugh escaped through her nose. "What's going on?"

"Oh, I don't know what's going on exactly, which is right where I need your help. I feel like there's something on him, but I don't wanna push into it with just him and me. I don't think that would be right. But I also don't think he needs, like, a big ministry time set up or anything."

"Have you talked to him about this?"

Detta paused a second. "We've been talking about everything. And he asks me to pray for him for all sorts of issues, so he's not hiding things. And I'm listening—you know—attentively. I think we both know there's something there. He asks lots of questions about you. I wonder if he has the same thought I have."

"That I should come over and see if there is something on him?"

"Well, that *would* be very helpful."

"When do you see him next?"

"Well, we're both retired. We can see each other any old day. When are *you* available?"

"I don't have anything today."

"Oh, well that would be wonderful. I could cook up some pork chops I bought yesterday. You wanna come to supper?"

"Have I ever refused?"

"Hmm. Maybe once when you were still a lost pagan girl."

"I was never a proper pagan."

"No, I don't suppose you were. Though not wantin' to come eat my food was surely evidence that *something* was wrong with you."

Sophie laughed hard. "I'm not denying that." And they ended the call still laughing.

Aiming to arrive at Detta's house a little before six thirty, Sophie hoped to get there ahead of Roderick. Was she supposed to call him that? Or Mr. ... What was his last name?

She parked her dented hybrid car behind a shiny gray sedan. That other car in the driveway wasn't new but had clearly benefited from a loving touch. Sophie ignored a hovering guilt about her scratched and dirty compact.

That frivolous regret didn't entirely block her view of the angels flying over Detta's house. At least two of them had come with Sophie, but hers usually didn't appear airborne like that.

"You trying to get my attention or something?" She squinted at a third flier. It didn't look familiar at all. Focusing on the spiritual traffic produced a view of Detta's guardians. They were both inside the house.

"Hello, Sophie." A large man with a ready grin met her near the back door. He held a kitchen garbage bag. Wiping his right hand on his khaki pants, he extended it to her.

"Roderick?" She was confirming the obvious and testing the use of his first name.

"At your service." His grin was topped with tight round cheeks that were clean shaven. He had a trimmed goatee that was peppered black and white. The hair on his head was a uniform gray. He clearly didn't color his hair, just like Detta.

Sophie reversed out of that thought. "Looks like Detta has you at *her* service." She nodded at the garbage bag.

"Small price to pay for a dinner at Detta's house. She's hardly letting me help at all." He rolled his eyes toward the kitchen door.

"You're a cook?"

"In one of my past lives, I was a cook. I still like to create in the kitchen when I can."

"But not Detta's kitchen."

"Oh, we all get set in our ways. Would be pretty hard to let someone else muck around in your kitchen the first time over."

Sophie knew right away why Detta liked this man. She also saw something that might have been what was concerning Detta. A pale shadow seemed to be hiding behind Roderick. As long as it hid behind him, Sophie wouldn't get a good look. But she forced herself to stop trying. "I'll let you at it. I should say hello to Detta."

He was staring at her a bit more intensely. Had he noticed her distraction? He didn't look worried. More curious. Gesturing toward the door, he let her pass. "See you in a minute." He headed for the side of the garage.

Sophie had never noticed the garbage cans there, in a sort of tight corral. Detta had never sent *her* out with the garbage.

"Hello, dear! Good to see you. You met Roderick?" Detta stepped up for a hug by the back door.

"Yes. Gotta love a man who carries out your garbage for you."

"Insisted on it. I can hardly get him to sit down. He's used to running his own kitchen."

"Leftover from when he was a cook?"

"Yes. Funny how you get a habit and carry it the rest of your life, no matter how long you live."

Sophie turned in time to see Roderick pass the window on the way to the door. A very distinct white figure was following him. A figure wearing a pointed hood. Despite herself, Sophie gasped and swore.

"Sophie?" Detta still held onto one of her arms.

Roderick arrived at the door just in time to hear Detta's exclamation. "What did I miss?"

Instead of hiding this time, the ghostly figure loomed over Roderick and leered at Sophie with a cavernous mouth and bloody fangs. Maybe it thought she would be intimidated.

She *was* struggling to get control of herself, but she wasn't going to back down. A fierce violence was rising in her. The sort of fighting urge she'd had in Hope's apartment. "There's a ... it's a ... spirit. It looks like ... like a Klansman."

"Oh, Lord!" Detta clasped her hands together and started praying in her prayer language.

Roderick just stood in the doorway, the screen door against his backside.

The Klan spirit swooped around the room. Its flight reminded Sophie of a crop duster. This one was spreading poison as it flew.

"In the name of Jesus, I command you to leave this house."

"It's not your house!" The thing hissed at Sophie.

She hated it when they spoke to her. But she hated everything about demons. This one particularly. "It's definitely not *your* house. Get out. Go where Jesus ... go where the true Lord Jesus Christ tells you to go." A flash of awareness that the Klan claimed Christian heritage crossed her mind in time to alter her command.

"Sweet Jesus!" Roderick fell to his knees on the doormat.

"Roderick!" Detta nearly fell next to him but grabbed one of his raised hands instead.

"Get it off me!"

This was a little disorienting for Sophie. The thing was still swooping over them, toasting the ceiling with red flames. But she knew what she saw didn't explain everything, including what Roderick was feeling. A silent prayer brought her an awareness of a rope tied to the old gentleman. It was around his neck. A noose. Sophie shuddered violently.

"Was ... was one of your ancestors ... lynched?" She was sorting her American history as she resisted the urge to duck below the diving demon.

Roderick nodded sharply. "I ... I believe so."

Sophie knew a veil of secrecy might have been dropped over a killing like that, but she felt pretty sure there was some connection between a lynching and Roderick's family.

"Detta, we need to break off any curse or claim on his family from the Klan and their murderers." She wasn't sure how to say it, but Sophie suspected Detta was on track with her.

"In the name of Jesus, I release Roderick from any claims by the Klan that have been passed down to him through the generations. I break all curses in the name of Jesus, all inheritances of evil and hate." Detta paused. "Roderick, I believe you have to forgive some folks you've never met. But you have to do it on behalf of your family line."

"Yes. I know you're right."

Sophie was glad Detta was handling that part. It seemed entirely unreasonable for her to ask Roderick to forgive that kind of hateful violence even if it was far in the past.

His voice quavering but rising in strength, Roderick broke off unholy ties with his family line and declared his family free from racist curses. And he pronounced forgiveness for those who had done horrible things to his relatives. He didn't seem to know the specifics, but Sophie could sense the genuine strain involved in letting it go.

She could see an increasing tautness in the rope between Roderick and the demon. And she couldn't resist any longer. Jumping, she swung her fist at that rope and watched it snap, though she didn't feel any sort of physical contact with it.

Roderick barked an exclamation that might have been a word, but not one Sophie recognized. Then all was quiet. The three of them stared at each other.

"I feel like it's gone. I can feel that." He struggled to his feet, Detta assisting.

She was nodding and grinning. Resting a hand on his shoulder, she said, "I feel it too. I knew there was something. And I knew somehow it didn't have to do with you directly."

He lowered his head, then raised his eyes to Detta. "Well, I knew when I was on my knees there that I was hangin' onto some very old resentments. I should have already brought those to the cross of Jesus."

"Oh, praise God. Thank you, Jesus."

Sophie smiled. She could smell something outside on the grill. "Pork chops?"

Detta clapped her hands and stepped quickly toward the back door.

Who Belongs with Whom?

Detta knew she would remember that battle in the kitchen for a long time. And she expected she wouldn't be able to forget the embarrassment of burning the pork chops soon enough.

"They're not burnt, Detta. They're blackened." Roderick had laughed and crunched into his chop. They had agreed to eat them like fried chicken—finger food, given the advanced state of blackenedness on one side.

Detta did catch herself looking at Roderick during lulls in the conversation, checking for the difference she had felt as soon as Sophie did that slashing thing with her hand. When Sophie explained why she did it, Detta had understood the snapping sensation she'd experienced during that peculiar ministry maneuver.

"I trust you, girl. And I've come to expect things to go a little different when you're fightin' demons. It makes sense to me that it would be different if I could see 'em."

Sophie had looked half convinced that her method was okay. But Roderick was beaming. Sophie had won another fan. And that was all to the good.

Detta had worried that Roderick was more skeptical about Sophie's gift than he was letting on. His church—Loretta's church—wasn't as apt to go for casting out demons as Detta's was. That was related to how she and Roderick had met in the first place. Folks from Detta's church trying to bring healing to Loretta, who was getting only sparse prayers for healing from her own congregation.

Wiping her hands on a paper napkin, Sophie watched Roderick for a couple seconds, then looked at Detta. "You two make a good couple. I see why you like each other."

Detta suspected Sophie was speaking more freely than she would normally, in the afterglow of victory. But the young woman also seemed to be working something out for herself.

"Thank you for saying that, Sophie. We get along real well, that's for sure." Roderick smiled expansively before picking up his iced tea.

Roderick was an easy man to trust. Something in his eyes was truer than most folks. But there was something else behind what Sophie did.

"What is it, girl?" Detta set her pork chop down. "Is this about you and Anthony?"

She could see Sophie laugh deep in her chest without making much sound. "You knew that just like I knew it was something with Roderick when you asked me for help this morning."

Detta let her head tip right, then left. "Not much mystery between us, is there?"

"I can see your angels." Sophie's tight smile, one that hinted at dimples in both cheeks, came with a little eye roll.

"So, what is it? What is it with you and Anthony?"

"I don't think I feel the same way about him as he feels about me." She glanced at Roderick but kept talking. "When I saw him with Priscilla last night, they just looked so much more likely than him and me. Priscilla is more normal. And she wants the kind of things women normally want."

Detta couldn't help recoiling and clenching her brow a bit. "You want those things too, don't you? Though it doesn't have to be with Anthony."

Sophie stared at her for a second, then took a deep breath. "You know, when you say it that way, I realize something." She reached for her glass of tea but didn't drink yet. "I think I was worried you would take it personally if I didn't want to be Anthony's girlfriend or something."

Shaking her head slowly and definitely, Detta checked for a scent of truth in what Sophie feared. "No. That's not even something that ever crossed my mind. I want the best for you two. That's all. And I can be honest and say I was never sure there was the kinda connection between you two that Anthony wanted. You seem more like brother and sister to me than anything."

Grinning even larger, Sophie reached over and took Detta's hand. "Does that make you my second mama?"

"You mean *madrecita?*" Detta checked with Roderick to see if this was getting to be too much for him. But he looked like a man fully satisfied with the company and the conversation. She had never seen him smile more contentedly. But maybe that mostly had to do with the monster Sophie had sent away.

They finished supper with a cherry cobbler, one of Sophie's favorites.

When Detta sent Roderick out with another load of garbage after dinner, she seized the chance to say one more thing to Sophie. "I know you'll find what you need, whether it's a relationship or just peace with being on your own. And you'll never really be alone, of course."

"How did you know I needed to hear that?"

"You looked sad even when we were joking around."

"I think I'm mostly sad about having to tell Anthony what I've decided. I never wanted to hurt him."

"Of course you didn't, but he'll recover. I've seen him do it again and again." Detta folded the dishrag and hung it on the edge of the sink. "I've seen him recover from losing his father too. And that recovery really only happened recently, you know. So, I think that will give him even more bounce back than he showed before."

"That's very reassuring." Sophie's gaze drifted toward the dining room door.

Detta suspected there was an invisible someone there who was visible to Sophie at just that moment.

Word of Hope

Sophie went for a run for the first time in at least two weeks. Labor Day morning was crisp and cool compared to the humid heat of August. She wasn't the only one out on the street. She had to shake off a scene with a petite woman running in front of a fat demon that seemed to be chasing her down the street. Though somehow Sophie knew the chaser would never really catch that young woman, she muttered a prayer for the stranger.

Tuning in to her own angel helped wipe away the residue of that regrettable scene. Her big guy was running beside her as she had come to expect. She recalled the time he caught her and kept her from getting plowed by a guy focused on his phone. She entertained a temptation to feign falling now, to see if he would do it again, but she suspected he would know the difference. He was probably reading her mind even now. Was he monitoring this nonsense? She glanced at him to find a rare, mischievous smile on his face. She panted a laugh despite herself.

Back in her apartment, Sophie showered and dressed in yoga pants and a long peasant blouse, anticipating a slightly cooler day. She crunched cereal and checked her phone. A message had arrived from Hope.

"I need to show you something."

California time would mean it was pretty early for Hope to be up and messaging. That worried Sophie. She initiated a video call immediately.

"Oh, hey. I didn't think you would get back to me so fast." Hope rocked in and out of the frame as she settled herself onto one of the chairs on her balcony.

A recollection of the moment when it looked like someone was about to throw Hope off that balcony flickered across Sophie's internal video screen, but the smile on her friend's face deflated the fright of that memory. "You said you wanted to show me something?"

"I don't think we established whether you can see angels over a video call, but I wanted to try."

"Really? You have a new visitor?"

"Yeah. I kinda feel like they're ganging up on me."

"In a good way?"

"*You* say."

"Where's the new one standing?"

"Floating, not standing. A guy-like one, over there." She turned the phone, and Sophie caught a shift in light but saw no clear figure.

"Okay. I can see something is there, but I can't see a clear outline of him."

"Weird. Well, it's something."

"You were worried?"

"Can you tell for sure that this one is good?"

"How does he make you feel?"

"Pressured."

"What do you mean? Is it that religious guy?"

"No. This is definitely a different guy. And the pressure is different." Hope settled the phone in position for a close-up that enlarged her nose a bit. It was a long, narrow nose, even longer in this view. "My angel girl says I should call my mom, and this guy shows up and holds his hand up to his ear like he wants me to call. My mom, I presume, not him."

Sophie snickered. "You think that's ganging up?"

"Well, I mean, yes."

"Ha. Okay, I get it. But doesn't it make you feel like it means calling your mom would be a positive thing?"

Hope blinked rapidly. "Well, if you think about it, they're not saying it's gonna be an easy phone call. An entire call with no shouting."

"Shouting?"

"I've totally lost it with my mom a bunch of times."

"*You* do the shouting?"

"My mother does not shout."

"Okay. Neither does mine. That can be a good thing, but I get your point. It's a really good point. Just because it would be good for you to call doesn't mean it'll be easy."

"I did grow up in church."

"I can tell." Sophie hesitated as a glow appeared over Hope's shoulder, then disappeared. "Did he just leave?"

Hope had already turned, maybe catching that flash in the little image of herself inset on the video app. "Yeah, looks like he's outta here. I guess it's mission accomplished for him." She glanced to the side. "My angel girl is out by me, catching the view. The sun rises behind us, of course. You saw that. And the neighborhood is lit in gold. These dudes seem to dig golden light."

Snorting another laugh, Sophie raised her eyebrows. "I think that just symbolizes heaven. That's my theory. It's, like, from the way they reflect the glory of God. I think it says in the Bible that angels stand in the presence of God even at the same time as they're talking to you."

"Wow. That gave me chills. Pretty sci-fi stuff."

"Yeah, them being in more than one place at a time."

"Or existing in parallel universes."

"Ha. Anthony could probably go on and on about that."

"Huh." Hope slouched a bit more. "You gonna see him today?"

"Yeah. I am, in fact. Not looking forward to it."

"What? Why not?"

"I gotta tell him today that I don't want a romance with him. Just friends."

"Oh, no. The two most dreaded words of all relationships."

"Just friends? Actually, he's more like a brother. So maybe I shouldn't say *just friends*."

"I advise against it."

"Clearly. Sounds like you have some experience."

"Maybe not so much, but enough to know the impact."

Sophie waited for a second. They were a bit off topic, but Hope had diverted. She could divert right back. "So, you gonna call your mother today?"

"Hmm. Well, maybe. Maybe I can do it without yelling at her."

"Like hanging up on her instead?" Sophie joked with a little hesitation, ready to retract any offense.

"Ha. There you go. There's always another option." Hope chuckled some more. "But, you know, going to my meeting is helping. The guy leading it is one of the pastors of that church. And he's pretty cool. An addict like the rest of us, but really grounded."

"Nice. That sounds great. So, you think yelling at your mom is off the table now that you're getting more grounded?"

"I said *he* was grounded. Not like I'm there yet."

"I don't know. I hear some real progress, Hope. You sound way better."

"Yeah, I guess I do." She took a deep breath. "I miss you. When are you coming out here again?"

"I don't know. What about you coming here? You could swing by after you visit your folks."

"Ha. Now I *am* getting ganged up on."

"I could try to send my angels over to make sure you comply."

"Do they ever go where you tell them?" Hope's tone was more skeptical than curious.

"Not exactly. I mean, not really. My best bet is getting on the same page as them. They take their orders from higher up the command structure."

"Uh, yeah. I get that."

"Anyway, I think you can do it. You make the call, and you can end the call, right?"

"Yeah. Theoretically." Hope pulled her knees up.

That pose somehow reminded Sophie of Kimmy. She wanted to call her next, to get caught up. "Well, I'll let you get to it. I need to call a friend who's a new mom and see how it's going."

"You ever think you could do that? Be a mom?"

Sophie let a sideways smile rise at the thought. "Well, not anytime soon. But seeing Kimmy do it has shown me it's possible for an old recovering addict."

"I forgot that you're in recovery. Your friends too?"

"A couple of them."
"There is ... hope, then."
"Yes, dear. There is hope."

What Did He Say to You?

Anthony sat on the park bench watching a little girl learning to ride a tiny bike, her mother stooping very low to help stabilize the tot. He could hear Sophie's stressed breathing even over the strong wind bending the trees. Her nerves made him nervous. But he knew what this was about.

"How's your mom doing?" Sophie glanced at him.

"She's fine. I think she and Roderick are for real. What about your mom?"

"Oh, she's good. She got reconciled with one of her employees who we think might have cursed her. All good now."

"Cursed her?"

"Yeah, sent her this back-pain demon."

Anthony snorted and shook his head.

"Hey, I just call 'em what I can figure to call 'em."

"Sure. I know." He let his engine idle. Sophie was stalling. They weren't here to talk about their mothers.

Sophie took a deep breath. She hesitated and scowled at the space behind Anthony and the bench.

He resisted the urge to turn and look at what she was seeing. He still hadn't completely banished that urge. "Something interesting?" He was reading her face. She didn't look concerned, only curious.

Waving one hand dismissively, she took another of those big breaths. "Sorry for the distraction. I really don't want to … I mean, I do want to talk, but I don't want to …"

"To hurt me?"

She huffed a laugh. "Yeah. That was what I was trying to say. But it didn't seem like the right place to start." She twisted her mouth apologetically, her eyes pleading a bit.

"It's okay. I know what you want to say. I get it."

"Do you? I'm ... I'm sure I've been confusing. Because I've been confused."

He nodded. "Me too, I'm sure."

"I mean, it got more clear to me the other day when I left you and Priscilla in the car. I saw you two, and I thought, you know, they would make a good couple. And that was disturbing at first, but I didn't really freak out at the idea. It didn't make me feel as bad as I thought it would. Or should. Or whatever."

"Me and Priscilla?"

"Yeah. You *would* make a cute couple."

Anthony couldn't help scowling. He didn't want to make this racial, but had Sophie just done that? "Me and Priscilla? Is this because she's black?"

Sophie froze. Her brow tightened and tightened some more. "What? No! That's not what I'm saying." She vented an exasperated breath. "No. I mean, that's pretty ironic, really. Because the thing I figured out is that you and me, I mean, at least for me, you and I are more like brother and sister. I mean, I was talking to a friend, and I realized I didn't want to do the 'just friends' speech because we're never gonna be just friends. At least for me. I think of you as my brother, or at least close to that. So that's why it just can't get ... you know, romantic."

Now he couldn't help grinning. Part of it was relief. To have Sophie suddenly go racist would have crashed his world. Another part was how much sense she was making even though she sounded more frazzled than she ever got when not wrestling with a demon.

Now it was his turn to take a deep breath. He felt more settled. Was that because they had laughed together? Was it because Sophie had finally said what she wanted to say and it wasn't so bad?

Sophie stared across the park.

Anthony broke the awkward pause with a random question. "How's Crystal?" A change of topic, obviously.

"Crystal? She's okay. She's gonna join a regular old church small group. No gurus, no drama. Just getting to know people and doing church with 'em."

"That sounds good. You gonna do that?"

Sophie looked a little surprised. Then she started nodding. "I should. Yeah, I guess I should. I'd been hesitating because I was thinking I might be traveling more. Might go with those demon chasers. But I'm not gonna. Not now, at least."

"That's probably good."

"Good for now." Her gaze drifted toward where that little girl had dumped her bike in the grass. The tot, wearing a bright pink helmet, jumped up from the lawn and fanned both hands with arms wide. She celebrated her survival with a laugh. The watchers on the bench both smiled at the scene.

"So, you gonna ask Priscilla out?"

He turned his head fully toward her to figure out if she was joking. She did have that playful smile on her red lips. "I might. Is this something one of your angels told you I should do?"

"Oh. I haven't been getting relationship advice from them much." Her eyes drifted out over the center of the green park. "Certainly not relationship advice for you." She turned back to him. "Probably that was just my idea. Pretty selfish, really. I wouldn't have to share my two friends with anyone new. Just keep it all in the family."

"That *is* pretty selfish." He offered his own version of that teasing grin. Then he shook his head. "She *is* a beauty."

"Right? See, I told you you'd make a cute couple."

He laughed. "It's not just about looks, of course."

She sobered. "Of course." She was tracking something over his head.

"Should I be worried about what you're seeing there?" He jabbed a thumb toward whatever she was focusing on.

She started to shrug, then winced for a second. "Sorry. I can't tell if that guy is related to you. He seems to sort of be waiting for something. I was trying to figure out whether it's you or me he wants."

"He? This is a new one?"

"Yeah. I don't recognize him. I wish you could …" She shook the rest of that thought away.

"I do too. I wish I could see them most of the time. Then I see you, like, freaking out over something, and I'm glad I don't have to deal with the stuff you see."

"Sure. Goes both ways." She was less focused on what she was saying than on the visitor she was watching. "Did you hear that? Did he say something to you?"

"What?"

"Just now, did you hear him say something to you?"

"Why?"

"Because he, like, came down and whispered in your ear."

"He what?" Now Anthony loosed his restraint and twisted in his seat to check for some flying guy whispering in his ear.

"You didn't hear anything?"

Anthony looked at Sophie again, shaking his head.

"Weird. I swear it looked like he said something to you."

"I didn't hear anything." Even as he denied it, he was testing. Was there something? Something other than the wind in the trees? He continued to shake his head slowly.

"But he must have wanted you to know something. To hear something." She turned from talking to Anthony to addressing the space above his head. "What did you say? Hey, what did you say to Anthony? Tell me, and I'll tell him. Hey!" She was up off the bench. "Where are you going? Wait." She stepped up onto the bench, reaching upward. "Don't go. Wait!"

Sophie jumped down and sprinted toward a dark brown building under the trees—public restrooms or a utility building. Sophie was chasing an angel again.

Anthony rose from the bench and found his knees weak. His first step was unsteady, and he wobbled one step before righting himself.

Sophie was reaching up and shouting, "Wait! Just wait! Can't you tell me?" Then she leaped up and appeared to grab one of the tree branches.

Anthony stopped. It wasn't a tree branch. What did she grab? She seemed to elevate unnaturally for just a second.

But that was impossible.

Then she tumbled into the grass and leaves beneath the tree next to the dark brown building.

He sprinted to her side. "What are you doing?" He landed on his knees. "Are you okay?"

Sophie looked up at him. She had a goofy grin on her face. "I almost caught him."

Anthony sat on his heels and leaned back. "Oh, my—" He decided to stop there. "You just about ... you are ..." He managed to keep editing.

She looked like she wanted to get up. He gave her a hand, and they both got to their feet.

She was laughing. Then Sophie imitated that little girl jumping up to show that she was unharmed by her bike accident. She fanned her hands on both sides and laughed at him.

And all he could do was laugh right back.

Sophie hugged him and kept laughing.

But an odd thought was struggling for Anthony's attention. An out-of-the-blue thought. He suddenly wondered if he should call Delilah Little. Yeah, he should give her a call.

But where did *that* idea come from?

Sophie was staring at him. Was she reading his mind?

Anthony was having a hard time reading it for himself. Or maybe just a hard time admitting what had just happened. He was pretty sure now what it was. And he was also pretty sure he wouldn't tell Sophie.

Not yet.

Book One in the series is available on Amazon: https://www.amazon.com/dp/B08NGRJ278

You might also enjoy, *Seeing Jesus*: https://www.amazon.com/dp/B00D8KZH0M

Sign up for our newsletter if you're interested: Subscribe | jeffreymcclainjones

Thank you!

Printed in Great Britain
by Amazon